# The
# Source of Light

# The
# Source of Light

## David Richards

*thistledown press*

Thistledown Press Ltd.
118 - 20th Street West
Saskatoon, Saskatchewan, S7M 0W6
www.thistledownpress.com


Library and Archives Canada Cataloguing in Publication
Richards, David, 1953-
The source of light / David Richards.

ISBN 978-1-897235-93-5

I. Title.

PS8585.I173S69 2011     jC813'.54     C2011-905349-7


Cover and book design by Jackie Forrie
Printed and bound in Canada

Canada Council   Conseil des Arts        SASKATCHEWAN              Canadian    Patrimoine
for the Arts     du Canada               ARTS BOARD               Heritage    canadien

Thistledown Press gratefully acknowledges the financial assistance of the Canada Council for the Arts, the Saskatchewan Arts Board, and the Government of Canada through the Canada Book Fund for its publishing program.

# The
# Source of Light

# Acknowledgements

Raymond Richards showed me the synchrotron at Canadian Light Source in Saskatoon. He explained as much as I could understand. The CLS organization is highly professional; the conflicts in this novel were pure fiction. There is no Hungarian Light-Source Team at CLS, that too was a fiction. Timothy Jantzen published a document called, "Synchrotron Radiation and MAD Phasing in Protein Crystallography." It is written at a level far above my chimp-brain ability to comprehend. However, it did give me a glimpse of the problems scientists face and let me come up with a plausible goal for Phillip. Michele Loewen's comments in "Understanding Proteins" actually make you believe protein researchers will one day shout, "There! That's the meaning of life!" John le Carré's books on spies, although not quoted in this novel, were certainly inspirational and are a delight to read. Finally, for you Badger atheists, and for those Phyllis faithful, there is Robert Wright's *The Evolution of God*. Wright will make you think through both sides of the whole God issue. For starters, read it before you decide on your soul's existence.

Braden Forer, Elizabeth Rotzien, Tina Rioux and Morgan Brososky very generously read the manuscript in its draft form. They gave me valuable advice on the characters and plot of *The Source of Light*. Your input was much appreciated.

"You and the Light" is from the book *Witness* and is reprinted with permission of Robert Currie and Hagios Press.

*To my brother Ray.*
*If you are charting the universe, building a homestead, or leading an armoured regiment in a desperate battle — he's the guy to call.*

## You and the Light

The light invents
the living room, lays
a rug on the waxed floor, one chair
squatting against the wall.
It stops the hands
of the clock at *now*, commands
the dark to huddle outside, waiting
for something to happen.
Held by the light, a novel
shadows the arm of the chair,
a single blade of grass
marking the final chapter.
Strong as water
in wind, quick as the crack
of a match, the light
can alter anything, invite
the night inside, hurl
the book and the room away,
but always it saves
the choice for you.

— Robert Currie, *Witness*

# CHAPTER 1

IF HE HADN'T LET BADGER GOAD HIM into proving the existence of God, he'd never have discovered that his mother was having an affair. Badger's experiment failed so God existed, but true to his nickname Badger stubbornly refused to admit defeat. So a win that was really a loss. Then of course discovering your mom is cheating on your dad appears on the surface at least to be another loss. A lose-lose situation.

Yet that's the whole point of that fortnight in May. On the surface it's so deceiving that it is scarcely worth consideration as evidence of anything. What we see is so rarely what we get that we might just as well ignore what we see. He was living proof of this condition. He was the grey man — boy more accurately — since he was only seventeen-years old. Anybody looking at him saw porridge that had cooled to the point of being almost, but not quite, inedible. Nothing to excite either good or bad attention. Light brown hair, dark brown eyes, medium height, medium build, medium complexion and a fashion sense that hovered between hair that was too long and too short. Slightly faded jeans or khaki denim trousers with beige leather hiking shoes (nothing as overt as hiking boots), and cream or pale blue cotton shirts were his unvarying choice. A solid 'B' student who was not a loner but whose few friends could never be described as buddies. Even his name was the most common of his generation, Michael, but reduced to Mike since one syllable is so discrete. He spent his time in high school much like a jackrabbit crouched in front of a snow drift. Visible if one looked closely but damned difficult to spot and almost impossible to flush.

On the surface he was a clear pool of water. Yet it was a sham. A contrivance to keep the world at bay. Anyone who cared to don goggles and snorkel to look beneath the grey boy's surface would have been surprised to discover a brightly coloured coral reef of rebellion, risk and fear. And so the lose-lose spring was really only a lose-lose on the surface.

~

"The Columbine School murders were okay by you?" Mike asked, irritated but trying not to show it. "Virginia Tech was just a culling of the herd?"

"Course not, definitely not okay. It was a gross violation of our biologic . . . ah, what is it again?" Badger ate a chip. "Yeah, violation of our biologic code. But there was nothing morally wrong. A couple of high school slackers more or less doesn't signify anything in itself."

Mike loaded the DVD and retrieved the remote. He spoke facing the TV. "One of those slackers died praying for forgiveness. Some of the slackers risked or lost their lives trying to save others. Surely there is a heroic story there, some kind of goodness."

"Praying, no." Badger paused, his face academic and thoughtful, no emotion otherwise displayed. "Trying to save others of the species, trying to stop the violation of the biologic code, yeah, that proves me right."

"It proves courage and love exist." He felt safe now and turned to face Badger. "Animals in the wild don't know courage or love — you said it yourself. So right and wrong exist for humans. The shooters were wrong, the girl who prayed was right and . . . "

"Try to understand me," Badger interrupted. "The heroes were responding to a genetically coded instinct to protect the herd; there was no moral right or wrong. It really is simple. They were no better or worse than the shooters except for the fact that the killers lost their anthropologic instinct and became a threat to the herd."

"Anthropologic? Where did you dig that up?" Mike sat beside Badger and punched his shoulder. "Surely you don't believe that. Come on, the Columbine shooters were nothing more than anthropology misfits? But human species so not much different from you or me?"

"Got it." Badger punched him back. "Now start the movie. Your folks will be home by midnight and it's nearly ten now."

Mike stared for a long moment. "Could you do it?"

"Do what?"

"Cull the highschool herd — be a Columbine shooter?"

"What! Are you nuts? Course not — that's sick, man."

"But you said they weren't much different from . . . "

"Genetically! Homo sapiens. Same species. But those guys are crazy." Badger returned his stare. "Badgers eat what they kill — never kill for fun. And this Badger is a lover not a homicidal deviant."

"There — *love* — you admit it exists. And what about beauty? What about poetry?"

"You hate poetry," Badger snorted and lunged for the remote. Mike held it out of his reach.

"Some people love it. And music and a meadowlark's song — what about them?"

"What about 'em?"

Mike took a handful of Doritos. "Humans love those things but there's no biological benefit — no survival of the species involved. So . . . if we get excited by music or birdsong for no reason other than the enjoyment of them, then there must be a reason for life besides keeping the herd alive. Good and bad exist, God exists."

"No, no, all wrong. Meadowlarks' songs mean they are horny. They're calling for a mate."

"But humans respond to that song — you love that song, birdwatcher boy. Are you going to hump a female lark? No. But you love that song — God gave you the capacity for . . . "

"Stress reduction!" Badger yelled. "Beauty, music, birdsong gives us pleasure which reduces stress which benefits us biologically. Some birds even mimic the songs of others to scare off enemies. One bird using two personalities to literally save its life. Now start the movie."

"Prove it." Mike obstinately refused to surrender the remote. "Prove it reduces stress — it does no such thing."

"With pleasure." Badger made clicking motions with his thumb. "I'm out Tuesday to video this one old lark. Sings his heart out but the girls probably know that he can't get it up anymore so they ignore him. Bring your dad's BP machine and I'll pick you up after school — we'll head for the coulee early to make sure we see him."

"Really?"

"Yes really. We'll put the blood pressure cuff on, listen to the bird song and watch our BP rates drop — stress reduction."

"Weird, but you're on." Mike pressed play. The movie opened with two bleached blonde women having a glass of wine at an outdoor café. They wore large fur coats and hats. They spoke with heavy Norse accents about the cold weather. Soon they were joined by two men also heavily accented who agreed the weather was cold. They should go to one of the men's apartment for a hot chocolate. There were long camera shots of them in a taxi driving through old fashioned streets. In the apartment all four of them sat on a couch drinking hot chocolate and talked about how warm and pleasant this was.

"God, this is awful," Mike said. "They can't really even focus the camera."

"It'll get better." Badger said confidently.

One of the men went off camera and returned a moment later with a plastic bag full of marshmallows. The words "Spanish Fly" were marked on it

"How much did you pay for this piece of junk?"

"Fifteen bucks," Badger replied, doubt in his voice now as the actors each took a marshmallow and dropped it in their hot chocolates.

"This will warm us up," one woman said, but the dubbed English audio did not match her lip movement.

"Oh, man I've been ripped off," Badger groaned.

"What's it called again?"

Badger picked up the DVD case. "*Swedish Spanish Fly Girls in Hot Black Leather.*"

"What is Spanish Fly?" Mike trusted Badger not to laugh at him if it was something everyone should know.

"A con." Badger pointed at the screen. "I think it was one of those phony aphrodisiac potions old guys bought before Viagra came along."

"I don't see any black leather . . . oh hang on, here we go." Mike turned up the scratchy volume.

"I am more than warm now. Now I am hot," one of the women declared as she shrugged out of her fur coat revealing the fact that she was indeed clad in a skin-tight black-leather jumpsuit. Within a minute, all the previously cold actors were warm enough to remove their clothes entirely.

"Some marshmallow," Mike said hoarsely.

"Yeah." Badger drank half his cola. "Black leather part didn't last too long."

"False advertising," Mike murmured.

"Eh?"

"Should be called Swedish Spanish Marshmallow Girls. Skip the black leather."

"Uh huh." Badger moved to the edge of the couch to get a better look.

~

"Want to fast-forward?" Mike asked, disappointed and bored but also anxious that Badger might think he couldn't hack it.

"Geez, yes," Badger said, relieved. "Twenty minutes of the exact same camera angle and the words 'Oh Baby, Oh Baby' repeated a hundred times . . . " He looked at Mike and laughed. "It's a pretty repetitive reproduction lesson when you come right down to it."

"See if we can find something better — or at least different." Mike hit the FF key and the actors sped up to a frantic pace.

"Now that is funny." Badger giggled. Mike shifted to slow motion, then FF again and they both burst out laughing. The actors changed positions. Mike hit play, but the show wasn't much better.

"Mike," Badger said softly. "You don't seriously think I'm weird enough to go Columbine do you?"

"No way, sorry Badger. Never meant anything by it — just debating — you know."

Badger smiled. "Good then. Let's forget it."

~

There were two large, empty coffee cans stacked near the inside of the garage door. One had several small soup cans inside it. This one rested partly on the lower coffee can and partly on the first flange of the door. When Mike's father activated the automatic door opener a half-block away, the door rose smoothly and quietly. Too quietly, hence the overturned coffee tins with subsequent clanging rumpus of flying soup cans announced his arrival.

Badger jumped, slopping cola on his jeans. Mike rose and went to the DVD player. He removed *Swedish Spanish Fly Girls In Hot Black Leather* and put it in its case. He picked a new one out of the rack, set it in the player and let the FBI warnings run by. Then he chose 'scene select', studied his watch and muttered "little over an hour, that should be near scene twenty two." He pulled up scene twenty-two, hit play and returned to the couch, deftly slipping Sweden into a thigh pocket on his pants. A line of charging American soldiers flashed up on the screen to the roar of gunfire and cheers. A gaggle of US jets screamed in blowing NVA soldiers to bits.

"What the hell?" Badger stared at him.

"My parents are home early. They don't mind me watching Mel Gibson slaughter Viet Cong but they wouldn't appreciate this biology porn."

"The cans?"

"Yes, early warning device. *We Were Young Once and Soldiers*". He picked up the DVD cover. "Is the fall back position for us."

"John le Carré strikes again." Badger held up his balled fist. Mike tapped his knuckles and grinned. "Choirboy and spy, an odd combination," Badger said.

"Altar boy actually, well, altar server to be exact."

"Can good Catholics watch porn?" Badger asked.

"Shouldn't, I suppose." Mike considered the question. "But we're all sinners and I can go to confession."

The side door from the garage opened into the basement a second later and his parents, Phillip and Phyllis, appeared in the family room.

"Hello Badger," Phyllis said, pulling her shoes off and wriggling her toes in the carpet.

"Hey, Mrs. S."

"Good movie boys?" Phil asked.

"Pretty fair, nearly done."

"Who left the recycle cans in front of the garage door?"

Mike shrugged.

~

The Hungarians were a lively bunch. "Mad Scientists" Phyllis called them. The dinner that officially welcomed them to Canada was not lively and it was bureaucratically late. The team had been in Canada nearly six weeks already. The Principal Investor – Dr. Janos Teleki – had been at the University for a year. The faculty lounge was decorated, gaudy, and overfilled with tables of compulsory guests. The food, predictably, was a Canadian effort to make foreigners feel at multicultural home. The caterers prepared Hungarian food that Canadians would like which meant it wasn't Hungarian in anything other than name. The Hungarians of course didn't want their own country's food; they wanted cheeseburgers and cokes. Janos Teleki was not just the Principal Investor lead scientist, he was the sparkplug of the Hungarian Light-Source Team. He was sweet talking Phyllis into ordering Papa burgers, fries and root beer from A&W and having a taxi deliver them to the dinner party.

"I'll do no such thing, Janos," she said in a loud stage whisper. Janos reciprocated with a quiet whisper in her ear. She blushed, snickered and took the money.

"He has no confidence in his English," she explained to Phillip's mildly disapproving frown. "He's a guest in our country you see, poor English . . . " She trailed off lamely, fingering the ten-dollar bills.

"Doctor Janos Teleki, brilliant biochemist on the leading edge of protein crystallography, can discuss the details of linear acceleration and particle physics in perfect English. I don't want to sound disloyal — I'm happy to be his Beam Line Scientist yet . . . " Phillip paused, a small grin emerging. "He can't grunt the words hamburger or root beer to a cab driver?"

"Not the same thing Phil! Talking science is hardly the same as ordering food in a social situation."

"Knows enough English to make you blush like a fifteen-year-old girl." Phil's grin subsided — his teasing banter had transformed into an angry crease of jealousy.

Phyllis' response to this was to retrieve her cellphone from her purse, smooth the snug black cocktail dress down over her hips, and march out of the dining room. Janos stared unblinking at her backside and legs. Phillip stared at Janos. Phyllis at forty-six was a shapely, Reubenesque improvement on Phyllis at twenty-six. The dress and heels were difficult to miss. The director's wife seated near Janos at the head table missed neither Phyllis' wardrobe nor Teleki's leering appreciation of it. Her undisguised frown made Phillip grin again.

The A&W order arrived in a large cardboard box. Phyllis, pretending embarrassment, bore it in and delivered it with the change to Janos just as the Hungarian soup was being served. Janos stood, took her hand, and called for attention.

"Please, my dear Canadian friends. Enjoy my country's food while we enjoy yours — a true cultural exchange!"

They all laughed. The director's wife started a flutter of applause. Janos bowed, kissed Phyllis' hand and clicked his heels together. Phyllis arrived back at her table breathless and flushed. "European creampuff," Phillip said. "He's ten years younger than you."

"Mmmm, yes, I believe he is." Phyllis dipped a spoonful of goulash to her mouth. "And very fit looking too — for a scientist."

Phil pulled his stomach in, held it rigid for a moment then let it slide back over his belt buckle. A man can't suck in his gut and hold it all night. He couldn't pretend he had the body of a handsome young Hungarian. "Fit for what?"

"Anything that comes his way, I should think, my dear." She winked one eye very slowly at him. "This soup is atrocious. I wonder if there is any more of that Hungarian Red left." She raised her glass and a waiter approached with a wine bottle to top her up. "We spend millions on an inner tube to create light but can't afford to leave the bottle on the table," she observed tartly.

"Don't let your Hungarian admirer hear you call it an inner tube Phyl, he'd get jealous." Phil slurped his soup. "Delicious!" He smacked his lips. "Teleki loves that inner tube far more than your little black dress."

Phyl glanced at the head table. "What? Do you really think a young man with his looks would notice an old mare like me?"

Phil leaned in to her ear and made a whinnying noise. She laughed, pushing him away. The director's wife gazed down at the Smith table then tugged at her husband's sleeve. "Phil and Phyl are at it again. For heaven's sake."

The director turned to her. "What's that my love? Having fun are they? Laughing? Oh, dear, I share your outrage completely."

She shot him a withering glare then turned back to make conversation with the Hungarian scientists.

∼

"I could have sworn I put those tin cans in the recycle box." Phyllis kicked the bedroom door shut with her heel and put her shoes in the closet.

"It really is of no consequence," Phillip said, watching her as she bent down with her shoes.

"I suppose not, memory must be slipping though."

"Not the coffee cans — Janos Teleki — a mere amusement, a trifle of a man. Intelligent yes of course, but not much else."

Phyl turned to face him, a grin on her face. "Why Phillip Smith, you are jealous." She reached behind her neck, fumbling with the dress zipper. "Golly, I'm almost blushing."

Phil snorted, angry that she had sensed his jealousy. He couldn't let her see it — he breathed in, trying to get past it.

"Janos Teleki was the life of the party." The zipper unravelled loudly. "Those dinners are so tedious — you've said it yourself — at least Janos made it fun."

"Janos this and Janos that." Phil parroted her. "Euro trash sissy. How could a red-blooded Canadian boy like me be jealous of him?"

"How could you not be!" Phyl shrugged and tugged her dress down over her hips. "He's handsome, swarthy, moustachioed, gallant and dashing like that cavalry officer in *Anna Karenina*."

"He was Russian." Phil watched the dress slide to the floor. "Moustachioed. Is that even a word?"

"Russian, Hungarian, who cares? He is gorgeous. Not that I personally find him attractive — but there is something about his face that seems oddly familiar." She made panting noises followed by a deep-throated growl.

The sight of Phyllis in her underwear snarling like a dog in heat, even in jest, made him uncomfortable. "Okay. Now I'm jealous." He laughed, trying to appear to be a good sport. "And I do feel sorry for the poor bastard. Brilliant man trying to do good work on a scrawny budget — constantly being harassed by Budapest over his expenses. Gotta admire his spirit."

"That's better." She put one palm on her hip and bumped it dramatically to the side. "But you don't have to worry. I prefer four-eyed, balding guys with a manly paunch and membership in the old-timers hockey league. That's my definition of hot." She growled again and reached out with her free hand to tug at his belt buckle. Phil backed up instinctively. Her hand dropped away as did her smile. She looked at him for a long moment and her shoulders sagged. He didn't move. She took a step back. Confused? Hurt? *Both likely,* he thought. He tried to think of something to bring her smile back but only heard himself say, "Long day, eh, Phyl? Pretty tired, ah, you know."

She picked her dress up and turned to the closet for a hanger. She sighed. His wife was attractive, especially in black underwear, and she was fun and smart and she wanted him, not Janos. He clenched his teeth, gritting till they hurt. Yet he made her sigh. She had been sighing now for well over a month but there was nothing he could do about it. He could create light multiple times stronger than the sun, more powerful than God's creation light. He made light for Janos but what could he make for his wife?

Only an hour ago at the dinner: Janos and Phyl whispering and laughing; Janos holding her hand, making a speech; Phyl admiring his fitness and savoir fair. Could she really be falling for Teleki? No, she was still his Phyllis, they were husband and wife — she had to love him, didn't she? Did he trust or doubt her? His head began to ache, blood pounding in his temples. He couldn't just turn away from her again — he must find a way to compete with Janos. That was it! Of course, so simple . . . his headache drained and he relaxed his gritted teeth into a calm smile.

Two large strides and his chest was pressed to her back, arms encircled her waist, his lips at her ear. "Mrs. Smith, you naughty thing," he crooned. "You tease a poor Hungarian man so far from home and not good Hungarian womens anywhere to be seen."

Phyllis' voice surged with relief. "Phil honey, I thought you'd . . . "

"Not Phil," he whispered. "Your old, flabby husband — pooh — who cares about him? When does he get home anyway?"

"Oh, he's working late again tonight, not home for another hour." She laughed. "Just what exactly did you have in mind?"

"Let me show you." He nibbled her ear. "I hope an hour is long enough."

"Janos?"

"Yes, Mrs. Smith?"

"Get the light will you?"

Phil flipped the switch and chased his squealing wife through the darkened room.

Mike locked his bedroom door, crossed the room to his dresser and opened the third drawer. He pulled up the thin plywood frame that covered the bottom of the drawer to reveal a neatly arranged collection of DVD's. Mostly movies his parents would frown at but only the one porn flick — on consignment from Badger — that could cause serious upset. He stowed *Swedish Girls* and replaced the false bottom, covering it with socks and underwear. Badger had been delighted to see the false drawer and had been full of praise for its construction, almost invisible. He'd insisted on hiding his *Swedish Girls* there. "More fun hiding it than watching it," he'd claimed when he left that night.

He unlocked the bedroom door, opened it a crack and wondered not for the first time if Badger was becoming a close friend, a buddy. If so, it was dangerous and unprofessional. He needed Badger as a cut out and had handled him as such, up till now. Showing him the false drawer; teaching him a bit of technique like tonight with the tins and the fall back DVD were all handy for recruiting and entertaining somebody like Badger. But now there were long stretches where he forgot Badger was merely his agent — useful only for running covert operations. Like tonight's debate over God's existence. Part of him wanted to be like Badger; he cared about Badger's opinion. Maybe time to ease him out, try to form a new operational cell before it became too painful. Yet Badger was so good and he lived openly in the real world. Mike could lurk in the shadows but his agent couldn't. If Smiley had taught him one thing it was that real operatives were real people and must work accordingly. He picked up *Tinker Tailor Soldier Spy* and let it fall open to read a page or two. It soothed him and cleansed the Badger doubts. Never strive for perfection; it's the worst possible give away. Mediocre on the surface, competence beneath, that's the ticket. He quietly thanked John le Carré and ended his brief ritual by putting the book back on its shelf. Almost like saying a decade of the rosary, almost religious.

His parents were teasing each other about something that had happened at the Canadian Light-Source dinner party. Mike idly flipped open the back of his stereo receiver and removed a cylinder from its hiding place. He clicked the tiny receiver dish open, turned on the power and aimed it down the hallway at his parents' room. He uncoiled a wire and fitted the ear piece into his left ear, tuning it for distance and volume.

" . . . you don't have to be. I prefer four-eyed balding guys with a manly paunch and membership in the old-timers hockey league. That's my definition of hot." She made a kind of dog snarling sound.

Mike stabbed the power off, shut his door quickly and folded up the directional receiver. God, they would be at it soon. Couldn't they at least wait until he wasn't home? He shuddered, remembering when he'd first got the receiver and had inadvertently tuned into their lovemaking. At least they weren't doing their amateur psychoanalysis of him. Listening to his parents' worried discussions about their loner, religious son had been more unsettling than their sex. But unlike the sex, he'd been unable to turn the receiver off — amazed at how little they really knew him and yet gratified by their ignorance in a way. He really had built his spymaster persona effectively.

He stuffed the device into the trap on the stereo and turned off the light. He lay in the pool of moonlight pouring through the window onto his bed. His eyes widened and his memory searched the moon shadows of the autumn night six months ago when he'd written down the car's license number. Badger had set up a fantastically successful operation yet Badger was completely unaware of his role in the whole thing. Yes, Badger could stay, and Tuesday he'd prove God's existence to boot. A half-stifled squeal echoed down the hallway. Mike covered his head with a pillow and went back to Cindy Foster's locker in the Big House last October.

# CHAPTER 2

CINDY WAS SMART AND ARROGANT. SHE WAS not particularly pretty but she was very popular. Not *because* she dealt dope, as Mike originally thought, but popular *in spite of* dealing dope. The other kids who sold pot and cocaine in various forms were generally looked upon as losers or dangerous losers who were nothing more than necessary evils. Hardly a step up from the twenty-year-old guys stuck in grade twelve who pulled beer from the liquor store for the price of a six-pack. It was Badger who had told him this and Mike confirmed it during his watch. The thing was, Cindy didn't *have* to sell pot, she did it as act of defiant, calculated rebellion. She sold only to her friends and only at cost, never for profit. She chose to be bad. The distinction set her above the common herd. If Mike or even Badger had approached her, they would have been at best humiliated, at worst slapped around by one of her friends.

Badger, unlike Mike, occasionally stood out in a crowd. He dated a grade-eleven girl for a few weeks till she dumped him. He went to some of the parties and had a larger circle of friends. He was Mike's social barometer and a pretty good source of entry level intelligence. It was Badger who alerted Mike to the fact that in addition to the ubiquitous pot and occasional coke, there had been an intrusion of crystal meth into the weekend parties. Mike knew instantly that this could be *the one*, his first real operation. Even Mike knew some of the kids who sold drugs and it was easy enough to watch them at school. He picked the most likely candidate, Ricky Gervais, and watched him for nearly two weeks. Obviously nothing more than marijuana passed through Ricky's hands. When Mike casually mentioned that he thought Rick could be the crystal meth seller, Badger had laughed out loud.

"Ricky G? You're not serious! No real drug guy is going to let Ricky move something as dangerous as c-meth. He's strictly low rent."

It was then that Mike realized his least likely pick, Cindy, was now the most likely. Smart, arrogant, selective, popular so nobody would dare shop her to the cops. He watched her for a few days and got his confirmation. She really was conceited and with that, careless.

The usual lunch hour chaos flowed down the hallway like river rapids. The inmates had their lockers opening, slamming, books heaved in or out, shouts, shoves, laughter all boiling like whitewater. And quiet, huddled and furtive stood Cindy with a kid from grade ten. She never sold dope to a boy two years her junior and would never sell crystal meth to her friends. She was flagrantly breaking her school pattern twice over so it had to be the hard drug. A quick exchange of cash and a palmed package told Mike the tale. Cindy's lips clearly mouthed the words, "Candy, man. Enjoy."

That had been easy. The tricky bit would be the dealer who supplied Cindy. The police wouldn't care too much about Cindy's small quantities of pushed drug but they would care about the dealer who distributed it. There were several problems now. One, they probably transacted resupply well away from the school. Two, the same could be said of Cindy's home. Three, Cindy had a car and Mike only had his mountain bike. A tough watch. He would have to pattern her outside of school and watch her until she broke pattern then follow her — on his bike unfortunately. As it turned out, Badger unwittingly caught Cindy out of pattern when it really counted.

"I'm going as Pacino, Scarface, should turn some heads." Badger adopted what he assumed was a menacing drug lord pose. "You should come — it's wide open."

Mike shook his head. "Thanks, but you know me and parties. Not my thing."

"Lots of female specimens ingesting alcohol, losing inhibitions." Badger licked his lips. "We owe it to the herd, man. We should be spreading our genes — you know a couple of alpha-dominant males like us — it's almost our duty."

Mike unlocked his bike from the rack and watched Cindy's red Ford Tempo pull out of the school parking lot. Badger followed his gaze. "Forget about her — way too dangerous — even for Alpha Dogs. Funny thing though. I heard she's coming to the party. She's usually too hip for open high school parties. College guys date her."

And it clicked. The puzzle piece out of place snapped smoothly home. Mike chewed his lips thoughtfully. The Halloween party. Good excuse to be out late, lots of customers, easy to see your supplier, great cover. "What's the deal with this party anyway?"

"McKennit's farm, twelve K west on highway seven, then eight K south. Parents not home. Machine shed, empty, enough to hold the whole school. Big sound system booked. MUST wear a costume or you'll look like a dork." He appraised

Mike's bland clothing. "Better show up with at least a dozen beer or ditto on the dork thing."

"Has to be beer?" Mike asked, his mind racing with plans.

"No." Badger squinted at him. "But for God's sake don't show up with a six-pack of Orange Crush."

"I was thinking vodka."

"Really? You? Mr. Teetotal, vodka?"

"Yeah." Mike swung onto to his bike seat. "I'm thinking martini, shaken, not stirred."

"James Bond, all right that's good." Badger smiled at him. "Need help getting the booze?"

Mike stared at Badger trying to decide whether or not to crack the door open a bit more. He pulled his wallet out and selected a card from under a flap on the side. Badger took the card. His mouth formed an 'O'.

"This is outstanding. The best fake driver's license I've ever seen. It's you, wearing glasses and nineteen years old. Arthur Guthrie?"

"Not fake. It's real," Mike said. "Issued by the government to Arthur Guthrie — they think he is real."

"Genuine, no shit, fake photo ID." Badger handed the card back. "I am in awe. How . . . "

"Never in a million years. This is indictable, not a photocopy toy, and I trust you to not say anything."

"Absolutely. You can trust me," Badger said earnestly. "Why Arthur? I mean pretty sad name when you could have picked anything like say, Nick Trout."

"Exactly. Who would fake their first name as Arthur? Nobody. So it must be genuine. Also, it was the given name on the best matching entry in the death register so I more or less had to go with it." He let Badger absorb this. He was quick with new ideas, adaptable without drama. "You want me to get your beer while I'm there? I'll hide all of it and we can pick it up before we go."

Badger nodded.

"I could use a ride to the McKennit's though," Mike lied casually. His parents never refused him the loan of a car but he didn't want that. He would need any cover he could get at the party and Badger's vehicle would work well. "I will drink very little — make it look like more. So I can drive home if you like."

"Deal." Badger scrutinized him. "I had you all wrong Smith."

"Thanks. That's the plan."

～

His father's old tux fit quite well. Phil couldn't squeeze into it anymore and Mike was filling out enough to take his place. He turned sideways to the mirror. The shoulder holster carrying a water pistol bulged just enough to be noticeable. Good, that would attract attention harmlessly. The extra pockets he'd painstakingly sewn onto the inside of the trousers below the waistband protruded slightly over his left and right buttock flanks. One pocket contained a silver flask. The other held a slim, hard-backed case containing a very small but very good quality pair of Bushnell binoculars. The hem of the jacket covered both rear pockets neatly.

The doorbell rang. Phyllis was already teasing Badger about his Al Pacino look when Mike got downstairs.

"In my day it was ghosts and Dracula and pirates." She clucked her tongue. "Now it's drug lords and license to kill spies. What do the girls wear to these parties for heaven's sake?"

"How would I know?" Mike shrugged. "I never go to these parties."

Phyllis put her arm around his shoulders and squeezed, pecking his cheek. "I'm so glad you let Badger talk you into going. You should get out more — maybe you'll meet some nice girls."

"I hope we meet some bad girls," Badger said.

Mike raised his eyebrows and shook his head, rolling his eyes toward Phyllis. She had only met Badger three or four times and he wasn't sure she would appreciate Badger's sense of humour.

There was an awkward pause, then she burst out laughing. "What a card! Phil — Phillip!" she yelled back to the kitchen. "Did you hear that?"

Phil ambled out to join them. "Yes, I heard — very funny."

"Seriously now," Phyllis said. "It's going to be freezing tonight. Have you got a coat?"

"The party is in a heated shed," Mike replied. "But I've got this." He took a knee-length black leather coat from its hook by the door.

"Oh no, that could be stolen." Phyl reached for it. "It's your one really . . . "

"Cool?" Badger suggested.

"I was going to say the one really nice — expensive — piece of clothing you own."

"I'll leave it locked in the van if I'm not wearing it." Mike smiled, reasonable and calm.

"Okay then. But the McKennit's have given permission for this party? Truly?"

"Yes," they lied in unison.

"And there won't be any drinking?"

"No," They chorused another lie.

"Ha." Phil snorted. "Of course there'll be drinking. For heaven's sake Phyl. You boys just be careful."

"No booze," Badger said softly. "But I do have a kilo of pure Columbian white to cut and move tonight."

Phyllis hooted. "See Phil. This boy is so funny."

"Hysterical." Phillip smiled. "Have fun guys."

◞

"Where's my Pilsner?" Badger asked as they pulled away.

"Dead drop at the bus depot," Mike answered.

"Eh?"

"In a briefcase in a locker at the bus depot." Mike fished the key from his pocket. "A dozen cans of Pil fit just right in my dad's old briefcase. Twoonie for forty-eight hour use of the locker."

Badger looked at him. "I have so much to learn in the art of deceiving parents. I thought I knew it all. What did you call it?"

"Dead drop," Mike explained. "One person goes in, drops off the merchandise and leaves. Then puts a sign up — chalk mark on a wall for example. Second person sees the mark, picks up later. No actual exchange or sighting. Very clean way of doing business. Mine was a modification of that basic idea."

"Spy stuff again. Your John le Carré books?"

Mike nodded. They drove quietly for several blocks. "My parents think you are great," he said. "They worry that I'm too introverted. 'A loner' my dad says. They're thrilled because they think I've finally found a good friend."

"What's that supposed to mean? We *are* friends." Badger shot him a frown.

"Yeah, sorry." Mike softened his tone.

"They watch this Columbine and Virginia Tech stuff on TV then get all weird about me being a junior psychopath." He pulled the water pistol out of his holster. "My mom actually tried this out, to see if it shot water. She didn't say anything but she was thinking."

"So if I bring you home drunk, with lipstick on your fly, they'll be happy." Badger crowed. "I'll be a hero!"

Mike smiled. "Something like that." Badger was perfect. A perfect alibi, a perfect cut out. And a good guy into the bargain — not that friendship really mattered but a bit of intelligent company was nice.

~

Badger jammed eleven of his Pilsner into a huge tub of ice and snapped one open.

"You drink twelve of those in one night?" Mike asked.

"Naw, I'd be sick if I had more than four." Badger sipped and made a face. "First one is always warm."

"Then why bring twelve?"

Badger laughed, then realized he wasn't joking. "You can't show up with six measly beer. Everybody has to think you're getting into it. Then if you don't, well, later on nobody really notices. Besides, most of the girls don't buy their own, so it's an in with them."

"Are we being watched?"

"Oh yeah." Badger nodded to the far corner of the shed. "Monday's rumours and reports being compiled right now."

Mike glanced over. The rafters of the shed were festooned with strings of Christmas lights. They connected to two large extension cables that dropped into an electrical box in the corner. A laptop sat on the box giving strobe interrupts so the lights blazed and dimmed in time with the bass. The music throbbed and the lights flashed in synch with it. Even the kids not dancing seemed to be jerking like puppets on musical strings. A small pod of costumed people lounged near the laptop, contriving to look bored, sharing a joint. He recognized a jock and girl from the SA with several others he didn't really know. "The Politburo."

"Who?"

"The upper crust — important people — reputation makers of what's cool and what's not?"

"Yeah." Badger grimaced. "All that and then some. So you'd better ante up."

Mike flipped his coat back ostentatiously and reached for the flask. Then he opened the briefcase and produced a litre of vodka and a litre of vermouth. He set them on the trestle table containing the ice and mix. He paused to be observed.

"What's he, Badger, your waiter?" Vanessa, dark hair, a strikingly curved figure and dark eyes sporting an industrial layer of makeup, appeared. Her friend, Angie, mousy brown hair, thin to the scrawny point, faded grey eyes and equally well-caked, giggled. They reached for Badger's beer. The flickering lights whipped their faces in and out of focus.

"Not cold yet," Mike volunteered, smiling.

They turned to stare at him. "And what business is it of yours, waiter guy?" Vanessa popped the can open and took a heroic slug. "Only supposed to be kids from our school Badger — where'd you get this specimen?"

"He sits two rows behind you in physics every single day, Vanessa," Badger said. "Monday to Friday. Two months this year so far."

Vanessa, predator of egos, turned her dark eyes on Mike, scrutinizing him. "Never seen him. You?" She inclined her head at Angie.

Angie took the proffered opportunity to look down her nose at Mike. "Never. And who comes to a Halloween party dressed as a waiter, anyway?"

Mike slipped his hand inside his coat and patted the water pistol. "Bond," he said, staring at Angie. "James Bond."

The girls stared back, not sure whether to sneer or laugh. Angie looked to Vanessa for a signal. Badger was edging backwards, cringing as though his mother had just shown up to take him home.

"Pouring Martinis, ladies." Mike continued calmly. He unscrewed the vodka. That held off the sneers for a second. He carefully poured some into the flask and added two parts more vermouth then screwed the lid on tightly. "One martini, shaken ... "

"Not stirred!" Angie burst out. She laughed and did not sneer.

"Exactly." Mike grinned, shaking the flask. He poured the contents into a plastic cup. "My apologies Angela, no olives I'm afraid. Let me know if it's dry enough for you." He took the can of beer from her hand and gave her the cup. She sipped, swallowed, and suppressed a cough.

"Well?" Mike asked. Vanessa had set her warm beer on the table, watching Angie. Badger was back, observing the girls closely for their reaction.

"Perfect. Just the way I like them . . . James." She took another, much smaller sip.

"Bullshit." Vanessa said. "She's never had a martini in her life." She pointed her chin at Mike unwilling to acknowledge him as acceptable yet. "He's mixing some crap up and ... "

"A Bond Girl who's never had a martini? Impossible." Mike interrupted before she could turn the tide. "You are a Bond Girl aren't you, Angela? I mean — your costume?"

Angie blushed. "Actually we came as hookers."

"Vanessa looks just like Halle Berry in *Die Another Day* — you know, dark-eyed beauty," Badger said, taking her chin his hand, turning her head gently to profile. "Yeah, Halle Berry to a T."

"Badger, you are so full of it," Vanessa said, tilting her head back. "But it's a pretty good comparison now that you mention it."

"You should try one of these V," Angie said, sipping again. "And by the way, how did you know my name is Angela?"

"Behind you every day for two months, physics." Mike raised his eyebrows inquisitively. "I observe." He shook the flask in Vanessa's direction.

"Why not. Make mine drier than hers."

~

"Oh man, I thought you were dead." Badger groaned, his pee splattering the tall grass behind the shed. "Vanessa had you in her sights. The martini was genius."

"Angie was the obvious target," Mike replied, unzipping. "She is the submissive sidekick. Once I got her the martini, Vanessa had no where to hide."

"Is that how you think? I mean." Badger burped. His voice wasn't slurred but it was disconnecting. "Do you see them as targets — figure all this out like some kind of contract hit?"

"Social stuff, parties, not my thing really. So I guess what comes naturally to others is kind of work for me." Mike admitted.

"Hey, no complaints here pal." Badger zipped up and slapped him on the back. "IF Vanessa lets her, Angie will eat you like a pizza."

"Eat me?" Mike was genuinely surprised. "Because she's drunk you mean."

"No! You really don't get it. Genius and stupid at the same time."

"Explain," Mike said.

"You made her feel special. She is like you said, Vanessa's puppet. But you let her move first, without the strings, made her the first martini, made her the Bond Girl — special, you know? Girls love that — feelings and crap."

"If you say so." Mike zipped up. "I just saw her as the weak link."

"I do say so."

Badger moved out of the darkness toward the shed, raucous with music and screaming partiers. "Here's the plan. We'll get the girls dancing, but gradually work apart from each other. With any luck I'll get the tasty Vanessa to forget she's here with Angie and you two can do what comes naturally." He hiccoughed. "Course Vanessa will never give it up for me — but I'll do my very best to keep her busy. She can be a good person if she wants to." He sighed. "We actually used to be friends when we were little — in elementary school."

Mike had to stifle a surge of alarm. This was a serious threat to the operation. He'd marked Cindy's car location in the yard outside the shed. He'd seen her palm drugs to two kids already and she'd been on her cellphone at least three times. She was surely getting ready to move, and soon.

"Yeah, great." Mike tugged at Badger's shirt sleeve. "Hang on a sec; you've had a few. Maybe I should have the car keys, eh?"

Badger dug in his pocket. "Okay. Oh. Wait a minute." He leered in the bright yard light. "You're not thinking designated driver — you're thinking like back of the van with skinny Angie."

Mike tried to leer back but ended up gritting his teeth. Badger pressed the keys into his hand, flinging an arm around his neck holding him in a head lock. "It's always the quiet ones." He bayed at the sky.

～

Mike dipped the water pistol into a cup full of pure vodka, filled it, and hurried back to where Badger was doing his "Badger Dance of Love" between the girls. They were shrieking with laughter as he imitated a badger doing pelvic thrusts at them. He raised his hands, stuck out his fingers like claws and snapped his teeth. He charged Vanessa who obliged him by backing unsteadily into the crowd. Angie hesitated, moving slowly to the music, vodka martinis leaving her uncertain. She slipped her arms around Mike's neck and he danced with her. Over her shoulder he saw Badger give the thumbs up and disappear into the dancing mob.

"Should we stick with them or just be by ourselves, Mike?" Angie whispered into his ear.

"James," he said, manoeuvring her to the side of the shed where Cindy and her friends danced in a closed musk-ox circle. She was on the phone again.

"Oh yah. James. Stirred . . . not martini," she chuckled.

Cindy closed the phone, put it into her small silver bag and began walking to the door. Damn, this was it! She was having trouble with the stiletto heels, apparently half the girls came dressed up as hookers, and hobbled to a bench to take them off.

"James Bond, that's me." Mike pulled the pistol out, desperate to get clear of Angie. "Guess what's in here?"

"Martini?"

"You got it." He aimed the pistol at her but she turned it back on him. He put the barrel in his mouth and obliged her by giving himself a quick shot. He swallowed quickly, shuddering. It was only his second drink of the night, so far he'd been able to mouth and spit or just have 7 Up. He aimed the gun back at her.

"Just like *Romeo and Juliet*," she said.

"Eh? What?"

"A romantic double suicide." She opened her mouth. He fired a hard burst to the back of her throat. She gagged, tried to swallow, then began coughing, retching, and in a moment he steered her outside where the night's beverages came up with tears and wailing ralphs.

Cindy swept out the door and past them, gingerly crossing the gravel lot in her bare feet. Angie's breath steamed white and fetid in the cold air.

"No more for you, Angie. Why don't you get back inside and sit down. I'll be right in to take care of you. Got to have a squirt first." He helped her through the door.

"Don't leave me Mike, James. Oh, God, I feel bad."

Mike drove out of the farmyard carefully. The fact that Cindy was gone meant nothing right now. He couldn't actually follow her down the grid road — too obvious. But he had to catch up to her on the highway before she got to the city. There were tail lights, pin pricks in the dark, well ahead of him so he hung back. They disappeared when the car turned onto the highway and Mike sped up. Badger's mom's van slewed on the gravel, not really a good chase vehicle, but excellent cover in the city for watching. Dark blue Soccer-Mom vans — a dime a dozen — nearly invisible.

He turned onto the highway and hammered the gas pedal getting up to a little over 120 before the vehicle started to shimmy. Thank God he was pursuing an old Tempo. Traffic thickened up as he neared the city. He had to pass twice before he caught sight of a red Ford. He pulled up close, confirmed the license number and noted the single blonde head as he passed. He roared nearly a half kilometre ahead of her then slowed. She passed him a minute later and he tucked himself behind her just as they reached Circle Drive. Plenty of traffic even at midnight. She wouldn't be suspicious until they moved off the main arteries.

She stayed on 22nd Street and drove due east without varying her speed. His worries about having to watch her on a quiet suburban street diminished — she seemed bent on going straight down town. Then just before the lights at 22nd and Idyllwild an old VW Bug pushed in behind Cindy. The VW promptly stopped and sat waiting to turn left out of the through lane while she disappeared around a jog in the road at 1st Avenue. The Beetle shot left through a stale yellow light and Mike whipped across, running the red. The Tempo was gone.

He slowed and forced his thoughts into logical order. She had been driving reasonably fast, not slowing or looking around when she crossed 1st Avenue as he now did. Logical that she wasn't going to turn on 2nd so he sped past it and slowed as he crossed 3rd, watching each direction for the Tempo. Nothing. No guarantee, but if she had turned she would have reduced speed and probably been in sight. He did the same at 4$^{th}$ and came to a stop at the T-junction with Spadina. He instinctively looked right to the grand old Bessborough Hotel and even started to turn right when the Tempo shape caught his eye going north vanishing against the dark backdrop of the river. ·

A couple of low riding pickup trucks swathed in chrome and cab lights charged, engines warbling loudly, south toward the intersection. Mike punched the gas, cranked the wheel left and beat them across. Their squealing tires and horns faded behind him. He followed Spadina north, ignoring the dark trees and dim river to the right, watching for a Tempo. He passed the entrance to the College Bridge with a quick glance and god damn! There was a flash image of an old Ford halfway over the bridge. He gunned the Astro Van up Spadina and hauled into the Mendel Art Gallery parking lot, back end slewing in a circle to get back out on the street. His headlights swung past a red Tempo parked in the corner near some trees.

Now what? The bridge or a quiet, dark lot? Had to take time to check. He took his foot off the gas and coasted as near as he dared to the Tempo, staring at the rear license. Cindy. He sped up and shot out of the lot as he had come in. To stop and park would have been ridiculously conspicuous. Hopefully to Cindy and her pusher he was just a kid in a van doing doughnuts in a parking lot. He took the next left, a quick right and pulled over. He grabbed his coat and threw it on as ran back across Spadina. Plunging through a fringe of bare willow bush, he half fell down the slope to the Meewasin hiking trail.

He stopped and caught his breath, letting his eyes adjust to the dark. Only a few metres away the river passed silently, its wet mud odour filled the air. Mike decided a creeping spy would fail so he must be a late night stroller. He shoved his hands into his pockets and began to walk slowly south, eyes raking the bushes and scanning the river bank. The gallery and conservatory loomed above him, he glanced up. A waning three-quarter moon was starting its descent, bouncing its bright whiteness off the conservatory glass but leaving the trail in moon shadow.

Two people sat on a bench five metres up the trail. One had a small gym bag. His heart began to pummel his rib cage. It was really going to happen, his first operation. *Don't look, don't look, don't look,* screaming in his head. *No eye contact for God's sake!*

He tucked his chin down as though against the cold and his hot breath puffed white before him. His eyes would not listen — would not be told — they flickered to the bench. Cindy faced him, her eyes on his face. Could she see him searching? Had she taken . . . no, she turned her attention back to the man facing her, nodding her head. Mike glared at his feet and walked past their murmuring voices. The trail bent ten metres further on and a grass bank opened on his right. He climbed halfway up the slope, careful not to be silhouetted against the moon, then doubled back to a leafless lilac hedge.

He carefully eased the binoculars from his back pocket and sat tight to the bushes. Moonlight passed above him and found a stretch of trail below. Cindy was clearly visible, her companion mostly in shadow. Mike couldn't hold the binoculars steady. He shook, but not from the cold. A grin took his face, refusing to leave. The hair on the back of his neck prickled. He was a dark shape in a black coat under cover and in moon shadow with clean surveillance of his target. A near perfect one man watch, almost unheard of among even professional watchers. This was textbook stuff — straight out of the MI 5 manual. He breathed deeply and settled himself then propped his elbows on his thighs and sighted the binoculars again. They were not light intensification glasses of course — he couldn't afford that — but they were good optics with wide lenses so they gathered light well. Cindy's profile was sharply detailed — talking, laughing, nodding. Her partner leaned forward and spoke. Wire-rimmed glasses, short curly hair, ball cap pushed back on his head, turtleneck sweater and a University Engineering windbreaker. Mike whispered the facts to himself. What else? A moustache and goatee! Christ he almost missed a major identifier. The subject leaned back into dark shadow. Cindy's head followed and they kissed.

Oh, no. A university man and a high-school girl. A "relationship". Mike's grin froze and died. Maybe this guy wasn't a pusher. Maybe he was Cindy's illicit boyfriend, too old and cool to be at a high-school Halloween party. She goes to the party but ducks out to see him. Her parents wouldn't know. It all fit. The subject took off his jacket, the engineering E flashing for a moment as he wrapped it around Cindy, hooker gear not very warm in late October nights. They closed, his arms encircled her and they began to kiss again. His hands dropped down her back.

Mike lowered the glasses, face throbbing in blush. Not a skilled watcher then, just a peeping Tom. U of S engineering men didn't push crystal meth onto high-school kids. He sat, not feeling the passage of time, staring up at the moon. Cold crept through his slacks from the frosty grass. Probably ruined the tux crawling around like an idiot. Might as well go.

" . . . money in a week . . . "

The words came clear on the night air then turned back into indistinguishable murmur. Money? He raised the binoculars. The gym bag was open in the moonlight on the bench. Cindy had two handfuls of small sandwich bags, inspecting them. She replaced them, zipped the bag and hiked the jacket up. Her hand disappeared down the waistband of her skirt and reappeared full of bills. The engineer took them and stuck them in his jeans pocket. They kissed and stood. Arm-in-arm they walked back toward the gallery, Cindy now carrying the bag.

Mike was up and out of the hedge like a startled grouse. He flew up the bank onto the Spadina sidewalk and strode toward the entrance of the Mendel parking lot. He stopped short, stepping off the sidewalk and away from the direct street light. Five minutes later, Cindy's Tempo pulled out and drove south on Spadina past him. A minute after that, a Jeep Grand Cherokee followed, its lone bespectacled driver smoking a cigarette. Mike drew the binoculars and aimed them at the pool of light shed by the next street light thirty metres away, focusing on the pole. The Grand Cherokee passed through his field of view: black on dark blue, gold stripe, license CKT 533. He fished a notebook and pencil from his coat, stepped under his street light and wrote slowly, neatly: CKT 533 Jeep G. Cherokee, 2002 to 2006, curly hair, glasses, moustache, goatee, smoker, U of S Engineering jacket. He paused, his grin came back as he wrote again. Crystal Meth dealer on the way down.

⌒

Vanessa hugged herself furiously. Angie huffed out her second round of dry heave spewing. Badger pretended to be angry so he could put his arm around Vanessa.

"You got her drunk and left her." Vanessa poked a finger at Mike.

"NO. I helped her outside to hurl then brought her back . . . "

"So where were you then? When we found her she was bent over in the corner, puking alone. She said you shot vodka into her from a gun — some fake murder-suicide game. What kind of sick bastard are you?"

Angie, seemingly on cue, retched loudly and began whimpering. "Oh God. I hate martinis. Can we go home V?"

"I was bad myself so I stayed outside — in the bushes you know — so I wouldn't make a mess ... "

Angie intervened with another loud, gargling, heave. "Let's go home," she sobbed. "To hell with James, Mike, whatever."

"Yeah, let's go, girls." Badger slurred his empathy. "I'll drive you home in V's car. This sicko bastard can take my parents' van back to them."

"You must be dreaming." Vanessa shrugged clear of Badger and helped Angie to her feet. "Don't ever talk to us again, either of you assholes."

The ladies departed, wobbling dangerously on their heels.

"Ah well," Badger sighed philosophically. "Not really worthy recipients of our genetic seed anyway, eh, Mike?"

⌇

Cindy, no previous record and from a surprisingly middle-class functional family, got a suspended two-year sentence and a probation officer. Not quite eighteen, her name stayed out of the papers. The same sentence went to two other girls, one only sixteen, from north- and south-end high schools. Terrance Wayne MacDonald — a third year U of S engineering student with no prior record, got two years less a day at a provincial jail. The judge said he had to serve time because he corrupted three minors and was pushing a particularly devastating drug onto high-school children. The real prizes had been Shane Eric Gauthier and Justin Wilfred Eberts, two men in their thirties and major suppliers of crystal meth — with substantial criminal records. The police had put surveillance on Terrence and caught the two supplying him.

Mike received his three-thousand-dollar cheque from Crime Stoppers at the guilty pleas, before sentencing. It came to P.O. Box 1348 rented by Arthur Guthrie and was made out to same. Mike deposited it to the account he maintained at the downtown Credit Union for Arthur, being careful to put on his glasses before he went into the auto teller just in case the closed circuit video tape was ever matched to his fake ID. An unnecessary precaution really, but fun to become Arthur Guthrie and leave Mike Smith behind for a while. He'd ordered the directional receiver and the wiretap kit from Spy House in Toronto, using the fake ID and P.O. Box. He paid for it from the Credit Union account. Always safest to keep Mike cut cleanly out of these things

These were among his most private, precious memories. Mike's most cherished and until Badger's arrival, his only friends, were his secrets. For some secrets, like the false bottom in his dresser drawer and the directional receiver, he maintained only a fondness. For other secrets, such as he gleaned from the wiretap on his mom's phone, he felt a proprietorial attachment — sometimes a guilty, unclean attachment. But the successful stalk and trap of the crystal-meth ring was lavished with a clean, pure love.

As the spring moonlight angled away from his bed he savoured the memory, polishing it in his mind's eye. Phil and Phyl were quiet now. He rose, undressed in the dark and slipped into bed, hoping for dreams of October moons and stealthy watches.

# CHAPTER 3

"Sure you won't need my car today?" Phillip finished his toast, washing it down with coffee.

"No, mine will be ready before noon tomorrow for work. I'll get the shop to pick me up then," Phyllis replied, a kewpie doll grin on her face. "I plan to be in all day today. Lots to do, some housework, bills to pay." She paused to check on Mike who was eating his cereal and reading a magazine at the same time. She made an exaggerated wink at Phil, lifting a spoonful of Cheerios to her mouth. "Just a lonely old housewife stuck in her boring routine today, no excitement at all." She crunched the Cheerios.

Phil winked back, without really knowing why. Phyllis had been so high spirited and full of good humour since the Hungarian dinner that he tried not to question it. He just played along, pleased that she seemed happy these days. No sighs at all. He winked again and blew her a kiss. Half the Cheerios sprayed back into her bowl, propelled by a loud guffaw that she tried to cover with a cough.

"Okay, Mom?" Mike lifted his head.

She nodded, stifling a laugh.

He went back to his magazine.

Phil laughed himself. His little family, happy and content, peaceful bliss. And today's meeting to discuss his new technique for illuminating protein crystal structure. He could hardly wait to get that going. Life was so unpredictably odd. Stress then bliss and no logical reason why the change. Even Mike, such a worry to them only six months ago, now with Badger, not a worry.

Phyllis was glowing red, but not from the Cheerios, and damn, she was winking again. He almost asked her what was so funny but he sensed it wasn't for Mike's ears. So he just winked back.

"Oh yes, thank goodness I'm only working three-and-a-half days a week." Phyl continued the inane discussion. "I need time to be the boring . . . "

*Another bloody wink!*

"Lonely housewife," she finished.

Phil, mystified, turned to his son. "What about you, Mike? Need a ride anywhere after school?"

He looked up. "No thanks. Badger's got his mom's van and we're going straight out after school to see his meadow lark."

"Right, yes, I'd forgotten." Phil loved the fact that his son was so full of thought and curiosity. "Prove God's existence," he said. "Nobody can say that you boys are afraid to tackle the big questions."

"Easy, peasy." Mike smiled back at him. "Badger's logic really falls down."

"Hey, don't be so certain. Badger has a first class scientific brain. Bit rough yet but it will come."

"Oh Phil, for heaven's sake. Badger's not an atheist." Phyllis scraped her chair back and stood.

"Yes he is," Mike said. "He doesn't believe in God but I'm going to convert him."

"Mike, honey, there are very few real atheists. Badger's not one of them." She smiled condescendingly. "Just saying 'I don't believe in God' doesn't make you an atheist. Badger has never been exposed to Christ's teachings. He has never studied religion in any way."

"And why should he? He doesn't believe in it."

Phil was nettled that his son couldn't see the simple reasoning in Phyllis's statement. Surely he was smarter than that. "You can't reject an hypothesis unless you first study it," he said. "Simple scientific process — state the hypothesis, perform an experiment to gather evidence, prove or disprove the theory — haven't you learned that in your physics or chemistry classes?"

"Yeah, good point Dad. He's always yipping on about empirical this and evidence that. I'll try it out on him."

"What about love, beauty?" Phyllis said, almost leering at him. "Am I not beautiful? Do you not love me passionately? How do you gather evidence to prove they exist Dr. Smith?"

"Mom!"

Phil shifted uncomfortably and took a drink of coffee, swallowing slowly, averting his eyes. Still, he couldn't deny that surge of affection for this family. Debating the big issues over breakfast. He found himself smiling.

"Look at the time." Phyllis turned her wrist watch toward Mike. "Don't forget I doubled your lunch in case your experiment runs late."

"Badger says the bird doesn't show up until nearly sunset but he wants to be there early just in case. So don't wait supper for me."

Phyllis looked back toward Phil, her eyes staring widely at him. "Hear that Phil?"

"Eh?" *What was with the eyes now?* "Yes, Mike might be late for supper but I'll be on time. Meeting will be over by four at the latest."

"I love it when you're home early. Just the two of us then, for the afternoon. Maybe a late supper." Had her voice dropped an octave?

"Sure you're okay, Mom?"

"Never better honey."

Phil stood and slipped into his wind breaker. Phyllis followed him to the garage door. He turned to kiss her goodbye. She took his face in both her hands and planted a long squirming kiss on him. They pulled apart, both slightly breathless. Phillip stared for a moment. Surely not? No. She couldn't still be expecting that, from me?

"Gotta go Phyl, see you later."

"Oh yes." She winked again, dammit. "See you later." She gave his bottom a pat as he went out the door.

~

Phil caught himself whistling several times that morning, *Four Strong Winds* then *Paint It Black*. Fran, his Beam-Line Science Assistant, crept into his office and began singing it, much to his simultaneous delight and embarrassment. He was flicking through the power point slides one last time to polish them. Phil's hard x-ray beam line was working on protein crystal analysis. The Hungarians were the Primary Investors on this line and would be its primary user. Representatives from the Users' Advisory and Scientific Advisory committees would be at the presentation as well as the big hitters — Executive Director, Director of Operations and his own boss, Len Edwards, the Director of Research.

"Anything I can do for you?" Fran asked.

"No, thanks. I think I'm ready."

Fran put her hand on his shoulder. "Of course you're ready. I just meant . . . "

"Yeah, I know." He patted her hand. "I can't tell whether I'm more excited than nervous or vice versa. I think this could have a real impact on future research, not just the existing teams."

"Len, Mr. Edwards, told me it was a quantum-leap forward in the use of our light."

"He did? He used the words quantum leap?"

She smiled. "His exact words. You'll wow 'em this afternoon Phil."

She left, singing in what she thought was Mick Jagger's voice. Phil turned away from his computer screen and tipped his chair back.

> And God said, "Let there be light;" and there was
> light. And God saw the light was good.
> — Genesis 3,4

The sign hung prominently above his desk. He never tired of reading those words, even toyed with the idea of getting them in the original Hebrew. God, then light, then life. A simple yet unbreakable logical sequence. It wasn't, "possibly God, maybe light, likely life." It was unequivocal, no hedging. He liked that, but didn't necessarily believe it. Phyllis and Mike were much more confident of God than he was. Which was why he had the second sign made to hang below the first one.

> Easier Said Than Done
> — Phillip Smith, Canadian Light Source

Phyllis thought it was arrogant at best, possibly even blasphemous. It got a chuckle from most visitors; young

Badger thought it was pretty cool. But it was true; arrogance was irrelevant; pride was well down the list of emotions he felt when he contemplated his work here. He and a relatively small team created light. Not by rubbing two sticks together. They boiled electrons from atoms, tore the basic building blocks of earthly matter apart. They surfed those electrons on microwaves, charging them from two-hundred-and-fifty-thousand volts up to three-billion volts of cosmic energy. The cavorting electrons whipped round the booster ring controlled by dazzlingly accurate equipment that bent and sped them up to more than ninety-nine percent of the speed of light until, like magic, photons flew and light appeared.

Phil closed his eyes, seeing the gun, the rings, the magnetic controllers wiggling and bending his subatomic river into light. His breathing became long, slow and very deep. His lungs seemed to inflate to gigantic proportions before oozing air out. He breathed so deliberately that he could hear his pulse inside his ears. He felt his life, which came from light, which came from God. He smiled. Phillip Smith, paunchy, impotent, old-time hockey player also created light. His synchrotron made light appear from invisible nothingness. And what a light, millions of times greater than the sun's light. It was wondrous. It was God-like.

He would never say that out loud.

But he thought it. Oh, yes. He dreamed it and his heart beat it and his lungs breathed it. Phillip Smith said *let there be light*, and by holy, holy miracles, the electrons obeyed him and there was light. And he, Phillip Smith, saw that it was good.

He opened his eyes and turned back to his power point slides. This afternoon he would explain — no, he would wow — the others with that light. They would see inside protein crystals — life really — like they had never seen before. As Janos was fond of saying, "to understand life one must understand proteins." One of Janos's protein crystals, subjected to Phil's hard x-rays, diffracted enough understanding to unveil the fundamental process of biology, of life. And they could use that insight to improve, no, to make life.

He got up and closed his office door then faced the signs again. "Phillip Smith, then light, then life," he whispered. Blasphemy perhaps, but not arrogance or pride. He had simply stepped into God's chain reaction as a fellow creator. Not God, but God's partner. These were Phil's innermost precious thoughts. And he savoured them. Some days he actually felt the divine genius inside and was able to produce divinely elegant ideas. Other days he was dark, painted black, and barely capable of turning his computer on. Today he was divinely lit and he would illuminate his colleagues with energy to spare.

He took his lunch from his briefcase, slipped a CD into his computer and shut off the office lights. The screen saver cut in and flickered randomly colliding coloured lights from the monitor. Music floated from his speakers. He ate Phyllis's egg salad sandwiches. What in hell was she winking at him for this morning? No matter. She was happy, Mike was happy and he was divinely lit. Would Badger prove that God didn't exist? Phil smiled, flipped his tie over his shoulder to protect it from pickle juice and crunched into a dill.

~

Len Edwards phoned just after lunch. "Sorry Phil, we'll have to postpone."

"What? No, don't Len. I'm all ready to go."

"Not cancel Phil." Len's voice grew an edge. "Don't go all defensive on me. Just postpone. I want this to go as well as you do."

*No you don't.* Phil's inner voice nearly escaped his mouth. *You're not the maker of God's Light. How could you understand?*

"Postpone till when? And why?"

"Hungarians got an urgent one from Budapest. Funding crisis of some kind."

"But they had their twenty-percent user funding in place a year ago. I saw the Memo of Understanding myself," Phil interrupted.

"I know, and Janos says it is just a miscommunication. He is certain he can sort it out but he has to get on it right now."

Janos Teleki: impudent, moustachioed, cavalry bastard. Perfect.

"And I didn't want to start you late or cramp the presentation. I want their full attention. It is only fair to them and you to reschedule. I've told Janos to come see you about it. Then you get Fran to rebook everyone."

Janos Teleki would come to see me. Pretend an apology. Reschedule, so what? So what if the new meeting came on a black day and not a light day? What if he wasn't divine on that new day? What if Phyllis started sighing again or Mike wore a long leather coat full of guns to school. It was all so unpredictable. So lacking empirical verification.

"Phil, you there?"

"Yes, sure. Bit disappointed Len. Ready to go but no sweat. I'll see Janos then let you know what we come up with."

Phil replaced the phone onto its cradle very deliberately, trying to keep the blackness from seeping out to smother his light. He was only partly successful. His divine inner sun was setting. His breath came shallow and rapid and a sour bile taste rose to the back of his tongue. He couldn't hear his pulse any longer. The dark was pushing back the light and that was tamping down his life. He closed his eyes and breathed deeply, fought back. Get Fran to jazz up some of the PowerPoint slides — he'd still wow them.

Tap, tap on the door. He ignored it. Tap, tap, tap. He turned to face Janos grinning and waving outside the office window. Behind and below the Hungarian, the south end of the ring bent into view. Phil opened the door and stepped out onto the walkway that ran the length of the mezzanine level of offices. Janos put his hand out, certain that North American men shook each time they met. Phil took it and Janos immediately clasped both his hands over Phil's hand and wrist.

"My most sincere apologies, Phillip. I was most anxious to hear your most excellent presentations today." His eyes actually moistened.

Phil retrieved his hand and backed up, reaching for the railing. He leaned against it. Hungarian Cavalry looked ready to start hugging. Phil crossed his arms over his chest.

"I understand it was unavoidable," he offered.

"Damn all the accountants and auditors!" Janos declared passionately. "They count all the beans, find a few missing, then threaten to stop the science of light. And the horror Phillip." He advanced — Phil shrank against the railing. "The horror is that there are no beans missing. They have lost my last report complete with all necessary wouchers but somehow it is now Janos Teleki's problem. Their incompetence, my fault."

"So can you straighten it out?"

"Yes, yes. We will get on the telephone and email and make it right. But I am so anxious to see your new technique presented. From what you have shown me already it could result in a gigantic leap forward. It actually hurts." He thumped his fist against his chest. "In here, dear Philip, to postpone today."

Phil's divine light fluttered up warmly inside. How could you dislike the guy? It would work out, of course.

"So we could reschedule . . . ?"

"Name the day. Anytime. Just not this afternoon, my friend."

Phil smiled. "Fine. I'll get Fran to contact the others and let you know what she arranges."

"Oh Fran. She is essential to the light team. How could we proceed without her, eh?"

Phil smiled again.

"Are all Canadian women so fine? I refer, of course, to your most excellent Phyllis. You are so lucky to have such a woman." Janos smoothed the tips of his moustache. Phil blushed. "At what does she work? I am sure she is good at her work, whatever it may be."

"She works part-time at the University Hospital. Used to be a fulltime nurse — neurology — but now she works the ward on a job share. Days only, really convenient for us."

"Neurology, fascinating. Why does she go part-time?"

"Stayed at home to raise our son and just got back with this part-time opportunity about four years ago." Phil shrugged, feeling like he was talking to a friend.

"Best of both worlds. Home and mother yet also important work. Excellent." Janos clapped Phil on the shoulder. "Every weekend can be, ah, your expression again?" He paused, thinking. "Yes, a long weekend. Mondays and Tuesdays off. Most excellent."

"We are lucky. Our son is turning out . . . "

"Sorry," Janos interrupted, shooting his wrist out and consulting his watch. "I am always apologizing it seems today.

But it is already night in Hungary so I must dash to talk to the bookkeepers." He grabbed Phil's hand and wrung it. "Good day, Phillip Smith."

And he was gone. Phil waved then dropped his hand. How silly. He faced the ring, sensing the energy pulsing through it, following the electron stream in his mind's eye and imagining its hard x-rays suddenly diverted off the ring and down a beam-line tube. The light in the tube now like an offshoot of a brilliant pinwheel racing to the hut at the end of the line to illuminate life for the scientists crouched there. He felt himself to be a streaking comet inside the ring. "Fly the son of a bitch, Phil," he said quietly to himself. "Fly it." He dipped and swooped his shoulder to follow his eye. Then he looked up, cleansed and happy.

He strolled down to the canteen, got an EatMore and Coke then climbed back up to the office platform. He gave the news to Fran who commiserated and promised to get the meeting back on as soon as possible. He rested his forearms on the railing, sipping his coke and nibbling the chocolate bar. He watched a man washing the second-story windows on the far side of the ring. A row of white CLS vans sat in the lot just outside the windows. Janos Teleki was crossing the lot, keys dangling from his hand as he made for the last van in the line.

Janos Teleki was on the phone to Budapest. But no, he wasn't. He had lied. A logic path assembled itself in Phil's mind. Janos didn't know anything about Phyllis's job — yet he did. "What do you call them — long weekends. Monday and Tuesday off." He doesn't know her job but he knows she gets Mondays and Tuesdays off. Phyl didn't need the car because she would be home alone all day. Wink. "Are all Canadian women so fine?" Smoothing moustaches. Burgers and tips and leers. Wink.

Phil had the keys to the Research van in his hand and was running down the stairs, still clutching the EatMore in his other hand. Phyl's smirking breakfast face came back to him. "Lonely housewife," he said bashing the exit door bar. "No wonder she's not sighing." He was halfway to the parking lot when he stopped abruptly. "Can't be," he said, staring at the keys. She loved four-eyed, old-time hockey players with manly paunches. She was the centre of his contentment and happiness and love. She wouldn't jeopardize that for a roll with some smarmy Euro trash . . . well, Janos wasn't that either. He was likeable but even so, not Phyllis. She'd never betray him, despite her sighing absence of physical love. And what about Mike? She couldn't betray him.

Janos' van swung onto Perimeter Road and pulled away. Definitely conflicting evidence. Definitely not on the phone to Budapest. Phyllis — no sighs and home alone. He hurried forward. This was easy. Just go find out. Simple experiment to test the highly unlikely hypothesis — prove it wrong — then not worry.

Back-end fishtailing, he shot out of the parking lot and onto Perimeter Road. Janos was turning right onto Preston well ahead of him. Phil squashed the gas pedal down. Strangely, there was no darkness. Potential anger, oh yes. Sweet, curious streams of it dammed up and waiting to either burst loose or subside. He breathed deeply and heard his pulse. He would shine a light on this sliver of life.

# CHAPTER 4

TELEKI'S VAN WAS GONE. PHIL HAD THE whole next stretch of Preston Avenue in sight and there simply was no white CLS cargo van on it. Slippery bugger, where could he have turned off? No matter, Phil knew where he was going and set course for home. Minutes later, he pulled into Brookdale Crescent. Hugging the curb he slowly cruised round the semicircle of bi-levels and stopped when his own piece of suburbia hove into sight. He killed the engine and clicked the seat back so his line of vision scarcely cleared the dashboard. Phillip Smith's eyes flickered across the window, front door and empty sidewalk then focused back onto the front door. Would it open to admit Janos Teleki into the bored, lonely housewife's home? His home. His blissful happy home. That bliss light would escape and a black vacuum would succeed it. He'd see to that. His eyes watered, but they did not blink. Phil lost track of time and space. For a physicist whose life's work is time and space, he cast it aside quite easily.

〜

"A rare treat this day," Badger said, opening the sliding door and pulling his backpack out. He puckered his cheeks and produced a startling burble of meadowlark song that fountained up then flowed away. Mike clapped. "Male larks have twelve different song variations, clever boys." Badger made a small bow then slipped into the pack and picked a tripod out of the van.

Mike drew the spring air into his lungs and held it there. Salad-green grass and fresh tree leaves all warmed by the afternoon sun — he could almost taste them. "It is a rare treat, this day," he said. "God's gift to us."

"Yeah, and after today you may regret all that time wasted on HE who isn't there."

Mike pulled his own pack from the van and put it on. "Think again son. I'll save you a pew, right up front and you can book the confessional for a couple of hours next Saturday. God does exist and He'll want a full list of all your sins. Man, the penance you're in for."

"Talk is cheap, choirboy."

"Altar boy."

"Whatever. Let's get set up."

Mike followed Badger down a trail trampled through knee-high grass. As they descended from the roadway the traffic noise faded. The bottom of the ravine held a serpentine creek, clear in the straight sections, choked with willows and cat tails on the wide side of the turns. Reaching its bank they turned east and followed its flow for nearly a kilometre as it wound away from the tarmac seeking to empty itself into the river. Mike edged around a sharp twist in the trail to discover that Badger had vanished. He hurried forward to the next turn, no Badger. Instinctively, he dropped to one knee and searched the path up and down. No tracks in the damp earth before him. Only his own behind him. He back-tracked to where there were two sets. But Badger's boot prints disappeared abruptly. He stopped, puzzled. Badger must have jumped straight up and out of sight.

The low branches of a squat maple growing beside the trail swept open as though hinged. Badger stood, holding a large screen made of thin wood lattice covered in sacking with skinny maple branches woven through it. Mike stepped through, trying not to look too impressed and Badger closed the door behind him. Heavier branches curved above them, willow grew thickly to the left and the great fat maple trunk guarded their right. They stood upon a circle of dry, packed earth. To their front lay the creek, fringed with grass. The hideaway possessed a perfectly clear view of the water, the far bank and the rising wall of the ravine beyond the bank. Blue sky edged the top of the ravine, delineated by the sagging posts and drooping barbed wire of an old fence.

"What do you think?"

"It's great — perfect cover." Mike turned 360 degrees, marvelling at the hide.

"It gets better." Badger lifted a green tarp from the base of the tree and retrieved two, khaki canvas camp-stools. He opened them up, set the tripod in front of them and began rummaging in his backpack eventually producing a digital camera and lenses. He fitted the camera to the tripod. Next came a small tape recorder wrapped in green duct tape. He set it on a rock in the grass fringe by the creek.

"Ready for Mr. Lark of the Meadow." He rubbed his hands, settling himself on a stool and rolling up his shirtsleeve. "Let's get a bench mark."

"If only Vanessa could see us now, eh?" Mike said, unzipping the BP monitor case.

"She'd get a gun and open fire. 'Terminal geek disease' — I think is her expression — merits the death penalty." Badger smiled. "But she is pretty hot. Best not think of her or I'll skew the readings."

Mike wrapped the cuff around Badger's arm and pressed the auto button. The machine hummed air into the cuff, paused and slowly breathed out.

"Too noisy for the birds?"

"Naw, nice breeze coming over the ravine should mask it. They won't spook." Badger touched the cuff. "What'd I get?"

"118 over 75, very good." Mike noted it and took another reading. "120 over 75." He took Badger's wrist and timed his heart rate. 96. Mike dug out Phyl's lunch and they split it, eating in companionable silence.

Preparation for a long watch often produces a short one. The bird arrived before the boys had even finished the snack. He settled on top of a fence post just opposite the hide. Badger got the binoculars out and confirmed him as an old bird — the frustrated male. He passed the binoculars to Mike who was unaccountably excited by the lark's appearance. He adjusted the glasses and the bird leapt into focus. Bright yellow upper breast but noticeably faded toward the lower belly and legs. It hopped so that the westering sun caught it full on one side and craned its neck as though seeking the warmth of the sunlight. His black, V-necklace glinted. He had come and Mike felt his heart patter not unlike the night he'd watched Cindy in the moonlight. The tape recorder clicked and Badger leaned back on his stool, obviously relaxing himself — cheater. Mike lowered the glasses and picked up the BP machine just as the first who-who-are-you flute-song fluttered across the creek.

Mike tracked the inflections. One series higher toned then two lower. Their world shrank down to the leafy theatre box occupied by the human beings and the vertical wood stage occupied by the feathered opera singer. Mike found his eyes half closing to the melody — his breathing stopped at the song, then resumed between choruses. He floated in a green somnolent state. Badger's finger touched his arm. Mike twitched, startled, then realized he hadn't activated the BP monitor. He hit the start button and carefully noted the results. 130 over 73. He waited for another aria to start then hit the machine again. 138 over 76. Taking Badger's wrist he counted a ten-second beat and multiplied by 6 to get 144. *How about that! God does exist.* He maintained a calm face. One more reading — 132 over 76 — then removed the cuff.

<hr />

"The damn cuff was on so long it probably backed up blood in my arteries. It was pounding to get through before the bird even showed."

Mike smiled, waving the notebook at Badger. "Empirical evidence. Trying to spin it won't work. The birdsong did not reduce either BP or heart rate. There was no stress reduction, no biological benefit."

Badger was not meeting his eye. He concentrated on the camera, reviewing the shots he'd taken of the meadowlark.

"In fact, you enjoyed the beauty of that bird so much your BP and heart rate shot up."

"Mild increase." Badger shoved his jaw out, obstinately refusing to admit defeat.

"SHOT up, I say. Proves your love for beauty and nature is a genuine emotion and does not make you healthier. Face it Badger, you took stress for the pure joy of it."

"That's it!" Badger set the camera down. "Good stress!"

"Aw, come on."

"NO. Seriously. There is such a thing, physiologically beneficial too."

"Then the experiment was a fraud," Mike protested. "No matter which way it went you have it rigged to win."

"I admit the experiment might prove something else exists — besides instinct."

"Such as?"

"Such as when I look into the other world I also admit that there is something different. Makes me feel like we're not alone, that there is some kind of, I don't know. A *plan* I guess."

"Other world?"

Badger spread his arms. "This. The others. Fartley Mowat coined that phrase. You could throw a rock from here and hit a carbon-belching car on the road, but right here among us, these others are still wild. Still alive. Not tame and arrogant like us." Badger knelt and pulled back some grass at the edge of the clearing. Ants trickled out. "These guys building shelter, finding food, reproducing." A grasshopper flung itself into the air. "Meadowlarks will hunt and eat him, then look for a mate and nest and create young and this fall migrate a thousand kilometres . . . ."

He stopped. He face burned red. "Uh-oh. Pretty sick, eh?"

Mike tucked the notebook into his pocket and cleared his throat. "I suppose not." He was close now. As close as he'd ever been to taking that final step of friendship, of bonding. He didn't need buddies. He needed contacts but Badger had crossed the line, waiting for him to cross over and meet. He could kid himself that it would only be a calculated move to keep Badger under control. But really, he was going to cross a line if this went further. The awkward moment stretched long. Mike looked at his friend, wanting to relieve the embarrassed tension, tell him it was a good thing to be a biology nerd. That he was safe as his friend. But he didn't. He somehow could not.

"Hey look! Here they come!" Badger darted to the edge of the creek. "Watch this, check this!"

Relieved, Mike stepped to Badger's shoulder and peered up the creek. "What?"

"There, just above the water, look at 'em come!"

Two dark-winged shapes skimmed the surface of the creek — their reflections racing just inches below them. First one, then the other straightened their wings and heeled over in a forty-five degree turn that shot them toward a cluster of cattails.

"Whoa!" Mike yelled, recoiling, certain they would crash. There was no airspace visible between themselves and the heavy brown cat tail knobs when both birds flipped over almost on their backs and cut clear, leaving one head swaying in their wake, fluff swirling in the turbulence. The birds rose, flapped hard then dove to the water, accelerating like small jet fighters on a bombing run. They levelled off just as they went by the hideaway, wingtips leaving tiny ripples on the water.

"Fly!" Badger shouted, his voice rowdy as a hockey fan. "Fly boys! Go on — go on!"

Mike involuntarily bellowed as the red breasts and dark heads flashed by not a metre from him. He was actually looking down on the two racers. They banked hard right, then left, then right again around a bend in the creek — gone.

"Those are two crazy robins." Badger leaned out over the water. "Watch now, they'll likely be back in a minute."

"They will?"

"Oh yeah — these two are nuts. Some kind of male dominance racing game. I got to know them about a week ago — seen them do this four or five times."

"You . . . know them?" Mike looked at Badger's face. Expectant, dark eyes lit, tip of his tongue wetting his lips.

"Yes, sure I know them. They'll be back, just . . ." He jabbed his arm downstream. "Here they come."

If possible, the robins flew even lower and in tighter formation, performing feats of airmanship and daring. Just as they reached the hideout, they came up over the bank, air thrumming through their flared wing-feathers as they careened bare centimetres from the maple trunk. Mike ducked, arms over his head as the two brown backs disappeared upstream.

"I'll have to get you to introduce me to your friends."

Badger grinned, shouldering his backpack and collapsing the chairs under the tarp. "Come on — they might be surfing — you gotta see this."

Mike stuffed the BP machine in his own pack and followed Badger — running as fast as they could down the creek-side path. They splashed through muddy dips and ploughed up small hillocks, panting and laughing — racing each other — leaping and elbowing for first place. Mike's runners skidded on a greasy patch of clay and he went down, sliding on his right hip — left shoe ankle deep in the creek. Badger crowed and raced on, Mike in hot pursuit. The ravine sank deeper now into the prairie, trees and roots and low-hanging branches slowed their pace. Finally Badger pulled up.

"Here. Look over there. Open spot on the coulee," he gasped.

The coulee wall facing them was tall — ten metres high — nearly vertical, and patchy with grass and open gravel where the face had slid into the creek.

"Wind funnels along the ravine, hits that wall and goes straight up on days like this. Robins ride it like an elevator sometimes."

Sweat prickled between Mike's shoulder blades and beaded on his hairline. A collection rolled suddenly down his forehead and caught in his eyebrow. His breath sounded full and heavy in his throat. Something was going to happen to him. He felt it but couldn't say exactly what it was. A robin flew up the creek, just above the surface again, but alone. It banked hard toward the face of the coulee then seemed to stand on its tail. The wings arched back, fully extended, red breast thrusting forward. Its sturdy head lifted and one dark eye found Mike's eye as the bird strained — its breath full in its throat and breast. Then up, like a rocket, spiralling lazily fifty, a hundred metres, maybe more into the blue sky, riding the updraft.

Mike craned his neck, felt his own breast swell, felt his own eye turn dark as his body seemed to spiral with the bird. The second robin appeared, soaring high in the wake of the first one. Mike felt the wind — spring fresh and full of poplar smell — it fanned his sweaty face. And he felt the pull of wings, the sudden giddy spinning ascension.

"My God. My God," he said, sitting down and looking away so Badger couldn't see his face.

~

"Might as well go up the old access road and walk back to the car from there rather than climb all the way back up the creek bed." Badger led them a few metres further down the ravine to where a wrecked culvert angled its rusty twisted rim out of the water, pointing at overgrown tracks graded into the side of the coulee. They started up, climbing quietly, then turned a switchback. The road was screened by trees here and rose on a much more gradual line to the top. Halfway between them and the top, a white Chev utility-van sat stationary in the track.

"CLS — Canadian Light Source," Badger read the decal on the rear door. "Your dad's work. What's it doing here?"

Perhaps it was the experience with the birds or perhaps it was his own instinct to spy but Mike knew that the van was wrong, implausibly out of place here in the wild. He put a finger to his lips, quietly shushed Badger, and led him into the fringe of trees by the road.

"Get your camera ready," he whispered. "We'll come up on the blind passenger side. Stay wide of the wing mirrors, quick approach then camera in the back window."

Badger uncased the camera, turned it on and took a test squint before giving Mike a thumbs up. "What do you think it is?"

Mike shook his head. "Could be anything from a slacker taking a nap on company time right up to selling stolen scientific equipment."

"Us? Bust a stolen goods ring?" Badger's eyes flickered to the van. "Excellent. Far out excellent. Let's do it."

"Okay," Mike snapped. "Follow me. Hand signals only." He let the espionage excitement in — why not — just for a minute, until they found a snoring technician. Besides, it would be valuable to gauge Badger's performance on a tricky stalk. Bent like paper clips they weaved carefully through the trees till they were opposite the passenger door. Mike lay down, Badger dropped like a stone beside him. Mike rose up on his elbows, motioned for Badger to stay put, then crawled on his belly to the road fringe. He did a slow push-up, then tucked one knee under his chest and rose, peeked across the door windows and dropped flat. Nobody in the front of the van. He rose again, confirmed his first sight, then waved Badger forward.

Badger appeared silently at this side. He glanced at his friend: flushed face, quick heavy breaths, but eyes focused on the van, camera hand calm. Perfect. Badger was just perfect. Mike rose and walked quickly to the side of the van, Badger at his hip pocket. They pressed themselves up against the paneling. Mike made a circular movie-camera motion and pointed to the back of the van. Whoever, whatever, they were about to discover was there. Badger should be able shoot through the back windows for several long seconds before they would be noticed and have to run for it.

"Oh, God Almighty, that's good. I can't wait anymore." A woman's voice.

"But you must not rush it, dear girl." A man's voice, accented.

"It's now or never, I can't wait . . . let me get up," the woman said. The van rocked slightly, tactile against Mike's back. A series of heavy, quick steps followed.

"That's it. Now we go. Without worries or holding back," the accent declared loudly. The van shook rhythmically. Badger squealed with suppressed laughter and darted toward the back window.

"No!" Mike hissed, grabbing his arm. "We're not Peeping-Tom perverts." He had to speak out to be heard over the thumping protestations of ecstasy.

"Oh, please man, just a few seconds."

Mike propelled Badger back to the trees.

"But it's misuse of company property. Not as bad as a heist but we should still tell your dad."

Mike dragged him up the road toward the top of the ravine. Badger was not perfect, but really, it was only a small amateurish flaw. Never waste resources on an operation that couldn't produce useful intelligence. A spying amateur sex movie was not on Mike's list of useful intelligence.

~

Mike leaned on the open fridge door, peering inside. "How about fried egg sandwiches?"

"On it." Badger dug the frying pan out from the bottom cupboard. Mike passed him butter and four eggs then began cutting bread.

"I still think we should have videoed them." Badger twisted the pan to spread melting butter. "Meadowlark calling for its mate — then humans actually mating." He cracked the first egg into the pan. "A biologic sequence observed natural and unscripted in the wild."

"All right, enough already." Mike poured milk into two large glasses.

"Groundbreaking video. National Geographic-level stuff but gone now." Badger salted and peppered the eggs. "Never recapture a moment like that. Probably way better than Swedish Spanish Fly marshmallow thingies."

Badger expertly dipped the pan and manoeuvred the eggs onto a spatula, flipping them in rapid succession. A streak of riverbank mud clung to his shirt sleeve. His eyes never left the task as he talked to the eggs. Mike was free to watch his movements. The thought of dumping Badger before he could intrude as a close friend surfaced again. But now it came to him as a stranger — illogical and foreign. Badger was his friend and he was Badger's. It was a state of being, and he felt no need to change it. He smiled at the thought and freed an impulse that only an hour ago he'd suppressed.

"Hey, the other world is good. I mean, I'm happy with it. I don't find it weird at all."

"So God doesn't exist?" Badger said quietly, shifting the eggs across the pan. They lifted and flapped in the bubbling butter.

"Oh God exists. I just wanted to say that being a biology nerd is actually cool — especially compared with pretending to be a spy." This last thought surprised him. Badger's face turned up now and his dark bird eyes settled on Mike. They watched each other unblinking. Mike found he was holding his breath, having just leaped off the diving board and now desperately hoping there was still water in the pool.

"Yeah. Good point. Except you are a spy, man. No pretending. That stolen goods turned cheap sex thing was excellent." He poked Mike with the spatula. "Still should have let me photograph them."

Mike smiled and held the bread up. They folded the eggs up in the slices and stood side by side over the sink, eating.

"Glad your mom wasn't home," Badger said. Yolk escaped his sandwich and plopped yellow into the stainless-steel sink. "This is the best, eh? Fried-egg sangies hand-to-mouth."

Mike nodded. "I don't know what's up with her. She was weird at breakfast. All giggly about being home all day — car's in the shop — bored housewife and ... "

"Hey! Check this out! It's the van." Badger leaned over the sink, nearly pressing his forehead to the kitchen window. A white Chev utility-van crept down the alley. The top half of the CLS decal showed above the Smith's back fence. It slowed, hesitated, lurched forward, then stopped. The passenger door opened and Phyllis Smith stepped down. She slammed the door, waved to the dark silhouette inside and slipped through the gate. The van's engine surged and it hurried down the alley out of sight. Phyl walked rapidly across the back yard and a moment later her key snicked in the lock. She stepped into the kitchen, closed the door and yelped at the unexpected sight of two boys, cheeks smeared yellow, staring at her.

"Oh my goodness, you gave me a fright." She pulled her cardigan, wrapping it tightly around herself. "I thought you would be out till dark."

"Got done early, Mom," Mike said, then took another bite of sandwich to fill his mouth rather than let it say more.

"That's good." She avoided his eyes. "I would have made you a proper supper."

"That's okay, Mrs. S. Got all our protein here," Badger said. "That, uh, Mr. S in the van there?"

Phyllis shot to the cupboard and began pulling dishes out to set the table. "Saw us did you? Yes, that was Phil. My car is in the garage and I simply had to get into work for an hour and he had the company van."

She scattered dishes over the table. "Here, come and sit down. I'll get you some cake."

She herded them to the table. "But you know Phil, Dad, doesn't want the neighbours seeing him use CLS vehicles for personal errands so he had to come down the alley."

"Oh yeah, I can see that," Badger said. "Covert op."

"What? Never mind. I'm off to the bathroom, back in a sec with your cake." She fled the kitchen. Badger sat. Mike chewed slowly, trying not to believe what he knew to be true. Badger fidgeted and put his sandwich in a bowl Phyllis had laid out.

"Hoo, boy. Some coincidence, eh? Your mom and dad out in a van — same time as . . . you know."

"Wasn't Dad in the van. Mom's sweater was inside out."

"What?"

"The tag." Mike touched the back of Badger's neck. "On her sweater was facing out."

"So she put her sweater on backwards leaving for work — in a hurry, like she said." Badger tried, gamely.

"No. It's fine. I caught the profile of the guy in the van — had a big moustache and maybe beard, no glasses — not Dad. It was my mom and that . . . person . . . in the ravine. Might as well face it. We just have to figure out what to do about it. Get some hard evidence then stop her? Or tell dad?"

He shrugged, his voice betrayed nothing of the boiling in his gut. His eye went to Badger's camera on the kitchen counter. Badger followed it.

"We?"

Mike tried to order his thoughts and failed. But one thing stood clear and certain against the chaos in his mind. Badger was in this with him. And it was the only comfort he could touch just now.

~

"So, God exists or not?" Phil tried to muster some enthusiasm for the debate, for Mike's sake.

"He exists." Mike kept his eyes fixed on the TV. He was watching but not seeing the program. Phil often did it himself. Home improvement shows with Phyl usually failed to penetrate his consciousness. But he liked her curled up, leaning into his chest with his arm wrapped around her shoulders. He could really let his thoughts free to roam anything from the light beam to that cancelled hockey game last December. If only they had been able to find some spare ice time to make up the game. He might have had a twenty-goal season. It didn't matter. Just being with Phyl was one thing that guaranteed contentment. Except Mike wasn't content; he was thinking but not happy. How did he know that? Fatherly instinct? Phil didn't fit that profile and he knew it.

Dishes clattered in the kitchen, Phyllis loading the dishwasher after their supper. A supper of silent, belly-eating guilt on his part. A supper of bubbly, lovely, gibberish on her part — as though they had just shared a long lazy Saturday with each other. She hadn't even noticed his tension. He'd noted the time when he'd pulled back onto Perimeter Road. Two hours spent spying on his innocent wife. Two hours waiting to see decent, friendly Janos Teleki not betray him. Two hours that were so strangely wrong and now difficult to even remember. Then back to work in a foul mood of unrequited revenge against a non-existent enemy. A snapping rudeness to Fran had added regret to his misery. A day that had started so clean and bright to end so dismally. And to cap it, a sullen son contemplating who knew what? Overwhelmed, Phil dropped onto the couch beside Mike and flicked his own eyes onto the TV. He should be light and happy but he wasn't. He was ashamed of himself. He needed something to keep the dark from coming and it was coming on hard now.

"All right, Dad?"

"Eh?" Mike had muted the TV. "Oh, yeah. Good, good. Just wondered how the meadowlark thing went."

"I was proved right, but as usual Badger tried to spin the rules."

"Badger wouldn't do that." Phil found himself studying Mike's face. A face that very rarely showed anything but a mask of indifference. But not now. Mike was nervous. Lip-licking, eye-glittering, nervous-coughing distracted. His son, the iron-faced boy, was letting it show. Phil wanted to know what it was. Perhaps he had a father's instinct after all. Mike wasn't concerned about the experiment, or Badger, or maybe even God for that matter. There was something to be learned from his son. Maybe something that would protect him from the shame of his mean suspicion of a Phyllis/Teleki liaison that spiralled him down. "Badger's science is pretty good. Are you sure he's not just interpreting the data differently?"

Mike stared at him and coughed. Lord above, for his son to clear the nerves from his throat twice in as many minutes, well, it must be something important.

"What is it Mike? It's not the experiment is it?"

Mike shook his head. "Nothing really, Dad. We got home early and made sandwiches in the kitchen and were eating them over the sink when one of your CLS vans drove down the back alley and I was thinking it might be yours but it ah . . . didn't pull in or . . . you know, just curious, you know. You're always worried about private use of company resources. Or whatever." It came in a rush and ended breathlessly. "Curious, about one of your vans in our back alley."

The back alley. What a fool he'd been to watch the front of the house. Teleki was too smart to come to the front door. Phil sat back, exhaling, no longer ashamed but shocked. Frightened. The streams of anger wanted out now; they'd apparently not gone away. Mike was waiting for an answer.

"Really? That is odd. Sure it was one of ours?" The clarity of his voice surprised him.

Mike nodded.

What did he know? Did he see Phyllis and the Hungarian hound together? Was he just curious or did Mike suspect something. No. Ridiculous. Mike lived in his own closed world. He'd be the last person to connect Phyl and Teleki.

"No reason for it to be here, then?" Mike probed, calmer now. "I thought maybe it was here to drop something off for you — or maybe you were in it."

"No. Nothing to do with me, son." Phil blurted out the truth before he could get his thoughts caught up with his mouth. Damn! He should have said it was his van — he had forced Mike to think farther. But now he had to know. Had Mike seen Phyllis and Teleki? If not them, then who or what had he seen? He looked away at the silent TV screen, then forced a smile as he turned back to Mike.

"I'll check on it tomorrow. Did you see who was driving?" Mike was gone. In his place was the deadpan mask — his own son playing the same game as he was.

"No. couldn't see inside." He clicked the TV volume up and returned to the program. "One thing that was really different today, Dad. I saw robins fly like jet fighters."

"Eh? What's that?" Phil tried to stay with Mike but his mind was full of the CLS van in his own back alley.

"Badger showed me. These two robins." Mike's hands curved through the air. "They flew like crazy daredevils. Badger sees them like a whole different world coexisting with ours . . . " His voice trailed off.

Strangely, the darkness was receding. It must have been Teleki in the van with Phyllis. He let the jealousy light up and burn. No more doubt — just evidence — data collection really. He'd figure out what to do about it later. Right now he needed proof. One more glance at Mike's serene face. At least he was spared this mess, thank God for that.

∽

Mike let the TV light ebb and flow across his face. It was soothing, almost like watching a fire. His father wasn't lying — that was certain — no clue about the van in the alley. God, he'd nearly lost it with Phil there a few minutes ago. Different when it's your own mom and dad, bound to be. He thought he'd had a pretty good game face but Phil's innocence had unsettled him. Well, put that in its place for future consideration. His own duty was clear now. He had to get proof of Phyllis cheating then decide what was best. Right now shattering Phil's innocence didn't seem like the best option. Using the intelligence to scare Phyllis straight would likely be the best approach.

Mike closed his eyes for a moment and Badger's face appeared. Badger would definitely know how to handle this. He smiled. Never thought the day would come when the handler would have to rely on the agent for direction. But this was hardly an ordinary op. He opened his eyes and glanced at his father, slumped on the couch inches away yet completely lost in his own thoughts. Probably dreaming up new ways to create light or score goals. At least Dad was spared this mess.

~

The phone rang and Phyllis answered. "Janos! Hello. Yes, he was disappointed but I'm sure he doesn't blame you. Friday night? No we having nothing on." She giggled. "Just an expression. We will be fully clothed."

She chuckled again. "It means we have no prior appointments. Oh, that's not necessary . . . "

"That's very thoughtful of you Janos . . . "

Mike listened with studied indifference. Janos? Friday? Could he be the one? He looked across to Phil. No change in expression. Phil suspected nothing of course. Mike went up to his bedroom and opened his notebook. Janos who? Friday night? he scribbled.

# CHAPTER 5

"GREAT NEWS PHYL! WE'VE GOT ICE FOR Friday night!"

"Tomorrow?"

"Yeah, and a chance for my fifty-point season."

Phil hurried through the living room, dropping his briefcase on the couch and wheeled into the kitchen. Phyllis was sitting at the kitchen table with a cup of tea in hand and frowning at an open cookbook. She glanced up.

"Ice? Oh, good. Do we need it?" She smiled vaguely and returned her attention to the cookbook.

"Need it?" Phil spread his arms wide. "Honey, we crave it — we lust for it — we've gone so long without it!"

Phyllis looked up again. "You're not talking about ice cubes for drinks tomorrow night?" She asked.

"Of course not." Phil unzipped his windbreaker and strode to her side. He knelt and clasped her hands reverently. "We are talking sacred ice; which is to say hockey ice."

"It's the first week of May, Phil, your league shut down over a month ago."

"Don't I know it. Nineteen goals and twenty-nine assists for yours truly. My best season ever. But get this; we wangled one more game tomorrow night against the SaskPower Team — bastards did a no-show last December remember?"

"Yes. I believe they were busy with trivialities like family Christmas, weren't they?" Phyl said dryly.

"Pussies. Knew we would crush 'em so they convinced the league to cancel instead of giving us the default win."

"Shocking corruption." Phyllis smiled up at him, humouring him. He loved that in her, when she indulged his crazy hockey enthusiasm.

"But the God of Hockey has smiled on us," he squeezed her hands. "The rink put ice back in yesterday for a hockey school that was supposed to start tomorrow night but it turns out they got the dates wrong — doesn't start till Saturday afternoon so they have open ice see?"

Phyllis' smile sagged. She pursed her lips into a sour crab apple expression. Phil climbed back to his feet ignoring it.

"So Budweiser gets wind of it, eh? He calls the league president and demands they cough up for one more night since we paid for that December game but never used it."

He pulled his jacket off and went to the hall closet shouting back over his shoulder. "Anyway, a lot of calls later he has the ice and a commitment from the 'SaskPower Sparks' — hah — should call themselves the SaskPower Farts." He giggled at this own light-headed joke. "Tomorrow night we get to strap on the blades again and . . . Geez, I shouldn't say it or I'll jinx it."

He returned to the kitchen using an imaginary hockey stick to swoop around a chair and backhand an imaginary puck at the fridge. "But wouldn't it be great if I got a goal to even out at twenty? Or an assist to hit thirty? Or both? Imagine, Phil Smith, a fifty-point season."

He stopped short at Phyllis's expression. He looked at the cookbook. *Fabulous Yorkshire Pudding — The Queen's chef tells all,* headed the page. Mike appeared behind him and pushed past to the fridge. "Nice shot, Dad — beat him on the stick side," said Mike. He pulled a juice box from the door shelf. Phyllis rigidly studied the magazine, ignoring his hockey moves. What was with her anyway? She usually laughed at his hockey talk. What was so important about that article? He looked over her shoulder. Yorkshire pudding. Oh yeah, and roast beef. For Teleki. That must be more interesting than his hockey game.

"I forgot, Phyl. Sorry." The light, bubbling and spurting inside him a moment ago now waned and cooled. Darkness crept up from his belly to push it aside. Friday night. In fact he had been brooding on it for two days now, dark and foul and angry every time he thought about it. But Budweiser's call had driven it from his mind and lit him up again. Janos Teleki wanted to take them to a Canadian steak dinner at the Keg as an apology for cancelling Phil's meeting. Phyllis had insisted he come to the house and bring some of his delicious Hungarian red wine. She would make him roast beef, Yorkshire pudding, mashed potatoes, the works. A real Canadian feast.

Phil stared at her, regretting the word sorry. In all likelihood that slime ball and Phyllis were ... at it. He couldn't bring himself to name the word. And here they were, bold as brass having a romantic red wine dinner in his own house, in front of him. By God, it was too much. She should damn well indulge his hockey obsession.

"Too bad. We'll have to postpone the Hungarian cavalry for another night."

Phyllis tapped her book. "Come on, be fair. You play hockey all winter and we schedule around it. It's spring — the Beer Caps can do without you."

"He cancelled my meeting. For no good reason I can think of." He glared fiercely at her and had the small satisfaction of seeing her blush. "So why not cancel him."

Phyl tried to meet his eye, but faltered. She went back to the Queen's Yorkshire pudding. "I know how badly disappointed you were, Phil. You have been like a grouchy bear and I've tried to see your side. But the meeting is set to go next week so surely . . . "

"So surely we can have the dinner next Friday. Let's say to celebrate." He bit the word celebrate off and spit it at her.

Phyllis rose silently and went to the wall near the kitchen window. She pressed one key and put the phone to her ear.

One key. Phil flinched. Teleki's number was entered on Phyllis' speed dial. He closed his eyes and forced himself to breath. How could she? Did she think he was stupid? No, she couldn't know he suspected her. Janos would have told her they were safe in a CLS van creeping down back allies. Mike pushed past him and ran up the half flight of stairs toward his bedroom, spilling juice on the way. Phil exhaled. Calm yourself. The time will come, but not now.

"Janos. Phyllis Smith here. Sorry to disturb you but I'm afraid I have a bit of bad news."

Her eyebrows pushed against each other and she fiddled nervously with the pad and pen attached to the phone base.

"As it turns out Phil has had something really important come up tomorrow evening so we'll have to postpone to next Friday, if you are free then."

She listened, biting her lower lip, staring at the floor.

"No, not his work exactly. Actually it's a very important playoff hockey game. You know Canadian men and their hockey." She forced a laugh.

"Yes. Oh, he told you the season was over? And that's true but this, um . . . " she looked to Phil, angry and hurt at being caught in the playoff lie. Then she brightened, smiling and turning her back to Phil. "You're so kind. Really, that is so very decent of you. Let me check."

She put her hand over the phone. "What time is your game?"

"We have the ice 8:30 to 10:00. Fifteen-minute warm-up then three straight-time twenty-minute periods. But I'm not going in late . . . "

She turned away from him again. "Perfect Janos. And again, thank you for being so understanding."

She put the phone back in the cradle and resumed her seat. She sipped her tea and studied the cookbook. "Yes, Queen's Yorkshire pudding should work nicely, I think."

"No problem then?" Phil asked.

"None. We'll have supper promptly at six pm tomorrow night. It seems Janos is dying to watch the 'Canadian Light Source Beer Caps' and is desperate to see you score a goal. So you can go at 8:00 to get ready, then Janos will take me at 8:45 and we'll watch the game together. Then we can all go out for drinks after."

Phil stared stupidly at her, knowing what would happen in his own home while he was putting his can and shin pads on at the rink.

"And," Phyllis' eyes glinted triumphantly. "Janos has insisted on taking us to the Keg next Friday to repay our generosity. Such a gent. The Old World sense of courtesy. Can't beat it, eh, Phil?"

Phil swallowed the fear and anger. Neither would go down. They surged up from his gut.

"So Smith gets his fifty-point season?" Mike was back, leaning against the dishwasher.

Phil nodded, then shrugged.

"I wouldn't mind seeing that myself." Mike smiled at him.

"Little roast beef wouldn't hurt either."

"But I thought you were going for pizza and a movie with Badger?" Phyl said. "And you never watch Dad's hockey."

"You never make Yorkshire pudding, and Dad getting fifty points doesn't happen every day, so Badger can wait." He grinned, almost challenging his mother.

"Great idea!" Phil sat heavily on the chair opposite Phyl. "Bring Badger to supper and the game if you like. You can all ride over with Dr. Teleki and Mom. Then you and Badger can have our car to come home after the game."

He looked to Phyl, expecting her protests. "Beef stretch to feed two young men?"

Strangely, she seemed relieved — happy even. "Sure. And Janos will get a kick out of Badger."

⌒

Mike watched his father stickhandle around the kitchen table and score on the fridge. He pulled a juice box from the fridge and turned to see the air go out of Phil. A tension between his parents leaped into the kitchen like an angry dog. He slipped to the side of the window and pretended to look into the backyard.

The next few minutes of Phil-and-Phyl-unplugged gave up a solid lead on the identity of the man in the van. Phyl's simpering schoolgirl delight at cooking for a scientist named Janos. Her disappointment about Friday. Her defence of Janos, then complete collapse when Phil challenged her about the cancelled meeting. It was strong stuff. His mom's lover was very likely Janos Teleki from CLS. The Beer Caps hockey team had unwittingly outed the bad guy.

Phyl went to the phone, punching one key. The guy was on speed dial! His mom had absolutely no spy-craft instinct whatsoever. The phone . . . Mike darted past Phil and went up the stairs two at a time. He slammed his bedroom door behind him and fumbled in his desk drawer for the headphones. He found them then quickly pulled the back cover off one of his stereo speakers. A tiny metal cassette case was mounted inside the speaker box. He jammed the earphone jack into the case.

" . . . then let me suggest an alternative my dear Mrs. Smith." The voice was strongly accented — eastern European, somehow familiar. The back of the van in the ravine, *we go now,* could be the same accent. "If you could manage an early beef and pudding dinner we could let Phillip go to his game. We follow later?" He paused. Was that a laugh? Mike strained to hear. "And watch the 'Beer Caps' gain an awesome victory. That would be greatly pleasurable to me and to you as well I think? And to repay you for cutting your dinner party short I insist on treating both of you to a great big steak with all fixings." His voice oiled the suggestion on her. "Next Friday."

"You're so kind." His mother gushed. "Really that is so very decent of you, let me check."

Mike could make out Phil's voice explaining the ice times. Then his mother came back. "Perfect Janos. And again, thank you for being so understanding."

Mike pulled the headphones off. Phil wouldn't suspect a thing. Phyl and Janos would be home alone for nearly an hour before the game. He could not make himself truly believe his mom would do this to his dad. *And,* he realized, *to me.* She was doing it to her son as well — her family. No, think, quickly now. "Sentiment later!" he said out loud. If, in fact, this Janos character was the culprit, he couldn't let this happen. Cancel Badger, stay home, go to the game. Then get evidence later. At least now he had a lead to watch for — that was something.

Mike checked his face in the mirror then went downstairs to save his mom from making a mistake — or another mistake. Was that it?

～

He hadn't eaten much for supper. Badger had agreed to the Friday meal and the game. Mike wanted a second set of eyes to watch Phyllis with Janos, see if Badger picked up on their collusion. If it was Janos cheating with Phyl then they could start a watch. But he needed a watch plan first. And for that he needed to think. Not at home. Not in proximity of his parents — too tough to stay focused and objective. He could use Arthur Guthrie's help on this.

He zipped his Guthrie glasses and hat into his backpack, announced he was going for a ride and slipped out the garage door. He accelerated down the crescent, leaning his bike into the curve at the end of the street. A quick shoulder check then he flew a semi-circle up onto Brookhurst and from there he weaved north and west toward 8th Street. A thick light from the setting sun cut nearly horizontal gold bands through the houses and trees. It flashed off his fenders and spokes, then disappeared in the shadows, then flashed again like a strobe light. His breathing came harder and he began a decade of the rosary in his head. *Hail Mary, full of grace, the Lord is with thee.* It ran in rhythm with his pedaling legs. Strong, clean, fresh. His bike seemed to float down the quiet pavement.

He finished the decade then: *Glory be to the Father and to the Son and to the Holy Ghost. As it was in the beginning it is now and ever shall be, world without end.* Perspective was everything, of course. The world, its beginning, without end. Our time was puny, insignificant. What we do with our time, now that is significant. He'd plan a watch, conduct it, gather evidence and bring Phyllis back into her family. *Amen.*

Mike popped a small wheelie up over the curb, coasted through the parking lot and dismounted near a steel guardrail. He chained his bike, put on the thick glasses and pulled a Yankees ball cap down close to his ears. He walked through the narrow gap between two buildings, turned right and entered the front door of the Greek Guys' restaurant. It was Thursday-night busy but there was a small table for two available near the kitchen door. He followed the host, a woman, dark skin, shiny black hair, very full figure. Late thirties but hard to tell in the dim light. She gave him a menu as he sat.

"Can I get you a coke? Ginger ale?"

Mike tipped his hat brim back and looked at her coolly, but said nothing. He opened the menu.

"Something to drink?" She prompted.

"Adele," he said, reading her name tag. "I think I'll have water for right now but I'll have a glass of wine with the meal."

She shifted her weight onto one foot.

"It's my first time for Greek food and I'm not certain of my ground." He said casually, John le Carré's intelligence officer, Smiley, in mind. "I'd like lamb but not sure if I should go with red or white. Perhaps you could . . . ?" He arched his eyebrows and raised the corners of his mouth into a condescending smile.

She leaned in closely, perfume subtle but present. A pudgy forefinger tipped in candy-apple-red fingernail polish tapped the menu. "I'd recommend the platter for one. And you might prefer iced tea with that."

He turned his face slowly, deliberately connecting with her dark eyes. She didn't blink. She wasn't going to back down. Excellent. A bit of a challenge. Mike Smith would have acquiesced and slipped into an iced-tea background. Mike Smith wouldn't even be here. He'd be at home in his room. Art Guthrie however could enjoy such an evening, relish it even. He extended his smile into a grin.

"Surely the Greek Guys don't drink tea with that."

She stayed close, not even flinching. "The Greek Guys are my brothers and they are both well over nineteen years of age. So they can have wine with heir meals." She smiled back at him. "They don't serve wine to minors, however."

"Admirable." Mike dropped his grin. "Why should any business risk its livelihood by serving liquor to minors, Adele."

She stood her ground, eyes now busy on his face. The longer the better, it was good practice. He held his Arthur Guthrie face quite well, keeping any underage nerves at bay.

"All right." She straightened up. "If you have decided on the platter then I can take your order. Would you like to reconsider the wine?"

"How can I?" Mike shrugged. "I still don't know what you recommend. Red or white? Sweet or dry?"

"Red, dry." She held her hand out. "But I'll need to see ID."

He complied with casual grace. "Of course."

She peered at the driver's license then at him. "I'm sorry, but I had to ask," she said stiffly.

"Adele." He returned the plastic card to his wallet. "No apology needed. I just finished finals — first-year Arts and Science done. So I'm treating myself. How are you supposed to distinguish between high-school senior and a U of S freshman?"

She pursed her lips as though swallowing a spoonful of sour medicine and left. He sat back satisfied. A Greek feast, a glass of red wine (that he wasn't really sure he'd like), and some long thoughts on watching Phyllis and Janos. So much more easily done as Arthur Guthrie.

Partway through the excellent meal, Mr. Garchinski came in with his wife and sat two tables over. She was young and pretty. Mike Smith was invisible to them. Art even got Adele to chit-chat, then pleased her with a twenty-percent tip on his Master Card before he left.

~

Budweiser stepped into the box, tipped his helmet back so the Bud, King-of-Beers-Crown decal stood on end. He shot water into his mouth from his bottle and spat it out.

"Pretty bad that the SaskPower Farts get more guys out to the game than the Canadian Light Source." He shook a glove off and picked up a clipboard, frowning. "We got the Pilsner line intact. That's good, those three young guys can do longer shifts." He looked up at three players wearing identical green helmets with a red and white Pilsner flag painted across the sides. "Then we got Guinness left wing, Boh right wing and me centering the second line. We'll have Coors spare in and out of our line — he ain't looking like no Silver Bullet tonight eh, Guinnee?"

Phil stood at the far end of the box with his chin resting on the butt end of this stick, staring into the bleachers.

"Guinnee. Something wrong, man?"

Phil started. "What?"

"You okay? Need more time to warm up?"

"Nah, got a belly full of beef and red wine, plenty warm already." Phil rubbed his stomach and smiled. In truth he'd barely managed to gag back a bit of meat and a couple of glasses of wine. Where were they? Nearly game time. They'd ditched the boys and were, no, he shook his head. No, that was silly. Janos and the boys had got along great at supper. He was safe, the boys wouldn't leave Phyl and Janos alone long enough for anything to happen. But then where were they?

"Expecting somebody, Guinnee?"

"Wife and son and Janos Teleki — you know — Hungarian guy from work. Said they'd show up tonight. Thought they'd be here by now." Phil yanked the door open and hopped onto the ice. He took two fast laps, pushing past some gliding Sparks then grabbed a puck and fired a wrist shot at OV, the goalie. The ref, a SaskPower guy, blew his whistle and pointed at this watch. The teams funnelled onto their benches, Phil scanning the nearby empty bleachers one last time before leaving the ice. Maybe this was better. He'd damn well get his two points tonight and wouldn't that be sweet when he finally caught them together.

Phyllis, tearful and begging forgiveness — Janos, red-faced and cringing, expecting the worst. But he would stand tall, cool, aloof, condemning their treachery. "While you loathsome creatures were betraying me, I was carrying the Beer Caps to victory. And a fifty-point season."

He took off his black helmet and rubbed his sleeve across the Guinness gold harps emblazoned above the ear holes. Sounded lame. Childish. This was real, not a revenge fantasy, not paranoia. The only woman he'd ever really loved, ever wanted was Phyllis. And she wasn't the tearful or begging type.

"Guinnee! Wake up for Chrissakes! Line change."

Faceoff in their own end to the right of OV. Bud got the draw, flicked it back to Canadian on defence, and Canee, quick as a weasel, darted behind their net then swung out wide. Phil chopped his blades into a sprint down the left wing and caught the Sparks' defenceman napping on the blue line. A quick, discreet elbow bounced off the Spark helmet and he was past, glancing back over his shoulder. Right on cue Canee, banged the puck off the boards knee-high and it came out clean past the Spark, rolling a few feet beyond Phil's stick.

Then Phil flew. Like an electron in the ring, accelerating toward the light. Phyllis, Teleki, cancelled meetings. "To hell with 'em!" a voice roared. His legs surged and he gathered the puck in with a quick tap to stop it rolling. The other Fart defenceman was coming on a converging course but Bud was riding him. No sign of Boh; no sign of anybody.

The cold air cut through his cage and past his glasses, making his eyes water. He could hear his own breathing, harshly sucking the crisp hockey air down deep.

"Screw 'em all!" the truculent voice bellowed again as Phil hit the enemy blue line at full speed, wheels smoking. The Spark goalie was out, blocking the whole net, but starting to fade back. Phil charged straight at him, no plan in mind, just smash into the bugger and cram the puck into the net. Goal wouldn't count, major penalty, so what. The goalie began to back peddle quickly but he'd misjudged Phil's closing speed. Instinctively Phil's shoulders twisted left, stick and puck with them, but his skates sliced a short arc right. The goalie moved with the fake while Phil swept right and there was the open net a metre away. Suddenly it was over — an open net — and nothing mattered. He tapped the puck in and let himself whip past the post, no effort to brake or turn, slamming loosely into the boards.

A series of strident hoots blasted from a plastic horn somewhere behind him in the stands. Phil lay on the ice, still loose, his left knee and shoulder joints aching. The caged light, red above him, was swirling gently clockwise. He closed his eyes.

"Wonderful goal scoring!" An accented voice from far away.

"Charged the goalie — this is rec-league hockey, man, and that's bull." An indignant Sparks captain.

"Never touched the goalie, not even close." Budweiser snapped back. "Tell your net jockey to untie his underwear and get back to work. It's one - nothing, Sparkie."

"Hey, he's not getting up." Boh shouted. "He hit the boards hard. Any of you guys know CPR?"

Skates scraped near his head showering his face with shaved ice. Phil opened his eyes. A green Pilsner helmet appeared above him. Pil One was listening to Phil's heart.

"Geez, Pil." Phil pushed him away. "You check for breathing and pulse, you can't hear a heartbeat through your helmet and my shoulder pads."

Phil sat up, flipped onto all fours and tried to stand but the ice tilted beneath him and he toppled over. Pil One and Boh hauled him up under the referee's instructions, one under each of his arms and he skated feebly to the gate. Phyl, the boys and Janos hovered anxiously, then followed, all talking simultaneously as Phil was borne to the dressing room. The dizziness passed and he was able to push through the door. He clomped across the wood floor to his bench and sat heavily, head leaned back against the wall, ignoring the babble of voices.

"Try to stop? Are you crazy? You scared me half to death." Phyl scolding. "You're not eighteen you know."

"Twenty goals Dr. S! Outstanding!" Badger gave a short toot on his red plastic horn.

Phil pulled the Guinness helmet off and brought the concerned faces into focus. "I'm fine. Just need a few minutes on my own."

"I'm not leaving until . . . Oh, good heavens — you're bleeding!" Phyllis whipped a hanky from her purse and pressed it to his forehead.

"Is small scratch from the edge of the hat when he hit the boards. Don't distress yourself, dear Phyllis." Janos took the Kleenex from her and dabbed Phil's head. "Very fine goal, Phil." Janos's touch was surprisingly gentler than Phyl's. A strange calmness seemed to flow from it.

"Mike, Badger, take Phyllis out, sit her down and get her a coffee." He saw the hurt flash across Phyl's face, but he didn't feel guilty. "Go on Phyl. Men's locker room. Janos will take care of me. I'm fine, really."

The door slammed. "I have intruded. Dear Phyllis is upset." Janos peeled the Kleenex back. "You have a first aid box?"

"It's okay, she's just flustered because both of us are here, at the same time."

Janos shook his head. "Sorry? Both of us?"

Phil pointed at the Red Cross box on the wall. "Never mind."

Janos retrieved a band-aid and a sterile swab. His fingertips were warm, soft and expertly firm while cleaning the cut then applying the bandage. "There — good as new." He smiled, eyes friendly and innocent.

Phil smiled back. Could he be wrong? No. Van, back alley, Mike had not been mistaken. Yet, even now it was difficult to dislike the man. He'd stand a better chance of catching them if Janos thought they were friends — Phyllis too. Lower their guards — they'd get careless — then catch and expose them.

"Care for a beer, Janos?"

~

Mike dropped a loonie into the drink machine and began punching the buttons for a large coffee, cream only.

"You sure he's the one?" Badger spoke softly, glancing back to where Phyllis sat outside the dressing room.

"I'd bet money on it. You heard the tape I made from the phone bug yesterday; she was like a teenie in love!"

"Yeah, the bugged phone. You have got to let me see how that works." Badger's face lit up. "I still can't believe you tape your parents' phone calls, man. That is just too weirdly cool."

Mike allowed himself a smug grin. "Keeps me one step ahead of them, most of the time anyway."

"So Janos might be our perp." Badger took the coffee from the machine, passing his horn to Mike. "She did sound pretty goofy but that doesn't make him the one for sure."

"You weren't in the kitchen. She was like an over-wound clock when Dad threatened to cancel dinner with Janos. Then he mentioned this meeting stuff and she caved. *He* doesn't get it because he suspects nothing."

"Poor sap." Badger checked the change return slot. "I like your old man. But then I liked Phyllis too."

"Phyllis couldn't risk any talk about Tuesday afternoon because she was out in that Goddamn van." Mike stopped himself and lowered his rising voice. "You watched them at supper, what do you think?"

They turned to walk back to Phyllis. "Oh, she likes him, but who wouldn't? Janos is a smart, funny guy. And I guess from an older woman's viewpoint, he must be good looking. If you like walrus moustaches."

"And." Mike tapped Badger with the plastic horn. "Remember I caught a profile of the guy driving the CLS van. Big moustache."

"We broke up their plan for tonight but we need better evidence before we bust her," Badger whispered as they approached Phyllis.

"Yeah. I got a plan. Talk about it later."

"Here you go Mrs. S." Badger gave her the coffee. "Hot instant coffee with fake cream from a plastic tube into a Styrofoam cup. It's an insult to the environment you know."

She smiled weakly. "Thanks, boys."

"I wonder how Dad is?" Mike pushed the dressing room door half open.

"Janos says he'll be good." Phyllis sipped her coffee. "And I'd trust Janos's judgment in just about anything."

Badger turned his back on Phyllis and shot his eyebrows up, mouthing a WOW. Mike twisted away quickly. God, what an amateur move. Badger still had a lot to learn. He put his head into the dressing room.

"Yes, I insist that is it. You were like a streak down a beam line — unstoppable. It is the truth my friend, not flattery." Janos sat beside Phil, a can of Guinness in his hand.

"Boards stopped me pretty good." Phil touched his forehead, then sipped his own beer.

"Yes, like a bug on the grill of a truck Mack, eh?"

Phil laughed. "Just so."

⁓

The window had to be two metres in diameter and was set high in the south transept like a perfectly round gemstone.

Spring sunlight refracted through the stained glass picking up gold from the crown, purple from the robe and green from the leaves to project them slantwise across the altar. Mike looked first to the window then let his gaze ride down the coloured light beams to where they stained his white alb. He loved this spot with its coloured God light. A sense of peace and courage seemed to well up around him. The soft hum of the regulars reciting the rosary drifted from the far end of the nave where they waited their turns in the confessional. Mike closed his eyes. Hot burnt air from a bank of votive candles came to him. It mixed with the ever present odour of the altar — a pocket redolent of incense and furniture wax. His first time serving mass — eight years ago — his little boy imagination thought it was God's body odour. He'd even told his mom he could smell God.

"Hail Mary, full of grace, the Lord is with thee. Blessed art thou among women . . . " He repeated the words with the regulars. Here, there was no fear. No fear of discovery. No fear of his mother cheating with Janos. (Phyllis no longer qualified as blessed among women). No fear that Phil was being horribly duped by Janos. No fear he was about to become the worst son and asshole in history. It was just sin and sin could be washed away.

He gave the credenze table one last quick scan — cruets, chalice, ciborium glittering gold and crystal. The Catholic Church at its traditional ordered best and simultaneously at its opulent, refulgent worst. He reluctantly genuflected, stepping down from the altar and out of the light. He walked down the north aisle to the sound technician station — a raised control consol where the various speakers, microphones and choir inputs were controlled. It was set at an angle to the north wall, only a couple of metres from the confessional. He sat in the swivel chair and unlocked the oak panels covering the controls, flipped them back and began to power up the systems. A quick glance showed Phyllis on the confession pew, old Mrs. Fitzpatrick in line before her. How awkward must that be for Fr. Fitz — hearing your own mom's confession?

Phyllis was on her fourth decade of the rosary, eyes closed, fingers massaging the beads.

"Lord forgive me," Mike said quietly as he pulled his receiver from his pocket and set it up on the console ledge aimed at the confessional doors. He unravelled the earpiece wire but found he couldn't put the plug in his ear. He was about to cross a line that should never be crossed, and it frightened him. Eavesdropping on his mom's confession meant betraying her, betraying Fr. Fitz, betraying God and in general being the biggest asshole in the universe — that self-description seemed to keep cropping up. He ran through the le Carré logic again, a mantra for the wicked; a *Hail Mary* wouldn't wash this one away. He had no choice. He couldn't launch his planned watch of Phyl and Janos based on the back-alley van and kitchen phone tap. He needed to know for certain she was cheating and he had to do this himself — no Badger today. This would never leave him. It would be like his October watch of Cindy, a private and personal memory to be hugged and cherished. Except this would be a memory to fester and hurt.

He waited for the confessional door to open, releasing its newly cleansed sinner, then forced the earpiece in and put his thumb on the tuning dial. Mrs. Fitz shuffled in and closed the door.

"Please, Mom, don't try to kneel." Fr. Fitz's voice was a clear, strong signal.

"Don't farce." Came the weak reply. Farce? No, fuss. Mike adjusted the tone up. "I can still kneel in church and I fully intend." There was a pause and a small groan. "There." A few deep breaths. "Made it."

Mike increased the volume a notch and whipped the earpiece out. Phyllis was finished her devotions and sat watching him, smiling innocence. His mom — a good Catholic — going for sacred confession then communion. He twisted the seat, flipping the choir input switches. He put the big padded headphones on and listened for the steady hum needed to blend with the main church speakers. That was it. No way he could eavesdrop on his mom and Fitz. He simply could not violate that innocent smile. He was wrong. Somehow there had to be an explanation as to how his mom came to get out of the van that he had seen rocking with fornication. Couldn't have been her. Not Phyllis. Too bad even if it was her, Phil was on his own.

He took the church headphones off. Damn. Phil, the trusting twenty-goal, old-time hockey player thought Janos was his friend, and Phyllis was his faithful wife. He couldn't leave Phil on his own. The confessional clicked open and Mrs. Fitzpatrick walked behind him. Phyllis's heels tapped and the door closed with a bang. He stared at the earpiece and felt sick to his stomach.

" . . . to the Blessed Virgin Mary and all the saints and to you, Father, that I have sinned. I was at confession a week ago, was absolved and took communion. I now accuse myself . . . " Her voice seemed to choke. Fitz was quietly patient.

"Father, I have been deceitful and committed impure — I guess adulterous, acts."

"Yes?"

"These are not white lies or flirtations, Father." Phyllis paused. Her breathing, shallow and rapid, whispered through Mike's earpiece. "These are mortal sins, not venial."

"Do not upset yourself," Fr. Fitz said calmly. "I'm sure it's nothing we can't put to rights."

"Oh, I fear it is, Father. It is like nothing I've ever done, even thought of doing before. And I'm so ashamed."

Mike's ear burned red and uncomfortable as though it wanted to spit the receiver out.

"What's worse, I'm afraid . . . I can't say it. You'll think I'm horrible."

"I'll think no such thing," Fitz said quickly. "You don't owe me anything in the way of details or apologies. This is between you and God. I can feel your remorse. I'm certain He can too."

"That's just it. I'm afraid I'm going to do it, lie and be immoral again. I don't think I can help myself, so my remorse is fake. Now I'm lying to myself." Her voice rose in pitch and filled the receiver.

"Please don't torture yourself. Perhaps a little explanation would help you see your way more clearly. I am a good listener and so is our Maker."

Mike could almost see the encouraging smile on Fr. Fitz's face. Phyllis was quiet.

"You know, even infidelity can be repented of. I've heard it all and He's forgiven all. If it helps, you can unburden yourself to me. I'm safe — I won't drop the ball."

"I've lied to my husband, Father. We're living a lie — or I am — for certain. I'm not sure what he thinks. But it involves a co-worker of his who is a really decent fellow and I am caught between them. I could get out but the consequences might be terrible. I'm not sure I even want out." Phyl's words ran together in a semi-coherent, gushing torrent of released guilt.

Mike pulled the earpiece out, shut his receiver and slipped it back into his pocket. He couldn't bear to watch her leave the confessional. He walked quickly back up to the altar and stood in his coloured God-light realigning the cross on the purifactor with the cross on the base of the chalice. He removed and replaced the paten, host and pall, fiddling to make them exactly even. He checked his watch. Fifteen more minutes for confession, then a half hour till mass. Couldn't face Phyllis, not yet. He'd go to the sacristy and wait for Fitz — no! That was no good. How could he joke around with Father knowing what he now knew about Mom and Janos? He needed time to get his game face back.

Mike dropped a quick genuflect and hurried through a side door to the children's quiet room. A tiny locked door at the back of that room led to a narrow rickety staircase that spiralled down to the basement and church hall. Technically, Mike wasn't supposed to have keys to the church but he'd taken the opportunity to copy a few of them two years ago when he'd been tasked to help the Christmas decorating committee haul wreaths and garlands up from storage. He always felt like Quasimodo or the Phantom when he traversed these back stairs and secret passages in the old church — especially with the skirts of his alb flowing behind him. He descended the stair well and let himself into the church hall but didn't turn the lights on. The dirty narrow windows at street level shed enough light for him to pace the linoleum floor.

The confession had been garbled and confused but no doubt Phyl was cheating. Didn't mention Janos by name but "co-worker" and "decent fellow". Who else? And how could she call a Hungarian gigolo a decent fellow?

Click.

The fluorescent lights began to flicker, then a second later, Mike stood exposed in their brightness. Footsteps sounded on the main staircase and the hall doors swung open. A young woman shepherded an older lady with a cane and uncertain steps.

"Okay, Gran?"

"Yes, fine." The old lady made her way to the women's bathroom.

"Need help in there?"

"No, thank you." A small chuckle. "Just help me back up the stairs when I come out."

"I'll wait right here."

Granny disappeared and the woman turned to examine the hall.

"Oh, God!" she yelped, putting her hand to her mouth when she saw Mike standing behind her. He retreated a few paces.

Angie. Physics, English, and drunken vomiter of James Bond vodka martinis.

They came and went occasionally — kids from his school — dragged to mass by parents or more often grandparents. Bored, sleepy, slouched in the pews. Nobody ever recognized him serving mass. They usually didn't recognize him when he sat beside them in class — Angie and Vanessa cases in point. School kids never connected the guy up front at the altar with anyone they knew at school. But Angie did, and short of diving behind the stacking chairs, he couldn't have avoided her. She was bound to know him, wasn't she? Her look of surprise changed to a laugh.

"You!" She walked toward him. "You scared me. Thought you were Jesus or God. You just materialized out of the dark in that get up."

"Sorry, you kind of took me by surprise too."

"So what is this? You some kind of apprentice priest?"

"No. I supervise the altar servers at nine o'clock mass every Sunday."

She surveyed the gown; a thoughtful look crossed her face. "Yeah, I guess I knew that, but still a surprise to actually see you in costume."

"You knew?"

"I found out after you got me skunked at McKennit's last fall."

"Hey." Mike spread his hands out palms up. "Nobody forced you or Vanessa to drink those martinis."

She laughed. "Actually you did hold a gun to my head as I remember." He didn't reply, probably best to say nothing. "Don't worry James Bond. I was drinking to impress Vanessa, not you." She reached out to touch the tunic. "Nice material."

Mike self-consciously tightened the cincture, hoping Granny would reappear.

"But afterwards, when Vanessa found a new best friend to bully . . . " she paused, looking him full in the face. "I realized I actually had a pretty good time with you and Badger — apart from barfing."

He laughed in spite of his game face.

"And Badger told me about your church thing and that you weren't a bad guy." .

"He never told me you talked to him," Mike said, regretting it instantly.

"I asked him not to tell you. I figured you weren't too impressed by a skinny, crying, fake-hooker nerd who got drunk and sick." She blushed.

"You were concerned about me being impressed? Your last words I believe were don't ever come near us again you . . . "

"Those were Vanessa's words, not mine." She smiled through the blush.

"Angie dear." Granny was back. "Let's go. I want to get a good seat."

"Is there such a thing?" Angie whispered to him.

"Rows H to J, north side, cushions on racks under the pews. Hardly anybody knows they're there. Save your butt from the hardwood." He grinned, then shocked himself when he winked. "Have a good mass, Bond Girl."

～

The sea of grey heads sprinkled with white rose for the start of the Eucharistic prayer. Angie's dark brown — he'd thought it was mousy brown, but no, it was dark, almost chestnut — her brown hair shone in the morning light. The kid on the bells wasn't paying attention. Mike tugged his sleeve and motioned him to the kneeler. They dropped for the transubstantiation of wine and bread.

"Take this all of you and eat it: this is my body which will be given up for you." Fr. Fitzpatrick's strong baritone turned the bread into body. Mike felt it like he always did. The chiming bells stood the hair up on the back of his neck. Christ's body, here for him. Redemption even for guys who bugged the confessional. Would Angie feel it? Would the power go to her? Would she let it in? He looked up for her face but it was lost in the congregation.

"Take this, all of you and drink from it: this is the cup of my blood, the blood of the new and everlasting covenant."

He would get a good look at Angie when she came up for communion, if she came up. Granny was Catholic but that didn't mean granddaughters were. Jesus! What was he thinking? Somehow his spine-tingling joy over the body and blood of Christ was being overrun by thoughts of Angie. He was better than that. He'd do a full rosary and five Our Fathers after mass — his own penance.

The Eucharistic prayer ended and he recited the Lord's Prayer without a single thought of Angie. The congregation rippled with noise and movement for the Sign of Peace. Mike shook Father's hand then quickly scanned the herd. There she was, leaning over a pew, laughing and shaking an old man's hand. Not that it really mattered of course but she did have a nice smile. He was glad to see her follow Granny up the centre aisle for communion. He wouldn't make eye contact but he could see how she behaved using his watcher's peripheral vision. A moment later, she took the host, stepped aside, placed it in her mouth, looked up and caught him staring at her. She grinned hugely. He grinned back. What was wrong with him? Leering at chicks during communion! Twenty Hail Marys and ten Our Fathers.

# CHAPTER 6

"You said it yourself!" Phyllis was indignant, but enjoying herself.

"Did not, pass the toast." Phil stuck his knife in the marmalade.

"What's the magic word?" Phyllis lifted the plate of toast and held it close.

"All right. Pass the toast, *baby*."

She extended the plate to him. "Was that so hard?"

He smiled at her. Breakfast peace. Thank God for a little breakfast banter, it had been a while.

"You said Canadians live on the edge of the wilderness staring survival odds in the face every day. You said . . . "

"Margaret Atwood said that," he interrupted. "And you made me read that illogical claptrap because you believed it."

"Don't blame this on Atwood — who is perfectly logical — or me! You said Canadians were victims trying to survive the dark forest."

"I parroted it to make you happy." He spread marmalade.

"Oh, give me a break. You were an uptight physics masters iceman who scarcely noticed the presence of other human life forms. Why would you suddenly become tactful and sensitive to a nursing student?" She put her palm under her chin and batted her eyes at him.

He shrugged.

"Come on, Phillip Smith — why would a science Titan bother to bend his intellect?"

"Grrr." He bit into his toast savagely, tearing off a piece and letting marmalade trickle down his chin. "Because Titan icemen need fire. And you, Phyllis Wolyschen, were burning pretty hot."

She reached across the table, got the marmalade on her fingertip and pushed it into his mouth. He licked her finger.

"Oh, Phil," she whispered, her grin flattening to a leer.

Jeez, too close — too much banter. He couldn't and he shouldn't let her think he could. He sat up rigidly in his chair.

"Anyway, my point is . . . " Phyl's finger crooked into a come-hither hook.

He ignored it, looking past her. "The point is that survival stuff might have been true twenty years ago, but not now. We are the creators now, unravelling any mystery we care to set our intellects at. This protein crystal analysis technique is huge. It puts us on the world stage."

Phyllis dropped her hand back to her coffee and sighed before taking a drink. "I know. Big meeting back on for Friday. Put yourself on the world stage."

"Us, on the world stage, us." He corrected her.

"You, on the world stage, you." She snapped back.

"You think I'm some kind of egomaniac, don't you?"

"No Phil." She set her cup down with a bang. "I think we were having some fun, enjoying each other's company, which hasn't happened too often lately. And all of a sudden this physicist materializes, boots my husband out of the room and proceeds to lecture me, again, on depth reversal x-ray analysis of protein crystal structure."

"Janos finds it interesting," he said quietly. "But not my own wife." Which was a stupid and petty thing to say, but he said it anyway.

"That!" Phyllis pointed her come-hither finger, now a dagger, at him, "is a cheap shot unworthy of even you."

He stood up, scraping the chair back hard against the wall. She did the same.

"And Janos, now that you've mentioned him, would never stoop to such a low thing." She turned to leave the kitchen. "He actually is a gent."

"Going to work now."

"Whatever."

～

Phil sat in his car in the CLS parking lot while the nausea passed. She was cheating on him; yet he was the one physically sick with regret over his behaviour. He'd have to figure out some way to bring this to a head before Friday or he'd never cope. And damn he'd promised himself not to argue, not bring up Janos. Phyl and Janos needed to trust him, not be wary. Particle physics was so easy. Wouldn't it be lovely if his only concern was depth-reversal light-beam analysis. There would be no fighting with Janos. But then Janos never leered at him over the cereal either. That was the real problem, wasn't it.

"Admit it!" He shouted. "Phyllis wants a normal guy. I'm a creator of life yet not even a man. Ergo, the Hungarian aristocracy is necessitated."

He thought of Friday's presentation. Maybe it was some kind of hidden block — like the boys and their crazy BP testing of meadowlarks. Maybe once Friday was over and his technique was approved for trial, then he could be what Phyllis needed. Maybe just ignore them till Friday. What could it hurt? Couldn't unwind the clock, last Tuesday happened, maybe others. She would still want me. If I had been able to chase her upstairs from the kitchen table with marmalade on her finger it would have happened. So what if Janos had been there before me? Logically, he and |Janos were not such different people and if it took the pressure off . . . NO! Janos could not be let in to take his place, even temporarily. It was insane logic that could end his marriage, maybe even end his life. He shook his head, got out of the car and slammed the door. "Son of a bitch, no! It's too late to pretend." To blow off the anger, he jogged for the main entrance doors.

⌒

Phil snubbed the receptionist's "Good morning," snapped at Fran's query about the hockey game and deleted a half-dozen emails from co-workers congratulating him on a twenty-goal season. He glanced at the clock, ten to eight. *Get a grip Phil, sort yourself, man.* Leaning back in his chair he breathed deeply then started subtracting the date — May 7th — from the clock. 750-743-736-729-722 . . . He let the arithmetic click smoothly in his head, perfectly based in four-four time, his foot tapping the rhythm. It was his mechanism for keeping himself in check and hopefully get Janos out of his head. Soon the numbers came by themselves with each tap of his toe and he began to think of the ring, then the beam, 652-645-638-631 Then the hut where Janos and his team refracted that beam to peel away the layers of material, searching . . . 554-547-540-533 . . . *Ah, yes. Peeling from the top eh, boys?* He smiled. *Let Phillip take you straight to the source, so elegant, so simple. Genesis.*

"Phil?"

It was Fran. He sat up, startled.

"It's eight-o-three." She didn't make eye contact. "You said you had to be at the Hungarian beam at eight — I was to remind you."

"Fran." He smiled genuine regret at her. "If I ever again snap your head off like I did this morning, please slap me, hard.

She regarded him coolly. "It's not funny Phil. I do have feelings."

"In that case, I sincerely apologize. I seem to be hurting everyone I care for these days." He shrugged. "Don't know why either." He looked up from his tapping foot, 414-407-400-393 surprised at his own candour. The arithmetic stopped.

"Well." Fran's tone softened. "I know this proposal of yours is loading you with stress. I guess I'll survive, apology accepted."

"Thanks." He picked up his laptop and stood to follow her out the door.

"I hear the Beer Caps won, four zip, and you got the winning goal."

"Got lucky there, eh?"

⟨∼⟩

Janos had seen the theory and the animation before, but Phil's latest "backsplash" had never been simulated in the actual beam hutch. So this was an exciting morning for all of them.

"To start the slate clean," Janos piped up the moment Phil arrived. "We recognize the problem. We must rotate the crystal during image collection to get the full 3-D view, but the reflection spots are then too close together to decipher the sequencing easily. So, we move the detector back to open the spots up, but then lose the x-ray light intensity due to atmospheric absorption. No synchrotron can solve this atmospheric absorption issue."

"Until now," Phil said, trying to sound clinical and not arrogant.

"Yes, until now." Janos spoke almost reverently. "The Smith technique keeps the beam intensity yet comes from behind, so not too close in reflection. The proteins that are life itself, that participate in every process in every living cell, are brought to light. We see the acid sequencing, Phil, we see life."

Phil flipped his laptop open, trying to keep his head from swelling under Janos's flattery. No, not flattery, true appreciation by an acknowledged genius in his field. He looked up and smiled at Janos.

"We need to leave the crystal strands intact and the detector steady. So we — you dear Phillip — will slice the narrowest of beams through the sub-atomic level then back light the desired material, leaving it pristine." Janos focused intently on the laptop screen, reciting Phil's technique exactly. "I understand how you serpentine the x-rays, excellent, but the depth reversal, what you call backsplash, I need to see."

"Minimal absorption with reflection at a distance." Phil tapped keys then drove the mouse. "Bounce these ones, or any ones you like, really, off the goal stick like so." He adjusted the mouse slightly. "And here she comes right back at us like an uncontrolled rebound. Then we pick our spot, net wide open, and . . . "

"Goal." Janos breathed the word. "Lovely my friend. Lovely. Again but with different reflections from the depth. May I try?"

"Of course." Janos was smart — a delight really — the way he soaked it up with minimal jargon. He got it. Janos, a biochemist expert in all things doing on protein crystal-lography, was also a dab-hand at particle theory and hard x-ray generation. The Yin, Phil thought. I am a particle physicist with a firm grip on protein crystal analysis, the Yang. In here, in the hutch, they were good together — undeniably good.

He turned the board toward Janos. "Here, you be God."

Janos looked at him. "I have no religion to speak of Phil, but please, not that."

Phil nodded. "Not God then, just scientist."

Janos smiled and shook his hand.

~

"Always the EatMore bar?" Janos set Phil's chocolate bar and coke on the table and sat beside him.

"Always. Phyl doesn't like me eating junk but there's not much she seems to like about me these days."

Janos coloured. "Not my business."

"Sorry." Phil unwrapped the EatMore. "Boring domestics shouldn't be brought up at work."

"Oh, no. I am very interested. I love you and Phyl. I want you to be happy but I will admit that I see tensions, and it worries me to think my two favourite Canadian people are unhappy with each other."

Phil returned Janos' worried frown with a shrug. "I'm sure it will blow over. Whatever is bothering her will eventually go away, I hope."

"Not my place to offer advice." Janos hesitated.

Phil leaned forward. "Please go ahead." The impertinent bastard was scoring Phyl and would actually now offer advice on how he should cope with that — solicitous hypocrite. Phil bit a large chunk off the bar.

"It is dangerous to hope for it to blow over. Should you not do something, be proactive?"

Inspiration comes at the most unexpected time and place, as a creative scientist Phil knew this very well. Janos had just done it here, in the coffee shop over soft drinks and chocolate bars. He must do something. His previous vague notion of following Phyl or Janos around until they made a mistake was next to useless. He must do something, set the agenda and take control. So easy. It appeared to him and he would act on it. No need to refine or second guess it.

"Maybe you're right. I can't do much before the presentation Friday. In fact I'll be here, going over the final details all Thursday evening." He tipped the coke back and swallowed, watching Janos's eyes. There was a flicker, a guilty but thoughtful glance aside. "Maybe a quiet evening all on her own would be good for Phyllis. Then I will be able to devote some proactive time to her once the meeting is done with."

"Surely you have your presentation in perfect order? You need a whole evening to rehearse?"

"Yes, but the night before the presentation I'll be preoccupied with it, bad company for Phyl. Better if I'm in here, rehearsing as you say. It will calm me and give Phyl a break."

"Yes, I see." Janos reached across the table and shook his hand. "A wise and generous plan. I am sure Phyllis will appreciate it."

The man's arrogance was his personality. He took Phyllis for granted already. Phil could see it in his casual manner. And he took it as natural that Phil should place the cuckold horns on his own head. Hand Phyllis over on Thursday night as a medieval peasant would serve his wife to a feudal lord. Well, by God, that arrogance was misplaced this time. No more compliant serf. As of yet Phil had not planned what he would actually do when he trapped and exposed them. That thought surfaced, troubling but not urgent. He'd do what felt right at the time. The tiny flash of satisfaction at baiting the trap was now offset with distaste. What was he doing? Setting up his wife with his friend? The word pimp nagged him.

～

Phyllis took the bait with fewer qualms than Janos had. She seemed relieved, as though some of the tension between them had broken. Yet, if anything, Phil was wound tighter than that morning fight at breakfast. She must have been missing Janos. Now she had the chance to be with him Thursday night while good old Phil slugged it out at work, that would be a relief. And she thought him so unsuspecting, so naively stupid, that she practically announced her intentions. Neither shame nor remorse in the tiniest measure. Just an overriding arrogance, like Janos.

～

"Looking forward to your dinner at the Keg on Friday?" Phil asked, pouring mushroom gravy over his potatoes.

"Sure, but I'll be happier that you'll have finally finished with that presentation."

Mike became alert. He forced himself to sit back in his chair and fiddle nonchalantly with his peas as though the dinner conversation was of the least, rather than the greatest, interest to him. The tension iceberg was shifting. Phyllis sat erect as a gopher watching for hawks, and Phil was practically crouched over his food.

"Oh?" Phil forked in a load of potatoes and chewed slowly watching Phyllis. "Anxious for my triumph?"

"Naturally, but you know darn well you've been like a bear with a sore tooth." She glanced at Mike. He turned up his blandest face then went back to spearing peas. This would be better done by eavesdropping but he couldn't justify disappearing so early from the supper table.

"Yes, I'll be happy for you and I'm sure you look forward to finally getting approval and funding for your own time on the beam line. I know the operations people want that money and it's stressful."

"It should be an open-net goal." Phil smiled. "But I'm not taking it for granted. I plan to stay late Thursday night. Rerun the whole thing just to be certain there are no loose ends."

Mike knew his mom was looking at him again, but he refused to respond. He methodically cut up his hamburger pie and dipped the pieces in gravy, willing her to reply to Phil.

"Surely you have all the details in order."

Phil jumped as though Phyl had yelled boo. Mike jerked his head up involuntarily.

"What is it?" Phyl asked.

"Nothing, nothing. Just somebody said the same thing today, exact same words."

"Fran?"

"No. Janos. Anyway, back to Thursday. I'll just be pacing the floor here so I might as well be at CLS working."

"Perhaps that is best." Phyl's body slumped back into her chair. She even exhaled as though she had been holding her breath. Mike risked a peek. Her cheeks were colouring and she was smiling.

"Then I'll phone Liz and see if she wants to go to the movies. You won't be home much before ten, will you?"

"Ten at the best. Do the early show, great idea."

Phyl tapped Mike's water glass with her knife. "Mike, honey?"

"Mmmmh?" He kept his eyes on his plate. My, that was well done — the barest display of exterior interest — even though internally he was receiving with all senses.

"You don't mind if I go out to see a movie Thursday night? I have been hoping to see this one on the big screen and you'll have homework and all?"

"Naw, no problem Mom." A faint nod of his head, so good to be in control.

"Goodie!" Phyllis bobbed her head as though in time to music. "I haven't been out with Liz in ever so long. We'll have fun."

"What's on?" Phil asked.

"Oh, chick flick, you wouldn't be familiar with it."

Mike tried to call Badger that evening but there was no answer. Tomorrow was Tuesday. They could set up the watch plan tomorrow night and rehearse Wednesday. Two rehearsals would have been better, but Badger was good. One would have to do.

~

A moment after Mike left the table, Phyl winked. "Remember what you and I used to get up to in the back rows of theatres?"

He grimaced. Was she cruel or just obtuse?

~

"Where have you been?" Mike caught up with Badger just as the inmates were shuffling into the chemistry cell for first period.

"Aw, don't ask, man." Badger's face turned sour. "My aunt and uncle, the retired ones from Elbow, Saskatchewan, showed up Sunday afternoon if you can believe it. I've been driving them to every Canadian Tire and Wal-Mart in the city so they can shop for all the useless junk they can't get in Elbow."

They reached their bench at the back of the room and dumped their books down.

"So you got to skip school yesterday?" Mike pulled up his stool and sat.

"They're nervous driving in the city and they don't get to see much of me, and my parents were too busy — so yeah — I got to *skip*." He made air quotation marks.

"Flashpoint," the chemistry teacher, began putting a formula on the white board, the room settled to near quiet.

"Phil and Phyl never let me skip school. I've got to do it on my own and be careful with cover." Mike flipped his workbook open. Flashpoint began working the formula, speaking loudly to the board.

"Listen," Mike whispered. "It's going to happen this Thursday night."

Badger was watching Flashpoint. "Eh? What's happening?"

"Phyl and Janos." Mike's whisper was louder than he intended. The kids at the table beside them looked over.

Badger turned, the chemistry problem forgotten. "You're not serious! Where? How'd you find out?"

Mike leaned close and tried to mute his voice. "Almost for certain. She'll meet him . . . "

"Bertram!" Flashpoint's deep bass voice jerked them out of their huddle. "Are you discussing my equation? And if so, let all of us hear what you have to say."

"Ah, no, not exactly, Mr. Fletcher." Badger fumbled with his lab book and pencil.

"Well, then I need you and . . . " Flashpoint stared at Mike, who shrank down onto his stool, trying to find cover behind the bit of apparatus on the bench. Fletcher took a step closer, peered through his glasses then picked the seating chart out of his binder and consulted it. "Oh, yes, Michael. I need you and Michael to pay attention."

Mike and Badger both nodded.

"Cold, Michael?" Flashpoint hadn't said ten words to him since the class started in late January. Now "Michael" seemed to be his favourite word. Every single prisoner was watching him. Their eyes invaded and filled him till he felt like he would burst.

"No," Mike croaked.

"Then please remove the leather coat. It looks expensive and we'll be handling magnesium later — don't want parents hounding me about damaged . . . "

Mike had the coat off and tossed into the corner before Flash could finish. What had possessed him to wear such ostentatious clothing to school? He could scarcely remember putting it on this morning. The teacher gave them each a meaningful squint then turned to the board. Mike stared straight ahead till everyone was back to work. Then he slowly swivelled his head around the class. One set of eyes — front-left of the room — were still on him. Dark brown hair above grey eyes. Angie. *Oh crap.* He smiled at her. *Double crap.*

~

Mike and Badger retrieved their English books from their lockers and made their way to the next class while Mike explained about Thursday night.

"So we follow them to the theatre and spy on them there?" Badger asked.

"Movie was likely just a cover — probably meeting Janos somewhere else. I'll have to check my tape from the phone bug when I get home today. Maybe we'll get lucky and find out their real rendezvous."

"What phone bug?" Angie asked, her voice practically in Mike's ear.

"Hey, Ang." Badger turned. She was following them so close she bumped into him. "You remember Mike?"

"Sure. We went to church together on Sunday," she said, stepping between them so they were walking three abreast. "What phone bug?"

"You went to church with Angie?" Badger reached in front of Angie and punched Mike in the arm. "You never told me altar boys dated."

"We ran into each other at church. She was with her Gran." Mike sped up, they were nearly at the English Twelve door.

"What phone bug? What are you guys up to?" Angie demanded, loudly.

"Phone bug?" Badger laughed. "What are you talking about?" He snorted and shook his head.

Angie pulled Mike's sleeve, making him stop. "Mike said he had to 'check his tape from the phone bug'."

"No I didn't." Mike set his face to deadpan. "Eavesdropping on private conversations often results in the listener getting it wrong."

"I did not get it wrong."

Badger laughed, Angie clipped the back of his head with her knuckles. They were blocking the doorway; the other prisoners were starting to push past them, Mike tried to slip away from her.

"You know, some people are starting to wonder about you two."

He froze, looked back at her. "Who? Wondering what, exactly?" Here was danger, exposure, unwanted attention.

"Bertram! Angela! Please come in and be taking your seats. You're causing a veritable log jam there!" Mr. Garchinski's good-natured bellow pulled them into the room. Badger and Mike got to the rear desks leaving Angie near the front.

"That was close," Badger muttered as they sat. "What do we do about her?"

"Stonewall. She doesn't have a clue," Mike said tersely. "She probably won't even remember it by the end of the period."

"I don't *know* about *that*." Badger flipped his notebook open. "She can be pretty tenacious."

"How *would* you know *that*?" Mike was genuinely surprised.

Badger shrugged and looked away.

Garchinski began to organize them into what he called a "creative stew." It was one of his favourite classroom exercises. They were given fifteen minutes to write at least a ten-line paragraph, in pencil, double-spaced, on a given topic. Today's subject was "An Old Man". It was to be physically descriptive as well as a personality sketch. It could be entirely fictional or based on a real person — your grandfather for example. Then each paragraph was put into an old, cast-iron stew pot, stirred, and each student then randomly drew another's assignment. In ink, they had to make two editorial suggestions: One identifying where the writer had succeeded, and one constructively criticising how to improve the piece. Any spurious attempt to humiliate or ridicule another person's work would result in the perpetrator's own piece being read out loud and cut to ribbons by Garchinski himself. Mike was completely distracted. After ten minutes all he had was: "His face had more wrinkles than an elephant's butt." He erased 'butt' and wrote 'trunk'. How did Badger know Angie was tenacious? He'd told her about Mike's altar serving but that had been months ago — after Halloween — hadn't it? Just how much had he been seeing, telling Angie?

"Two more minutes my young creative geniuses." Garchinski checked his watch. "Let your pencils run free."

Mike scribbled madly in large letters about an old man's failing eyesight and his anger at losing his driver's license. The old man was thinking of taking revenge on his eye doctor — no, optometrist.

"Time's up! Into the stew!"

They jostled around the pot to drop off their papers. Groans and shrill laughter bubbled around the stew. Although nobody admitted it, most of them liked the break in routine for creative stew. Garchinski lifted the full pot up and carried it through the crowd, making them reach up into the kettle to draw blindly. Mike waited his turn. A folded piece of paper pressed against the back of his right hand. Angie's arm touched his arm lightly. Her left hand hid the paper and pressed it against him again. He turned his own palm to meet hers and took it. She never looked at him, then drifted off to make her selection from the stew. Back at his, desk Mike slid the note under the assignment and unfolded it.

*What telephone bug? Tell me at lunch. Meet me at the picnic tables outside. This is your last chance.*

*A.*

A skull and crossbones was skilfully etched below her initial. Mike reached across the aisle to borrow Badger's eraser and left the note tucked under the corner of Badger's notebook. A moment later, Badger took his eraser back and the note appeared in its place. He had added his own message below the skull.

*I told you she was tenacious.*

~

The May sun really did bring out the chestnut — deep chestnut — colour of her hair. An observable fact and nothing more. Mike chewed his ham and cheese sandwich slowly, elbows propped on the picnic table. Angie was across the table, turned sideways, questioning Badger and gradually boxing him in.

"Don't you dare try to deny it. We are past that." She glanced briefly at Mike. "I clearly heard him say the telephone was bugged and recorded."

Badger opened his mouth, hesitated, then folded. "Suppose you did. I have no idea what it's about either, Ang. Ask Mike. He's the one you seem to think is a spy."

"He doesn't speak!" she shrilled, glaring at Mike now. "He eats that damn sandwich and drinks his little kindergarten juice box but he DOES NOT SPEAK!"

Mike smiled benignly, sucked grape juice up the straw, swallowed, then took another bite of sandwich. He'd instructed Badger on the silent stonewall technique but Badger just had to talk to girls. No doubt another biological imperative. Anyway, it was a good move for Badger to play dumb — shift her focus. Mike knew he could block her and she would have to give up. He couldn't be cracked by the likes of Angie. Normally he enjoyed stonewalling people, watching them squirm in frustration, but this time it felt wrong. He found himself regretting it. He could talk to Angie — would like to talk to Angie — make her laugh and smile rather than make her cross.

"You guys think you're so clever." She took her watch off, clicked the mode to timer, and set it on the table.

"You have just two minutes to tell me about the phone tap or . . . "

"Or what?" Badger smirked, confident of victory.

"Or I'll tell Vanessa that you are planning to go Columbine." She fixed Mike with a hard stare, grey eyes roaming over the leather jacket.

"Ha!" Badger dismissed her with a wave. "Who would believe you? Not her — you've told us she's not your friend. That's a pretty lame . . . "

"They already think it," Angie said calmly. "Vanessa-and-friends have been pestering me to get close to you, to find out."

Badger stiffened, head snapping to Mike for help. "Oh come on. Why would they think that already?"

"Long leather coats, weird martinis, water pistol shots to the mouth." She touched her fingertips, counting the points scored. "And that's just the Halloween party. Then this church obsession; you two heading off somewhere with BP machines and binoculars; secret who–knows-what goings-on."

"You've been watching us." Mike felt the thrill of the hunted spy. He was astounded, truly. And strangely, not very upset.

"It speaks," Angie said. "Keep going."

"Nothing else to say." Mike couldn't give in so easily. He fiddled with his juice straw. "So you have some observations that we are eccentric. There is really nothing 'Columbine' in it." He paused, watching her face. She was firm, staring at her watch. "You don't have anything to go to teachers or police with."

"Teachers? Police?" Angie hooted. "Don't make me laugh! I'm talking to Vanessa, and she talks to everybody. It would spread to every kid in school and then to all their parents and then come back to the teachers from concerned parents. And then you two would be on the hot seat with every . . . " her voice rose loudly and her arms shot out to embrace the whole school.

"Oh, crap," Badger's shoulders sagged. "She's right, man."

Mike had already decided they were beaten so now it was time for damage control, containment. "How much does Vanessa know?"

"Nothing really, no facts. She's waiting for my confirmation," Angie replied, instantly dropping her dramatic arm gesture. "She trusts my ability to get inside on this."

"Trusts?" Mike sucked on the dry bottom of the juice box making ratcheting sounds.

"She thinks every kid in this school is dying to serve her. She has an ego the size of the football field." Angie reached across the table and yanked the straw from Mike's lips to silence the sucking noise. "She treats me like dirt, then thinks I'll do anything to be her friend again. Actually, that tactic works with a lot of people."

"But not you," Mike said quickly.

"No."

"Then why *are* you reporting to her?" Mike intended his tone to be one of a hard-nosed interrogator. Instead it sounded like a concerned friend.

"Well, boys." Angie grinned, looking from one to the other. "That's just the point isn't it? I'm not reporting to her if you tell me whose phone you're tapping. How you do it. And why."

"Aw, shit. She's got us," Badger said.

Mike would have preferred a more dignified surrender but "aw shit" was an accurate assessment of their predicament.

"Okay. We think my mom is cheating on my dad. We're bugging her phone conversations on the kitchen phone at my house — she doesn't use her cell much — to discover when she'll meet her lover. Then we plan to mount a watch, get pictures . . . ."

"Hang on!" Angie's cool exterior shattered. "You're going to photograph your mom and another guy actually, uh, you know, that's sick."

"NO!" Mike barked. "Just pictures of them meeting, going to a motel, maybe kissing. Enough evidence that I can confront her and force her to break it off before Dad finds out."

"What if," Angie's voice softened. "Mike, what if she doesn't want to break up with this jerk?"

Mike's stomach cramped, the table seemed to tip backward, dizzily. He stared at her, offended by the notion.

"Naw." Badger shook his head. "You have to know them. Phil and Phyl are good to go. She's just bored and following her urges with a younger male. She'd never leave Phil. It's pure science for her."

"That's what I thought about my parents before my dad left." Angie's eyes had not left Mike. "What do you call them? Fill and Fill?"

"Phillip and Phyllis — Mike's parents have the same nickname," Badger said. "It all started last Tuesday when we were at the coulee bird watching."

Angie listened to the whole week's events. Mike gradually unclamped his stomach as he watched her. No smirks, no giggles, just the occasional pained squint or murmur of sympathy. When Badger finished, she turned, reached across the table and touched her fingers to the back of Mike's hand. By God that felt good.

"So you won't tell her?" he asked.

"Tell who?"

"Vanessa, of course," Badger said.

"Oh, Jeez no. I wouldn't give that bitch the time of day."

"You have to tell her something." Badger looked over his shoulder at the smokers' cage where Vanessa and her ladies-in-waiting were pretending to enjoy their cigarettes. "We'll have to come up with something for you to tell her."

"No, we won't," Mike said, a sudden bright revelation welling up inside him. "It was just Angie all along, Vanessa never asked her to spy on us."

"Eh?" Badger turned back to face Angie. "You bluffed us?"

Angie pulled her hand back quickly. A half-apologetic smile appeared.

Mike held his hand up. "Well played, Bond Girl."

Angie high-fived him. "Don't call me Bond Girl."

"Whatever you say, Bond Girl." Badger elbowed her.

"I want in." Angie elbowed him back. "On the watch, Thursday night."

"You're in," Mike said, too quickly. You had to improvise, be flexible. That was the hallmark of a good spy. He was still thinking of how warm her hand had felt resting on his. Spying was as much art as science. This must be the art part, he thought.

⁓

"Janos Teleki speaking." The tape was not great. Mike made a mental note to upgrade the recorder.

"Hi Janos, is this a bad time?"

"Dear Phyllis. Not at all. For you, anytime is not bad."

"Oh, Janos." Phyl laughed, Mike thought she laughed playfully. "I don't want to interrupt anything important."

"Please, Phyllis. It is only William with his beam-line reports and he is nearly finished. Tell me why you called."

DAVID RICHARDS

"Only to confirm that you are still free for dinner at the Keg on Friday night. I made reservations for seven-thirty. Is that all right?"

"Oh yes. Naturally. I look forward very much to it."

"Then I'll let you go and see you Friday."

Angie leaned over the kitchen counter, staring at the tiny recorder, listening intently as Janos and Phyl said their goodbyes.

"That's no good," Badger said opening the fridge door. "Who wants a coke?"

Angie shook her head. Mike turned the recorder off then took a can from Badger.

"No mention of a Thursday-night rendezvous." Angie straightened up and looked inside the cupboard again. "Sure this thing picks up all the conversations?"

Mike nodded and examined the recorder counter dial. The figures were so small.

"What do you call this?" She reached into the cupboard and retrieved the SaskTel box.

"That's just a fake cover to hide the tapping device." He moved next to her and reached in, his arm brushing hers. "This unit here has three jacks. One on this wire goes through the small hole I drilled in the bottom of the cupboard and fits into Phyl's phone base." He touched the base. "The phone conversation comes through that wire into this beige box where it is fed out on this wire and jacks into my mini recorder. That's why it's called 'Beige Boxing' — not really wiretapping or bugging. Then the real signal goes back on this third wire to the regular phone jack in the wall. The two people talking have no idea their conversation is being siphoned off to the recorder."

He smiled. Angie shrugged. "Simple enough. Kind of sleazy isn't it?"

Badger laughed. "Spying's a nasty game, Ange. Losing your nerve already?"

She shook her head. "And your parents don't suspect anything?"

"I just hid it under this SaskTel cover, why would they pry it up?"

She looked at Mike as though he hadn't showered for some time. He examined the counter dial on the recorder again.

"Hang on, one more call here, I think. Yeah, a short one."

He adjusted the tape reader and hit play.

"Janos, it's me again. Has William gone?"

"Who?"

"William was there when I phone earlier. Surely you remember?"

"Oh, yes, he is much gone my dear — we are speaking lonely now."

"Thursday night then. Back row of cinema number four, the Galaxy Theatre. Seven-thirty show."

"I'm loving when you give orders." A husky laugh. "I am obeyink your every command dearest woman."

"Then obey this," she said sternly. "Come in after the show starts so it is too dark to be recognized. I'll be in the back row, left end."

"And Phil will be at work?"

"Yes." Phyl breathed deeply into the tape. "No interruptions there."

"What is name of movie?"

"Doesn't matter, you won't see much of it."

Janos growled. Phyllis laughed. They hung up.

"What a deal," Angie said, wide-eyed. "This is enough evidence right here. Yet . . . "

"What?"

"Sounded like two different men." She wrinkled her brow. "Play it back again, Mike. Both calls."

They listened again.

"See? Two different men," Angie said.

"Easily explained." Badger hit the replay button. "This first one is Janos with a person in his office so he has to be on his best behaviour — thus best English." He tapped the fast forward into the second message. "And this one is Janos being the forbidden fruit."

"What?" Mike stopped the tape. The second message though necessary, was more than he wanted to hear.

"The exotic European — he's deliberately overdoing it." Angie explained. "Playing the sexy Euro guy to entertain your mom." She blushed.

"Exactly," Badger said. "What the shy Angie is trying to say is that the second call is their sex game, role playing. Pretty common among burnt-out old people."

"Okay, enough, Badger." Angie held up her hand and stole a glance at Mike. "God, this must be awful for you."

Mike tried his spy face, but only partly succeeded. "Can't afford awful right now." He smiled his thanks for her sympathy. "Got to get some hard evidence and put an end to this mess."

"At least it actually is at the theatre. I was dreading a cheap motel." Angie smiled back at him.

"Yeah, I've got a dandy little light intensification camera with an infra-red finder." Mike brightened at the thought of showing Angie another piece of his equipment. "Should work well in the show. Couple of pictures — this tape — and we're done."

"Course, you'll have to train Angie on the camera," Badger said.

"Me? Oh, no, I'm the rookie here."

"He's right Angie. They're going back row left so we can't get behind them. Have to be a near side shot and if Badger or I try to get close enough we'll be spotted."

"Oh, shit. Can I quit?"

"Sure, but then we'd have to kill you, Bond Girl." Badger half shut his eyes and sighed dramatically.

⁓

"Yes, I do remember, dear Phil." Janos smiled — ingratiatingly, Phil thought. "And you are positive that there is nothing I can help you with, for your presentation?"

"No, thanks pal." Phil slapped Janos's shoulder and the thought struck him that had they been hockey players, and had Janos scored a goal, then he could give him a tap on the butt. All above the belt in the office, though. "I'm better off here tonight."

"I just feel so guilty for cancelling your last meeting." He grabbed Phil's hand and began shaking it. "You were, what is it American athletes say — you were peaking. And I have made it so you must peak again."

"Couldn't be helped, eh?" Phil pulled his hand free. "You had an emergency conference call to Hungary right?"

"Yes, most regrettable. My superior demanding details on our progress with the beam line."

"Really?" The familiar angry darkness churned up from Phil's gut. "I thought it was your accountant questioning some of your financial reports?"

"Oh no, dear friend. You are mistaken. Last Tuesday was boss, not the bean counter."

*You arrogant bastard, you were out with my wife and you don't even have the courtesy to keep your lies straight.* "Ah, micro-managing. How irritating," he said. "I'm lucky Len leaves me pretty much alone. As long as I do my job of course."

Janos insisted on shaking his hand once more. "I have to say this, Phil. I feel proud that I am to be associated with your new procedures — that Hungary will be the first partner in this venture. We are not God but," he pointed skyward, "by God we will make others take notice of the results we'll achieve by using the Phil Smith Backlight Technique."

Phil could not muster the contempt he should have felt for such a pompous speech. Why? Because the man was genuine; you could feel it, see it. The creeping darkness of a moment earlier drained away. He found himself longing for Janos Teleki's friendship — not his downfall.

"Thanks buddy. That means a lot."

Janos beamed.

~

"Janos Teleki was looking for you, again." Fran arched her eyebrows.

"Found me. We went for a coffee."

"He's always looking for you." Fran turned from her computer screen. "And he must shake your hand fifteen times a day, a bit creepy, like he's stalking you."

"Nothing so sinister, Fran. He's just really keen on my new process — hey — you know he's already given it a name. Guess what it is?"

"'The Phil Smith Backlight Technique.' He told me when he was here looking for you."

"Well," Phil said. "Do you like it?"

"As compared to what?"

"My name was 'A Depth-Reversal Light-Beam Analysis of Protein Crystal Structure With Sub-Atomic Implications'."

Fran paused as though weighing the two options. "Much as I hate to be disloyal, the 'Phil Smith Backlight Technique' is sexier — better for marketing."

"Yup, that's what I thought. It could pull some really serious research teams to us at CLS, good marketing. But if you want marketing — I did come up with a really, really good title . . . just a little hesitant about mentioning it."

"Why?"

"A bit too flashy — not scientific nomenclature," he said awkwardly. It was the Teleki effect, shaking him up, making him over confident.

"Now I am intrigued," Fran said. "What name would so violate scientific nomenclature that it would cause you to blush?"

"No, I shouldn't. You'll think me some kind of Prima Donna."

"I already think that, Phil, in a nice way though. You are a Prima Donna of physics."

Phil knew physics — it was his lifestyle. Something to put on, wear around, live with. He often forgot that others saw his work as fantastically complex, something wonderful and other worldly. Fran's simple compliment surprised and warmed him. Phyllis used to talk that way to him, about him. But not much anymore.

"So, what did you come up with? I'd really like to hear it."

"The 'Genesis Technique'," Phil blurted out, blushing again.

Fran watched him for a moment. "I love it. Creating light to study life to ultimately create life — am I right? Genesis, the beginning of creation?"

"Exactly. You got it perfectly."

"I have helped prep your reports and presentations about five-hundred times. So a bit is bound to rub off. Even on a regular IQ plodder like me."

"You've got a mathematics degree and a top-class brain, Fran. No false modesty," Phil said. "CLS doesn't hire plodders."

"Thanks Phil." It was her turn to blush. "I think I do get a fair bit of it. The biology stuff using protein crystals is where I bog down.

"Do you get the four macro molecules — nucleics, proteins, carbs and lipids?"

"Sure, the big four that differentiate us from rocks."

"Janos and his boys are zeroing in on proteins. They build crystals — like chains — which are solid proteins bound in repeating sequences. They want to see each link in the chain so they can figure out what it is. If they can do that, then they will know what gives life to the chain and thus the cell and thus the organism. The meaning of life, Fran. A biggee."

"Why in hell couldn't Janos say that?" She spread her arms wide. "So your super light lets him see the atoms and structure in the proteins."

"I knew you'd get it." Phil stretched his arm out and slapped her palm in a horizontal five.

"Janos started dumping amino-acid-peptide-bond-crystallography who's-your-father on me and I gave up. If you can explain it so I understand it, then you'll do fine at tomorrow's meeting with the really smart guys."

"Just to be safe, I'm coming in tonight for one last run through — settle the nerves."

"Hopefully the creepy Teleki won't show up to interfere. He comes in late and stays locked up in his office till midnight some times.'

"Are you serious? How do you know?"

"Andy, the commissionaire, told me."

"A really dedicated man of science?" Phil asked.

"Maybe. But he often leaves early only to come in late — why keep such odd hours? Creepy I say."

Phil retreated to his office. Surely they're not at it here, at CLS, in Janos' office? No. How could he sneak her past the commissionaire? And anyway Phyllis was home every night. God this was making him paranoid. But the theatre, or wherever they ended up, wasn't paranoia. There would be no mistakes tonight. He'd stick to them like glue and then bust in on them and then . . . well, then there would be hell to pay. He regretted calling Janos "buddy." Fran was right. The bastard was a creep who seduced honest women.

# Chapter 7

"WHERE'S THE CAMERA? DON'T TELL ME YOU forgot it?" Angie sounded hopeful.

He opened his leather coat and pointed to a Velcro strip near the bottom hem. "Movie ushers get nervous of people walking into their theatres with cameras — don't like hijackers. I'll give it to you when we get inside."

"Forget the camera!" Badger laughed. "Good one Angie. Hey, you're dealing with a couple of pros here, girl. We expect the unexpected. The real question is, are you ready and steady?"

"I'm good," she said tersely.

"Gotta be calm. Like us at the van last week. Stay focused. You get too nervous and ..."

"Easy big guy." Mike put a hand on Badger's shoulder. He needed Angie calm not Badgered up. "Nerves are good." Her grey eyes really were striking. And even though she had her hair tucked under a ball cap, the rich brown of it cascaded in a pony tail out the back. He moved close to her, lowering his voice "Nerves show you're alert and on. Just keep your game face and you'll be okay."

She took a step that brought her inches from his face. A scent came — some kind of herbal hair shampoo — really nice. Maybe it was a body wash. Man, herbal wash, rubbed all over . . .

"I'm good, Mike, really. I want to do this for you if it is what you truly want. It's not a game you know." Her eyes searched his face. "This could really screw up your family."

"If we are right, it's already screwed up. This is my chance to fix it — scare Phyllis off Janos."

"Maybe. Or maybe you'll just blow it apart and then she won't have a chance to quit on her own."

Mike returned her look. She could be right. How do you know what's right? It's the fog of war. Figure your best plan on the facts you have and get on with it — John le Carré.

"What's the call?" Badger was close and whispering now. "Go or abort?"

Mike felt his face slide into its familiar banal mask. "We go. We get the pictures at least. I can always change my mind later about how to use them. Keep our options alive, get the best intel we can right now, while we have the opportunity."

Badger punched his arm. "Yeah. No second guessing now." He looked at his watch. "I'm up." He made a fist. They copied him and tapped knuckles. Badger jogged out of the parking lot and around the corner to the main entrance.

Angie still stood close. She put her hand on his arm and rubbed it gently. "You're right. Get the pictures, then do a rethink. It'll be okay."

Mike kept his face straight. But his hand disobeyed a direct order and went up to cover hers. She took it and squeezed. They stood together quietly, holding hands. Mike had never held hands with a girl before. If only they were going into that theatre to watch the movie and hold hands and smell body washes.

~

A tiny part of his brain had clung to the idea — hope — that Janos would appear at CLS after supper and insist on helping with the prep. That Phyllis really was going to a show with her friend. That Janos could be *his* friend. He drank a half litre of coke and ate a chocolate bar waiting for Janos. By six forty-five, the tiny flicker of naïveté was extinguished. Phil signed out and drove home. By seven, he was parked, lights out, on Brookdale Crescent just between his house and where the back ally joined the crescent. Sneak out the back or use the front door, didn't matter. He was swallowing every few seconds, tapping the steering wheel and whistling a tune he couldn't name.

The garage door powered up. Back-up lights flickered from inside the garage and Phyl's car crept out onto the street. She shifted gears and drove out of the crescent. Phil started his car, breathing hard, and followed.

"Calm down for Chrissakes!" he shouted at himself. Phyl turned north onto Boychuk Drive, drove rapidly to 8th Street and almost lost him when she turned west on a stale green light. A Super-8 motel sign loomed on the right. She slowed, indicated and shifted to the right lane. "Jesus. A Super 8! Cheap bugger — not even a decent downtown hotel." He heard his own voice, recognized it, and chuckled. But Phyl drove past the motel and a few minutes later turned into the Galaxy Six parking lot. "What the hell? They really are meeting at a movie?" He parked three rows behind her then rummaged in a gym bag on the passenger seat. "Okay, okay, I'm ready for that — no problem." He pulled a ball cap out of the bag and jammed it on. He traded his wire rim glasses for the black plastic horn rimmed sports glasses he used for hockey. Finally he retrieved a small Ziploc plastic bag. He opened it and gingerly lifted a fake moustache — like a dead caterpillar — holding it close to the dash light. He peeled back the reverse-side tape exposing the damp makeup glue and carefully stuck the insect onto his upper lip. He combed it flat, examined himself in the rear-view mirror and saw a stranger. Excellent. Even a bit of irony — using a moustache disguise while stalking the moustachioed Hungarian.

Phyl was nearing the entrance. He hopped out of the car and jogged in behind her. The pervasive odour of hot popcorn, a swarm of noisy teenagers; rock music. Why weren't those kids doing their homework? It was a school night. He bought popcorn while Phyl bought her ticket. He kept his back to her as she passed by. He followed, stopping short of the attendant taking tickets. He pretended to read the Coming Attractions billboard, munching popcorn.

"Cinema four, on your left. Starts in ten minutes," the kid said.

"Thanks."

Phyllis hurried on, no backward glance. Phil returned to the kiosk and queued for his own ticket. By the time he entered cinema four, the previews had started. The theatre was black, light flickering on the scatter of faces intent on the screen. He climbed quickly to the back row, centre, and pulled his popcorn up to his face, fingering it into his mouth one kernel at a time. His eyes rapidly scanned the rows of seats, mostly empty. No Phyl. No Janos. Take your time. He sought each patron one by one. Fat guy with little kid, no. Couple of teenage boys, no. Three young girls, talking, cellphone lights flashing while they texted. He worked his way through the seats. No Phyl. Had he misheard? Cinema four? A young woman to his left shifted in her seat, leaning forward to examine what — a phone — in her lap. Beyond her sat Phyllis Smith. Alone, no girlfriend. She turned her head, looked over the young woman's back, and stared back at him.

Phil dove his fist into the greasy tub and stuffed a wad of popcorn into his mouth. Had she recognized him? No. Impossible. Ball cap, black glasses, moustache, dark room. He peeked at her. She was stretching, eyes on the screen, arching her back, arms extended. She wore a very tight black sweater so her torso was nearly invisible but the movement was pure come on. Phil swallowed and tried to control his suddenly shallow, rapid breathing. It was going to happen. Teleki would come in any second, and what were her words from supper the other night? *Remember what you and I used to get up to in the back rows of theatres?*

"Not tonight, by Christ. Not tonight," Phil said into his popcorn.

The young woman glanced at him. He ignored her, ignored Phyl, ignored the movie just now starting. He focused on the entrance, waiting for his prey. The half litre of coke swelled in his bladder, damn. Best go now — quick pee — then back. They'd be here re-enacting Phil Smith's youth. As he descended the stairs a raucous, shoving clutch of boys with two squealing girls, pushed past him.

⁓

Mike was sideways in his seat, back to the wall. Extreme right-lowest seat in the right-hand section. His dark coat was draped over his body, hiding his legs that were slung over the armrest. Bunnyhug hood up, he was almost invisible in the dark but had a view commanding nearly the entire seating. Badger was in the same seat, lower-left extreme. Overlapping arcs of observation. Perfect. Angie back-row left. Phyl hadn't given her a second glance when she'd arrived just before curtain and shuffled past her to the far-left seat.

Headscarf, sunglasses, raincoat, Phyllis was a caricature of the cheating housewife. Once seated she'd removed the glasses, wriggled out of the coat and pulled the scarf off shaking her hair free with dramatic waves of her head. Then she sat back, tousled, tight sweater, waiting. Angie, breaking discipline, had shot him a despairing look just before the light dimmed.

Well into the previews a man with a ball cap and popcorn arrived and sat near Angie. Mike stiffened, straining to see the face but it was permanently stuck in the popcorn. Not Janos — no move toward Phyllis. Just as the movie began a group of noisy brats pawing two girls arrived and started up toward the back row. The popcorn, ball cap guy pushed past them and left. The kids hit the back row and spread out, jostling past Angie. They filled all but one of the seats separating Angie from Phyllis. Angie leaned forward looking past the now grappling kids toward Phyllis. Then her head swivelled rapidly between Phyllis and Mike.

"Be cool, Angie," Mike whispered. "Sit tight, Phyllis won't stay there — let her go."

Angie half stood.

"No. Ange, no," Mike murmured to himself, willing her to stay. She looked for him, there was nothing he could do but trust her. "Come on, remember what we said." He closed his eyes trying to project his thought. When he opened them, she was sitting again, watching the movie. "Good girl. Well done Angie Bond Girl." Mike grinned into the darkness.

Phyllis stood her ground for less than a minute then gathering up her coat she edged past the kids and Angie. She hesitated briefly, scanning the theatre, then moved down a row and right, into Mike's sector — where she resettled. Mike counted slowly. In the event of a target move, Angie was to give a full two-hundred count before following. He hit two-fifty when Angie, during a part of the movie shot at night, glided behind and to the right of Phyllis. Perfect. Best possible set up. Those kids were a God send.

Phil checked his appearance in the bathroom mirror. Not a master of disguise but plenty good enough. He left the bathroom slowly, looking down the concourse for Janos. Didn't want to test his cover by a face to face meeting in full light. The entrance to cinema four was deserted. He hurried across and darted up the tunnel toward the big screen.

Conscious of exposure, he climbed quickly up the left aisle to his seat. Halfway up he looked for Phyllis and saw only the noisy kids. Phyllis was gone, as was the young woman. Phil stopped and searched the theatre. Damn kids must have spooked her. Not back left, must be back right. There, one row down from the back. Okay, go get the popcorn, sit and watch the show for a minute to look natural, then maybe move a few seats to the right. Phyllis would actually be easier to see now that she was down a row. Then when Teleki arrived, the real show would commence. He changed seats and settled himself low, peering under the brim of the cap. His eyes locked onto her, they did not blink. Exactly like the last time he'd parked outside home, waiting for Teleki to appear. His breathing shallowed out. His heart, slow now, thumped regularly. He could hear it. Darkness crept in once more and he welcomed it — no light needed for this evening's work.

Mike turned his observation to the entrance almost the instant the ball-cap man re-appeared at the bottom of the screen. This time he was profiled against the movie screen, moustache easily visible, as were a pair of phony-looking glasses. It *was* Janos, in a joke of a disguise. He stood, hands in pockets, looking to the back left corner of the theatre. He started up the left aisle, hesitated and stopped. Then he resumed his climb slowly, peering into the dark, searching for Phyl. Upon reaching his seat he picked up his popcorn. What was their game? Why the double entry and hesitation? Maybe they were being cautious, waiting to see if Phil was following them. It's what they should be doing — watching their back trail. Two minutes later, Janos crossed over, taking the seat beside Phyllis. The target was in place. He put his arm around Phyl and she curled under it to kiss him.

Mike turned his head. They were no longer "targets." He was no longer a watcher. This was dirty and nasty. He couldn't watch. Neither could he leave. It was up to Angie and Badger now. He was out. Angie had known this would happen — he hadn't — or at least he'd denied it. He tried to watch the movie but it was blurry. He was crying. Not sobbing, but his throat ached and the tears wouldn't stop. *Lamb of God, you take away the sins of the world: have mercy on us*, he prayed, pulling the hood down over his face. He thought no more of spying.

As it happened, the whole thing worked exactly according to plan. Angie got a half-dozen pictures. Phyllis left about twenty minutes before the end of the movie — Janos ten minutes later. Then Angie dropped the camera in Badger's lap on her way out. Badger left as the credits rolled. Mike, eyes dry and sore, stumbled out when the lights came up.

~

Phil believed his mental state was what they called conflicted. He'd been so confident that Teleki would meet his wife in cinema four. They would behave like naughty teenagers or they would leave for their real rendezvous. He'd been prepared for both eventualities. He'd not been prepared to sit for nearly an hour and a half while his wife watched a movie serenely ignorant of his presence. What in hell were they playing at? Then, just before the show ended, Phyllis had put on her scarf and coat and simply walked out. No Janos.

The whole thing seemed to be over in an instant — a nothing — as though he'd slept through the movie on his own. He was aware of a profound sense of relief. Maybe, just maybe, he was wrong about them. She could be his wife. Janos could be his friend. Or more likely, Janos had got cold feet. He'd stood her up. Arrogant prick, of course that was it. He'd already grown tired of her. He'd just show up, or not, at his pleasure. A raging, illogical anger replaced the relief.

"Don't be absurd. You can't be insulted that the man seducing your wife doesn't behave like a gentleman." He said it out loud to force himself back into some kind of normality, or at least reality. "Think, what else could it be?"

The movie was reaching its denouement. The hero racing against a ticking clock to save the heroine from the villain who'd abducted her. "Damn!" Phil was up and out of his seat and loping down the steps two at a time the instant the revelation unfolded itself. The movie was a dodge. Phyl had left early to meet Janos somewhere else. While he'd sat in a confused stupor she'd given him the slip. He ran through the deserted concourse and barged past the people lined up for the nine o'clock show.

Twilight, soft spring air. The parking lot nearly full. He ran, dodging and twisting through the cars. Maybe they were doing it in her car. No. A CLS van in a secluded area, yes. A busy, well-lit public car park, no. He reached the row Phyllis had parked in — her space was empty. He raced up it and down the next row only to arrive at his own car panting, sweating and raging oaths. Half of the ridiculous moustache had detached itself. He tore it free. The other half was well secured and stung. He swore again. What a jackass. His wife and Janos now somewhere in the city performing foul, obscene . . . He kicked his car door and was rewarded with a burning fire in his big toe. They would be laughing and mocking his inadequacies.

Phil breathed deeply, searching for something to grab hold of — a life preserver. He was drowning. His left foot came up lame, the toe throbbed. Couldn't go home and face Mike. Only one place to go — he'd head for the light — the ring. God's light, Phil Smith's light. He got in the car and drove for the Canadian Light Source. He could think and find a life jacket there. As he drove he glanced at his watch. Eight fifty-three. Cinema number four. His brain began ticking by fours: 853, 849, 845, 841, 837, 833.

~

Mike went home because he had to. Angie and Badger wanted him to stay with them, go to Badger's place and hang out for a couple of hours. "Decompress," Badger had said. But he could not. He had to go home to see her, talk to her, take the reality of his mom at home and force it up against the cheating bitch, Phyllis. He'd not confront her. No, he'd run off some hard-copy photos for that, prep himself. Perhaps even leave it all as Angie still urged. But for now, he had to be home.

He opened the front door. She was just leaving the kitchen, blowing on a cup of coffee to cool it.

"Hi honey. Where'd you get to? I thought you were going to stay in doing homework?"

Hair tousled, naughty curls bounced on her shoulders and the back of her neck. *You shook your hair out for him, you cheating Phyllis bitch!*

"Over at Badger's." He showed her the textbook he held in his hand. "Got some help on a couple of biology questions."

"I've just boiled the kettle." She pointed back into the kitchen, black sweater taut, straining, as she extended her arm. "Like me to make you some cocoa or tea?"

*Whore! Black sweater, groping, disgusting Phyllis whore!* "No thanks, don't bother. I'll get myself some cocoa."

"It's no bother. I'll make it for you." She disappeared into the kitchen. He stood for a moment, let his face crumble into a grimace of rage and swore the foulest words he could think of just under his breath. Then he rebuilt his face and went into the kitchen. She was putting a marshmallow into his cup. He sat at the table and she put the cup in front of him.

"Remember how I always made you cocoa at bedtime when you were a little boy?" She smiled at him. Happy, secure, flannel pajamas, hot cocoa with a melting marshmallow, Mom.

"Yeah. I loved it, especially when the marshmallow went all mushy." He smiled back at his mom, genuinely, no game face. It was Mom he wanted. *Here she is, accept her,* he thought. He sipped his drink, biting half the marshmallow and chewing it. She ran her hand over the back of his head, smoothing out his hair.

"Then Dad would read you a story, changing it, to include the effects of quantum physics on the Berenstein Bears picnic."

He laughed. She laughed. The three of them were good together. Angie was right, hang on, don't upset it.

"How was the movie?" he asked. Why had he done that? What was wrong with him? Couldn't he stand to be happy?

"Not bad. More of an action-adventure thing than I thought it would be."

He shrugged Phyllis's hand off his neck. Set his cocoa down. "How did Mrs. Prentice like it?"

"Oh, you know Liz." She turned her back to him and picked up her coffee cup. "She's a real movie hound; she loved it."

*Don't turn your back on me and Dad, you lying Phyllis liar, liar!* He wiped his own hand over his hair and neck, scraping off the feel of her touch.

"I'm tired. Think I'll take this up to bed." He stood and walked for the stairs.

"You okay, Mike?"

He kept walking. "Just great. Thanks for the cocoa."

"Night honey."

He didn't turn or answer Phyllis. Maybe his mom would come back if he got into his pajamas and drank his cocoa in bed.

# CHAPTER 8

JESUS WEPT. HE HAD B.O. COLD SWEAT sprouted under his arms and started to trickle into his shirt. He hurried to the washroom, hobbled by a swollen and painful big toe. He pulled his shirt tails clear of his pants, got his hands soaped and reached up, scrubbing his armpits. Then a rinse, then dry with paper towels. His shirt was wet now but at least it didn't stink. He hurried back to his office and threw his sports coat on. No sleep last night. Couldn't eat more than a bite of breakfast while Phyllis prattled on about the movie and speculated — kindly he had to admit — about the sure success of his presentation. Kindly, that is, for somebody with a poorly made-over hickey on her neck. God, he'd nearly screamed when he'd seen that. Then rush into work and stare all morning at his notes without seeing a single word. Suddenly hungry, he'd scarfed two EatMores and a large coke. Now he felt sick and stank. Jesus wept, Jesus wept. He was stumbling in nearly opaque darkness. How could he inspire anyone with his vision of light? Genesis Technique. Might as well call it Three Stooges Technique.

"Good luck, Phil." Fran at the door, grinning. He managed to pull his lips back over his teeth, hoping she's see it as a smile of confidence.

"Thanks."

"You won't need it."

"What?"

"Luck. You won't need luck. They'll approve your backlight procedure on the spot."

"Mustn't count our eggs before they're chickens — I mean hatched. Into chickens. Or not, if you're over confident."

Fran's smile subsided. "You don't look very good. Are you ill?"

*Jesus wept, no! I'm going to puke or crap my pants or just fade into darkness.*

"Me? Right as rain. Better get going."

He fled.

He was talking too fast but at least he was on track. The PowerPoint slides were good, really good, and he was smart enough not to read them to his audience. As each illustration flashed up he gave a ten-Mississippi count of silence then began talking about it. Not brilliance but solid. Janos caught his eye from the end of the long glistening table. A discrete thumbs up and a quick smile. It helped. He slowed his patter, inserting deliberate pauses. Bastard was actually with Phyl, just last night . . . no. Today he must be friend Janos, not bastard Janos.

Okay, next slide introduces the notion of inserting the beam on a serpentine wavelength. Give each member of the committee some deliberate face time. Be inclusive, Fran's very good advice. The darkness was edging back, a glimmer of lit-up hope crept into its place. He wasn't sweating anymore. Len Edwards, Director of Research, was midway down the table, intelligent face above a striped short-sleeve dress shirt and polka-dot tie — the beloved office attire of engineers. His eyes flickered across and down the screen. Phil turned slightly, smiled, and addressed Len.

"I know this will be of special interest to Dr. Edwards. This is likely the best part of the procedure from a purely scientific process point of view."

Len nodded thoughtfully. "Gonna show us how to stickhandle that beam through the matter eh, Phil?"

"Should be a guaranteed shot on goal, Len."

A flutter of laughter rippled about the table. Phil breathed it in and it was a balm. He breathed out confidence.

"Oh, yes. The hockey metaphor," Janos said a bit too loudly. "I saw Doctor Smith score a goal actually on ice and on my x-ray line. Both very impressive!" Janos beamed, head swivelling left and right.

Phil tried for eye contact. *Too much Teleki* his raised eyebrows said.

Janos missed the signal, bobbing his head in a near sycophantic fever.

"Doctor Teleki is too kind," Phil interjected, in control now. No need for Janos's support anymore. "But I do believe that this technique will allow us, once sufficient depth has been attained, to flare back such a high degree of light as to illuminate the very meaning of the structure being studied, without any absorption loss."

"That's a tad vague, Phil. Can you be more direct?" Len asked.

"Well, not to put too fine a point on it, I think we will see what makes these crystals tick. Why they live, how they live."

"Surely you're not suggesting an illumination capable of revealing new subatomic information." Hard and quick, from Stu McCulloch, the Linear Accelerator Scientist.

"Not at this point, of course." Phil, slightly nettled, pointed his clicker at the screen. "But once we see the penetration model achieved, I will demonstrate . . . "

"I get it, Doctor Smith," McCulloch snapped. "But my question still stands. How can you be so confident your procedure here," he pointed at the screen. "Will lead to such vastly superior results — in fact, defeat the absorption problem?"

"We've done some testing, naturally." Phil made an effort to speak calmly — professional to professional. "And the Hungarians have been good enough . . . "

"Hold it a minute." McCulloch stood, chair swivelling away. "You're not authorized to test yet. And certainly not using Canadian CFI money granted to foreigners — no offence, Doctor Teleki."

Janos smiled an innocent no-offence-taken back at McCulloch.

"I don't think I have violated any funding guidelines." Phil pointed his clicker at Janos. "But preliminary testing is allowed under the Memo of Understanding so long as the cost comes from the users' twenty percent. And the Hungarians will be the first for this so . . . "

"First users, *if* we give approval." McCulloch was borderline belligerent. "Right now the Operations vote is not a given."

Phil suddenly awoke. Stu McCulloch was here to sink him. The petty son of a bitch. His own request for Operating and Maintenance funding to upgrade the LINAC had been denied. But kill my project, and he might get his hands on this dough for his beloved accelerator. God, he'd not seen it coming, and nobody had warned him. So, there must be other votes in doubt.

"I didn't mean to imply otherwise." Phil ran his eye toward the executive director, hoping for top-dog support. The ED stared hard at the screen, arms crossed, body language not good. What the hell? Was he already sandbagged?

"But I am confident the results we've predicted are conservatively achievable." He locked onto McCulloch, ready to drop the gloves if need be.

"Conservative! Really? Let's try to apply some restraint." He smirked.

"I have light that would make God envious and I have the means of shedding it in the cause of great science, gentlemen." Heat rose darkly up Phil's torso. By heavens he'd not be bullied by this greedy, jealous arse.

"God's Light!" Stu turned to the executive director. "Surely we're not doing a Higgs Boson search for proof of God!"

Phil bit his tongue. How had he let that phrase out? He'd played right into Stu's game. He looked quickly to the director who was now trying to avoid eye contact with both men. "What are you saying, Doctor McCulloch? I'm not sure I see the relevance, you know." Phil felt himself in a verbal stumble, trying to regain his professional balance but knowing he looked like a clown.

"Are you denying knowledge of the Higgs Boson search?" McCulloch was now in open sneer mode.

"No, of course not. I mean, not denying. I have heard of it. But what has that got to do with my procedure?" Phil exerted every bit of self-control to stay rational. *Don't let this guy get to you, go around him.*

"Higgs Boson." Stu leaned forward, stuck out his jaw, and placed both hands, palms down, on the table. His gaze swept round the members coming dangerously close to hijacking the presentation. Nobody was looking at the screen or Phil. "The God Particle — the answer to why matter exists in excess of anti-matter," he said dramatically, forearms flexing. "Thus why we, or anything exists. The Large Hadron Collider — a seventeen-mile accelerator ring in France and Belgium — searching for the key to creation." He turned and stared significantly at Phil. "I suspect Doctor Smith, perhaps on an unconscious level." He smiled to show his well meant intention. "Thinks he is chasing the same Holy Grail. We have heard him use the term God Light and then there are the signs hanging in his office . . . "

"What in hell are you suggesting!" Phil's voice shot across the table, too late to recall it or tone down its insipient hysteria.

"You've lost your objectivity, Phil. It does happen, it's insidious." Stu's face smoothed into a concerned colleague veil.

"Don't be ridiculous!" Phil jabbed a finger at the now ignored PowerPoint screen. "God's Light is a slang phrase that I would never seriously use. And I'm not in any way trying to emulate the Hadron Collider in France. There are no collisions." He whirled back to face the director. "You can't seriously be thinking that I'm on some sort of God quest."

"Well, Phil." The director coughed and blushed. "Doctor McCulloch and I have had occasion to notice changes in your behaviour over the last couple of weeks."

"But you've never said anything to me. You two . . . "

The director held his hand up. "Please, Phil, it's not a conspiracy — it's a concern."

"I am illuminating protein crystals to understand their creative functionality." Phil spoke each word carefully. The director was now calling him 'Phil' but everyone else by their formal title of Doctor — a really bad sign. He had lost control; he must regain it or risk losing the whole thing.

"Sure Phil," Stu murmured. "Anything you say." He rolled his eyes up. The director sighed sympathetically.

Phil lost his struggle for control. "Those cowboys in France are building a seventeen-mile ring to search for something that may not exist!" He screeched. "And if they do find it, they might start an anti-matter reaction that will create a black hole that'll suck Europe up its own ass! That has absolutely nothing to do with the Smith Backlight Technique!"

He panted, cold sweat coursed down his ribs, his vision tunnelled through encroaching darkness. He tried to step back from the table, get some distance, but caught his left foot on a table leg and fire leapt up from the injured toe. "Damn and blast!" He yelped, staggering. "Damn it all!"

"*Smith*, Backlight Technique?" Stu pretended confusion. "I didn't know we'd advanced so far as assigning personal-credit nomenclature, did you Executive Director?"

"That was me." Janos stood slowly, eyes squinting to focus on McCulloch. "And it was a trivial gesture of friendship that should not be of any concern to a meeting of this stature." His English was precise, almost no accent. "Why would you, Doctor McCulloch, be so negative towards a process that has not even been fully presented yet?"

Stu squinted back. "Free country, Doctor Teleki — we question and probe without fear of rank or politics. Let me explain. It is a rigorous system of ... "

"I understand your reference to my country's unfortunate political history of intolerance and suppression. I also understand the scientific process. What I am not understanding, my dear Stu, are your petty references to signs which are hung." His accent crept back. "In some person's office or the herring red in France and Belgium."

"I meant no offense to the Hungarian team." Stu lost the staring contest with Janos and turned to the director, shrugging his shoulders.

Janos flipped rapidly through a binder lying on the table in from of him. "Here it is." He looked up, shot Phil a conspiratorial wink, then faced the director. "Contract parameters and budget guidelines from our initial bid request approved by CLS Users Committee more than two years ago."

He cleared his throat and began to read. "Any research arising from existing procedures and consistent with initial research goals shall be encouraged by host and Principal Investor. Any additional costs must be paid from the twenty-percent user contribution." He looked up from the binder and stared at the director. "Doctor Smith's procedure most certainly meets this guideline, if we are allowed to hear it."

Janos tapped his chest. "I am Principal Investor; I am most encouraged, and," he paused for effect. "It is Hungarian money that so far paid for the extra testing. We are not . . ." A glare at Stu. " . . . attempting to obtain free research from Canadian Light Source optimization or O&M money."

McCulloch dropped into his seat like a shot duck. The director's face flushed claret. He began to speak but Janos cut him off.

"May Doctor Smith proceed?"

The director exhaled in relief. "Of course. Please let us do carry on." Janos resumed his seat and turned his attention to Phil. Phil, eyes prickling with tears of gratitude, drew a shaky breath and turned to face the screen, composing himself.

"Yes." He coughed. "The flare back projection as illustrated here."

Phil's world was full of light. He was not even sweating. His heart was flying the ring — twisting, banking, and soaring. The man who shed the light and sent him flying was the very same man who had given Phyllis a hickey in the cinema less than twenty-four hours earlier. He would defer that hideous contradiction for later examination.

～

"The Hungarian Light-Source Team, a toast!" Phil raised his wine glass, grinning broadly.

"NO, please, you embarrass me," Janos said, clearly pleased with the gesture.

"I insist." Phil tapped the table. "Lady and gents, I give you the best damn science team at CLS — the Hungarians — and their peerless leader, Doctor Janos Teleki."

Mike dutifully muttered, "Doctor Teleki," and drank his iced tea. Phyllis, seated across the table, took a largish swallow of her wine and laid her hand on Janos's arm, giving it a congratulatory squeeze. Then she turned to Phil, put her arm around his shoulders and pulled him close for a loud kiss on the cheek.

"What was that for?" Phil asked.

"Why for creating an effective back-light technique to enhance the study of protein crystal structure."

"But you were fed up with that."

"That's not all." Phyllis raised her glass. "And for being a modest, generous genius who toasts others in his own moment of triumph."

"That," Phil said, returning her kiss, "is tempting fate. McCulloch raised a doubt; the committee reconvenes on Tuesday to decide whether to proceed with my project or not. It's not in the bag yet."

"Oh, McCulloch, pooh-pooh." Janos reached across Phyllis, his shoulder and arm pressing tightly into her as he extended his opposite hand to Phil. "Shake on it, my dear Phil. I am not afraid to congratulate now. They will proceed."

Phil grasped his hand and pumped it. Phyllis put both her hands over theirs, practically rubbing herself onto Teleki's arm. "You really put the boots to McCulloch with your twenty-percent Hungarian money." He raised his glass again. "To Hungarian research with Hungarian dollars!" he cried.

"Euros my friend, but Euros most gladly and well spent," Janos replied. "I did not give my boots to anyone. Another Canadian expression, I assume?"

Mike pasted a smile on his face and gritted his teeth. Poor Phil, unsuspecting sucker. So pathetically grateful for a bit of help at the meeting that he doesn't even see his own wife being groped in front of him. Their voices turned into a bubbly static as they went for another toast to Phil the Genius, then Teleki the Saviour, then Phyllis the Best Wife Ever. Mike flinched when Phyllis touched Janos's wrist; then again when she shook her hair free of her collar and her curls brushed his cheek. God only knew what was happening under the table out of Phil's sight. Each gesture was a slap to be taken on his father's behalf. A slap that he must return with a smile. *Turn the other cheek*, he thought. The toughest thing he had ever done. He would be printing the digital photos tomorrow but he'd promised to meet Angie and Badger to talk it over before confronting Phyllis.

Right now, chewing his lower lip in humiliation and rage he felt like showing the pictures to Phil then ramming them down Phyl and Janos's throats. Not to scare Phyllis straight, but to hurt her like she was so happily hurting her family. Angie may have been right; maybe Phyllis didn't want to be warned off. Maybe his own mom wanted to leave him and Dad for this ridiculous moustached seducer.

" . . . the prime rib, Mike?" Phyllis, smiling over the top of her menu.

"Eh?"

"Will you go for your usual, prime rib, honey?"

Mike stared at her, repulsed at the "honey" from this phony bitch. He looked at Phil. "What are you having, Dad?"

"Thought I might try the liver and onions."

"Then that's what I'll have," Mike snapped. "I don't have to eat prime rib every time I come to the Keg, do I?"

The three adults looked at him, an awkward silence settling on the table.

"I was only joking, son. Who in their right mind wants liver and onions at the Keg? I mean, I doubt it's on the menu."

A corner of Mike's conscious self called for him to control his temper but being caught in dad's liver-and-onions joke seemed to make the whole thing even more intolerable. "Maybe I'm not in my right mind." He focused on Janos. "Maybe I want to eat liver and onions rather than prime rib. Do they eat a lot of liver in Hungary, Doctor Teleki?"

Janos half grinned, not sure whether this was another joke or not. He waved his hands. "I'm not knowing really, yes, I suppose, but why such a question?"

Mike didn't know why. It was a stupid thing to say but the ferocious surge of rage wasn't logical. It just demanded that he do something. He turned on his mother.

"Maybe you and Doctor Teleki should share a surf-and-turf for two, Phyllis." He flipped his menu open and pounded his fist on it. "Then Dad and I could just eat whatever you tell us to eat, eh? Prime rib for us, was it?"

Phyllis' eyes widened. She put her napkin to her lips and sat back heavily, frightened of her own son. Mike fed on it. He banged his fist on the menu again and a waiter came hurrying into his peripheral vision.

"Well Mom? What's wrong? You and Teleki lost your appetites?"

"Mike!" Phil took his fist in his hands. "What in hell has got into you? Are you all right?"

Mike opened his fist, gripped his dad's hands and dropped his face to stare at them. Tears, embarrassing cry-baby tears stung his eyes. *God Almighty, please don't let me cry.* Some of his anger flowed into his father's innocent hands; he squeezed tighter and tapped off another layer of rage. A deep ragged breath — no tears — okay. He looked back up at the ring of worried faces. The waiter hovered silently just beyond Janos, twisting his apron in knots.

A robin suddenly flew through Mike's mind's eye — followed closely by another one. They banked, dipped and flashed low over water, riffling its surface. Then the clear bubbling delight of a meadow lark's song welled up inside him. He thought of Badger and his other world of ants and birds; of Angie and her sympathetic grey eyes. He released his clamped jaw then opened his eyes wide and relaxed his face, shoving the last of his emotions down.

"Sorry, I, ah." He looked at his mother. *You'll be sorry tomorrow,* he thought. *But one on one, not in front of Dad.* "Mom, Doctor Teleki, I just don't know what came over me. I really do apologize."

"Should we go home, an early night?" Phyllis reached tentatively forward and touched one fingertip to Mike and Phil's hands, as though testing to see how hot they were.

"No. I truly need some beef, just hungry I guess, but I promise I'll be fine," Mike said, fully confident he wouldn't lose his game face again. "Maybe the thought of liver and onions freaked me out." He smiled. "You know, temporary insanity."

They all laughed much too loudly, eager to band aid over the unpleasantness. Mike whipped the menu up and pretended to study it. Pretended not to notice the anguished looks of fear his parents exchanged.

~

There was energy in his son's fist. A surge of energy that was being transmitted into his own hands. Phil sensed it like a mild electric current. The notion again surfaced that he might be more of a father than he thought. Mike was furious and at the same time frightened almost to the point of tears but certainly not over a joke about liver. Mike's fist changed to an open hand that gripped desperately like a drowning man might grip a rescuer's hand to keep his head above water. Mike was humiliated. He was angry with Phyllis and it seemed Janos, but what had triggered it? And why Janos?

Phil watched Mike's face intently — dark brown eyes glaring. The normally inscrutable face now taut as he stammered some insincere apology and struggled to regain his composure. The emotion seemed to pulse through their hands. Phil did not know why, but at this moment he was convinced that his son loved him and needed to be rescued — so he squeezed Mike's hand and absorbed his humiliation.

The electric current died. A poker-faced boy replaced his needy son and he slipped his hand away from Phil. He studied his menu. Phil was shocked by the sudden transformations. Smiling happy, then rage, then shame, then a controlled mask of indifference in the space of ninety seconds. Mike's words 'temporary insanity' rang in his ears. His worst fear. The nightmare of a teenaged loner overwhelmed by some kind of insanity, gone savage and violent. He looked to Phyllis and saw his fear reflected back. And something more. Guilt perhaps. Mike had been deliberately hostile to both her and Janos. Could he possibly know about them? Sense it? No. Ridiculous. Mike had problems, but teenage-boy emotional problems. Phil picked up his own menu and broke eye contact with his wife. He glanced over the rim of the menu at Mike transformed. If only I could turn Janos and Phyl's treachery on and off like that. Remove the complications of Janos as his saviour and Phyllis as the best wife a man could have.

Darkness began to creep in around the edges of the menu. Liver and onions more appropriate than he'd thought. What if the committee rejected the Genesis Technique on Tuesday? What would he do when he finally caught Janos and Phyl at it? Could he weather two such calamities or would the darkness take him once and for all. And would he take them with him?

〜

Badger's bird-watching blind was an impressive bit of workmanship. Mike could understand Angie's surprise when Badger melodramatically pulled the camouflaged screen back to reveal the cozy hiding space beneath the big old maple tree. But she went overboard and it roused his suspicion.

"Oh," she said. "My," she said. "Gawd!" she squealed. "This is just awesome." She twirled around as Badger replaced the screen, grinning smugly. He removed the tarp and set up folding chairs. "This is like, just awesome," she said again.

"Beautiful morning like this." Badger opened his arms expansively, "and we might get a look at the aerobatic robins."

"Really?" Angie enthused. "Like, that would be too wicked."

Mike fingered the envelope in his thigh pocket. A half-dozen pictures of Phyllis and Janos practically devouring each other in the theatre. A glance at the pictures had been almost more than he could stand. He'd let Angie and Badger see them of course, but he couldn't examine them closely without feeling sick to his stomach. The envelope was heavy, at least if felt like a dead weight on his leg. He pulled it out. Angie and Badger both let their eyes flicker to it then dart away.

"So tell me where these birds of yours will appear, Badger." She walked to the edge of the creek and Badger followed her closely, pointing out the usual flight path. "That is so cool. Birds flying like fighter planes you say?" Her head swivelled back and forth, pony tail whipping behind it, looking up and down the creek for the robins.

"Okay, what is this?" Mike asked, irritated that they were obviously performing to a prearranged script.

"What's what?" Badger shrugged, innocently.

"Angie sounds like Vanessa at a Valley Girl convention and you're acting like Professor Doolittle."

"I do not sound like Vanessa. And that screen thingy is like, awesome, so why shouldn't I say so?"

"That is your fourth 'awesome' and about your tenth 'like'. You pride yourself on never using those two words."

She didn't argue. Her eyes dropped down to the envelope in his hand.

"Well?"

Badger fidgeted, moved one of the chairs, then moved it back and sat down. "We had a talk at my place on Thursday after the movie," he said. "Let's sit, huh?"

Angie squatted, leaning her back against the tree trunk, Mike sat in the second chair.

"Talked about the pictures?" Mike prompted.

"Yeah." Badger looked to Angie, neither seemed willing to go farther. The leaf-green space fell silent. A distinct plop, followed by a splash came from the creek.

"What was that? A beaver?" Angie half rose to look down stream.

"Muskrat most likely," Badger said.

"Oh."

"And what did you decide about the pictures?" Mike tapped the envelope.

"It's your family so your decision, not ours," Badger said. "But we do have advice, or I guess an opinion, and you said we should discuss it, so here we are."

"I think I have to shove these pictures down Phyllis's throat and let Phil see what he's got for a wife," Mike said, the Keg dinner-anger spiking up. "But I do want to hear you guys out too." He turned toward Angie. The ponytail and sweatshirt looked good together. Actually just about anything she wore these days looked good. "So what's with the Valley Girl?"

"We decided to be as upbeat as possible." Angie leaned forward. "We, me especially, really worry about confronting Phyllis and particularly Phil. Once you do that, it's like a line that you step over and can never step back from. So we figured if we met here, calmly, natural and all, then if we were cheerful and ah . . . "

"Upbeat." Badger supplied.

"Then at least we could set the stage for both options rather than just being all gloom and doom," Angie finished.

"Manipulate me with upbeatness? That was your plan?" Mike was taken aback by their naïveté

"Not manipulate." Angie blushed. "We are your friends."

Her unblinking grey eyes met his, honestly, he thought. He returned her look and found himself smiling.

"It appears to have worked. I feel pretty 'upbeat'." He made quote marks with his fingers. "But only because that had to be the saddest excuse for spy-craft acting I've ever seen. It was funny. Man, you guys are weak. I mean, you couldn't manipulate a . . . "

"I told you it wouldn't work, Ange." Badger pointed at Mike. "The guy manoeuvres his parents, all the teachers and several government agencies. We're not going to trick him into being so damn cheerful that he won't show the pictures to Phyllis!"

"Oh yeah, like you had a better idea." She shot back. "You want to know what his plan was?" She turned to Mike.

He laughed. "I shudder to think."

"He wanted me to distract you." She stood up and put one hand on her hip, shoving it out at a provocative angle. "Then he was going to grab the photos and camera and refuse to give them back unless you promised to take a week to cool down before going to your mom and dad. Talk about a crude, macho, bullshit plan."

Badger now stood up. "That plan would have worked, Miz Feminist." He waved his arms at her. "He's already half goofy for you. If you showed the right plumage, he'd do anything you said! But look at you. Old jeans, baggy sweatshirt, and no makeup. You couldn't have distracted . . . "

"He's half goofy over me?" Angie said it quietly, turning to face Mike.

"Uh oh." Badger sat down quickly.

Mike knew he should have been thinking toward a logical disconnect from this dangerous emotional trap. But he'd gone blank. He tried to force a thought — any thought — into his head. He looked at Angie. *Hail Mary full of Grace*, he prayed to himself. This was trouble. Would she burst out laughing? Mock Him? Did it matter? Yes, it did matter a great deal.

She didn't laugh or mock. She simply stared at him and he stared back.

"Actually, your, uh, plumage, is pretty darn distracting." What in hell was he saying? What was happening? A songbird wittered its shivering call from the maple branches above them.

"Yellow warbler," Badger said. "Female, I think."

Angie's face turned up into a smile. "How did I ever get mixed up with you two?" She shook her head. "I mean, spying on people; taking pictures of your mom making out; eavesdropping on phone calls; and now discussing my — geez — plumage, in a bird-watching blind." She burst out laughing and sagged back against the tree.

"Nobody forced you to be here." Badger stuck his jaw out defensively.

"Oh, hey! Don't get me wrong, boys. This is where I want to be." She slid her back down the tree and sat at its base. "This is real, no matter how bizarre, it's real. We're here for some pretty serious business. We should discuss the pictures and Phyllis, but first." She looked back at Mike. "First, I guess I want to say to Mike that I'm really happy you like my plumage. But that's for another, better day, right?"

Mike swallowed a tremendous lump of anxiety and nodded vigorously.

"Okay, I saw Phyllis and she's doing wrong." Angie steered them back to business. "But your dad still loves her and she might even love him."

"How?" Mike fumbled the pictures out of the envelope and they scattered on the ground. "How could she love him and do that?"

Badger scooped them up and glanced at them. "Crap. Poor Phil."

"Exactly." Mike took the photos back. "What about Phil who still loves her even though she's cheating on him and me and wrecking our family?"

"Showing Phil these won't solve anything." Angie said with conviction. "He'll be crushed and maybe grow to hate the woman he loves. Crushing and hating never produce a good thing."

Mike felt himself wanting to agree with her. His parents in love, Phyl misbehaving but still his mom, still Phil's wife.

"So my question stands. How can she do this . . . " Pausing, he slapped dirt and bits of leaf off the pictures. " . . . and still love him?"

"Don't know," Angie said flatly. "Doesn't matter really. Janos seduced her, flattered her, she's angry at Phil for his hockey and work addictions, but deep down she probably still loves him."

"They're the happiest old farts I know," Badger said. "My folks hardly ever laugh and have nothing in common now that the young are nearly raised. Phil and Phyl are always, or *were* always, acting like best friends."

"So I do nothing?"

"Let it run its course." Angie knelt at his side and took his hand in both hers, speaking urgently now. "If I am right, this Janos guy will get tired of her or go back to Hungary and she'll wake up and see what she almost lost. It will be over and nobody gets hurt."

"Too late." Badger interrupted. "Mike already feels like she's kicked him in the cojones."

Angie shot him a dirty look and squeezed Mike's hand to hold his attention. "And if I'm wrong, and she does betray him, leave for good." She drew a deep breath. "Well, then it is bad and it hurts — but no worse than if you expose it now. At least my way there is a chance. Show those pictures to Phil and it's over now."

This was the third time she had held his hand and Mike realized that her hands were always warm. So comforting. But not particularly soft. Not girly hands puttied with fruit-flavoured lotion. It occurred to him that Phyl would probably like Angie. In fact both his parents would be overjoyed if he had a girlfriend. Guys with girlfriends don't go Columbine. Could Angie really be his girl?

"What about Mike? He's got to suck it up for the next year till Teleki goes home?" Badger asked.

"Yes, he does."

"But you should have seen them last night, at the Keg. Touching and laughing and toasting. That bastard and my own mom in total-bitch mode. Phil not even knowing what they're up to." Mike spat this out like bile, his stomach sick with the memory.

"My folks fought a lot but I never knew my dad was going to leave us till he did — so I can't say I understand exactly what you're feeling but." Angie's voice trembled. "But you've got to handle this if you can. If it could make things better."

"I don't think I can," Mike said quickly. "I nearly lost it at the Keg. I can't. I know I can't hack that over and over again for a year."

"Then how about this." Angie let his hand go and stood. "Go to Phyllis like your first plan. Leave Phil out of it and go to Phyllis. Show her the pictures." She began pacing the small blind. But not shouting and threatening to force her back. That won't work. Let her know about how hurt you are — what you guys just said."

"That she's kicking him in the *cojones* and she should stop," Badger declared.

"You could word it better than that, but yeah. Let her know the hurt she's causing but then back off, leave her for a few days. She still loves you and Phil; she'll see the right thing to do." She clapped her hands together. "This could work; maybe it's even the best way to go."

"All right, I'll go now. If she's alone at home, I'll do it."

"Wait a minute, think your words out before you leave," Angie said.

"No. I'm ready." Mike turned to leave then turned back to face them. "Ah, I don't know how to say this but you two are the best, really."

So much for the spy handler with ice water in his veins. To hell with it anyway. "I won't forget this, what you guys are doing for me."

"It's name is friendship, Mike." Badger grinned. "But from a biologic imperative to preserve the mating family unit. Don't go all mushy on me."

Angie smiled so sweetly he could almost taste it. "Before you go, I have to ask. What government agencies have you manipulated?"

Mike fished his wallet out and showed her his Art Guthrie driver's license and social insurance number card.

"The real things?"

He nodded. "Badger can explain."

# CHAPTER 9

"EYYYEE DON'T KNOW HOW TO LUUUUUV HIM!" Phyllis's quavering tenor shot up, reaching for a soprano level at "love him" but failed the summit and warbled back down to her natural depth.

Phil opened one eye and squinted at the clock: 08:30. He closed the eye and snuggled his head back into the pillow. Fresh sheets and pillow slip. Still crisp and clean against his skin. Nearly nine hours of sleep — dreamlessly vacant. When was the last time he'd slept so well? When was the last time he'd slept in even a half hour on a Saturday morning? Was that coffee? He sniffed and focused. French Vanilla, from the fresh ground beans. Phyl must have put it on the timer then gone to shower. Her rendition of the *Jesus Christ Superstar* love song crescendoed again, drowning out the sound of the rushing water. He smiled. She had sung that song at the top of her lungs in their honeymoon suite just before they made love on their wedding night. Got a call from the front desk to pipe down — so she sang it again — or tried to before his impatience got the best of him. Then it became their little intimate joke. She would hop in the shower; sing, "I Don't Know How to Love Phil," then dash out half wet and naked to . . .

"Oh, damn!" Phil sat up, heart pounding.

Phyllis, shower, love song, Saturday morning sleep in. The thoughts whipped through his head and he knew what came next. He couldn't face the certain disgrace of that. Nor could he reject her again and watch the disappointment. Better run for it. Into the closet, pull on sweats, socks, grab running shoes. But she was with Teleki now. Why would she want me? The singing ceased. No time to take a chance. He darted to the bedroom door. The shower stopped running. Blast! Wallet and car keys. He hustled back to his side of the bed, grabbed them and turned just as Phyl, wrapped in a bath towel stepped out of the bathroom. God, she looked good. Dark wet hair, shiny and slick on the curve of her neck and shoulder. Eyes bright, mouth open, smiling. A very damp towel clinging . . . maybe he could.

"You're dressed! Did my singing wake you?" She laughed, humming the tune, extending one arm dramatically like an opera star.

"Yeah, but I loved it. Just like the old days."

"Not that old." She pouted, then winked. "Seems like yesterday we were on our honeymoon."

He edged toward her, cursing himself. Why bring up those memories? Maybe she had been just singing in the shower, but now he'd got her thinking.

"Coffee smells great. Thought I might zip out and get Saturday papers — a *Globe* and a *National* — maybe a couple of Danish pastries." He waited for her face to fall, the sigh, the sagging shoulders.

She clapped her hands together. "Oh, goody. A lazy Saturday morning over coffee, Danish and papers. We haven't done that since before hockey season."

She smoothed the towel over one hip. "I ate too much at the Keg — maybe I shouldn't have the pastry. What do you think?" She looked at him but not as the coquette, just as a self-conscious woman in her forties.

"That," he said pausing in the bedroom doorway, "is a ridiculous question. I'll bring you two Danish and you'll still be the definition of svelte."

She smiled. He left, confused. That whole episode should have ended sweaty in bed, with him mortified and useless. But she seemed genuinely happy for morning coffee and nothing else. Could it be Teleki's influence? She is well satisfied? He strode through the house puzzling over these Saturday circumstances and stepped into the garage. Mike was just coasting in on his bike.

"Out to the gym, Dad?"

"No. Papers and pastry, back in twenty minutes. Where have you been so early?"

"Met Badger at the ravine, nothing doing really."

"Want a Danish?"

"No thanks. I ate breakfast before I went."

~

The hairdryer stopped its high-pitched whine and a moment later, Phyllis breezed into the kitchen humming a tune from the old JC Superstar opera.

"Hi, Mike. Up early for Saturday. Had breakfast? You just missed Dad, he could have brought you a doughnut."

Mike sat at the table. "Already had breakfast and been out to the ravine. Saw Phil but didn't want a doughnut," he muttered.

She shot him a quizzical look then began pulling mugs and plates from the cupboard. "You okay?"

"Why shouldn't I be okay?" he snapped.

She turned, setting the cups on the counter. "Are you angry with me?"

He glared at her, pictures hot against his thigh, scarcely able to contain himself. She needed that cheery Saturday smile erased. She had no right to cozy coffee and buns and newspapers the morning after flirting with her boyfriend, right in front of her family.

"Why would I be angry with you? The perfect wife and mother. According to the toasts made last night."

Her face hardened. At least that stupid grin was gone.

"All right, that's enough. You did your best to ruin your father's special dinner last night now you're being downright ignorant with me and I'm not going to take it."

"ME!" Mike lost his slim grip on self-control. He was conscious of it drifting away and knew he should grab it back but a chirpy Phyllis had pushed him too far. Angie's advice was good, but he couldn't do it. "I ruined dinner?" His fist pounded the table top. Phyl jumped. "You and your boyfriend are pawing each other right in front of Dad, and *you* think *I* ruined the evening?"

Phyllis shrank back, almost cowering like a hunted animal for a second, then recovered herself. "What on earth are you saying? Make sense, boy."

She never called him "boy." She never berated him. But he'd never yelled at her before. A corner of Mike's mind went calm, analytical. She was acting a part now. He was out of emotional control. This could go horribly wrong. He thought of Smiley and John le Carré. Make it happen on your ground. Regain the initiative. Phil couldn't come home to a mother-son battleground. He simply had to regain his composure or the whole operation would be blown clean away. Angie was right, Phil didn't need to know yet.

He sat quietly with these thoughts, listening to her breathing, waiting. He put his spy face back on and grappled his self-control back into harbour. Phyl walked toward the fridge, paused, then backed up to the counter. Good, he was calming; she was beginning to spook.

"Let me rephrase." He put his hands, palms down, on the table and leaned forward. "I know you are having an affair with Janos Teleki. That is a simple fact. I know that even Phil will eventually figure it out. I know that when he does, it will destroy us all. I don't want it Phyllis. I want you to break it off with Teleki. You're hurting me and you'll crush Phil."

Perfect. Exactly as it should have started. But the next words stuck like a bone in his throat. He coughed and tried again. "If you love us . . . your son and Phil. You will stop now."

"Michael." Her voice was strong, clear. "I don't know how you got such an idea. Of course you would be angry, if that were true, but it's not."

"Don't lie, Phyllis. It's a time waster and Dad will be home soon. I want this resolved by then." He actually felt a ripple of satisfaction with that line. This was better. He was back now, in charge.

"I'm not lying." She took a threatening step toward him. "And I am still your mother. You can't interrogate me with that tone, boy."

Boy again. Good. She was still acting, but it was shaky. He shrugged, smiling. "You are not my mother when you cheat on me and Phil. And I am not interrogating. I have the answers already. I know what you are."

"You know nothing! This is ridiculous." She was close now. Anger obviously being faked. She turned her back to him.

"You have picked up some silly idea and made it into a dark fantasy and I want you to stop."

It occurred to Mike, as he pulled the photo envelope from his pocket, that she was reverting to her old fear of him as a high-school shooter. That was not part of her pretense of innocence. Time for the pictures.

"Phyllis, turn around please."

She turned and he dealt the first photo like a playing card, face up on the table. She glanced at it, looked away, a then quickly looked back. He dealt the second one. It seemed to draw her toward the table. The third one she reached for slowly and picked up. The phony anger dropped from her face. She put her free hand over her mouth stifling any conversation. She didn't bother to look at the other three when he laid them out. She stared at the one in her hand, as though hypnotized by it. The kitchen clock ticked long, slow seconds. The collapse into tears and remorse Mike had hoped for didn't happen. Did she not believe her own eyes? Or did she not feel remorse?

"I saw who was driving the CLS van the Tuesday before last when it dropped you off in the back alley. I saw the moustache. I asked Dad if he had a van out but no, he hadn't."

Her eyes shot up, fearful now. A reaction he could work with.

"Don't worry, he didn't know why I was asking. I never mentioned you or Teleki."

Her face relaxed. She gazed back at the picture as though it was a shot of a family holiday. That's it? As long as Phil doesn't know she's content with the situation?

"Badger and I were in the ravine that day. We saw the van, heard what was going on! Don't give me the silent treatment. I want you to break this off with Teleki or I will show these to Dad."

Angie said no threats but he had to get something going.

"Badger! He knows?" Her hand dropped from her mouth. "Has he seen these pictures?"

"Yes, but he's cool. He likes the both of you and won't say anything. You should know that I'm not bluffing. I'll go to Dad if you keep . . . "

"Oh, Lord. What a mess. What a complicated pile of shit. And my poor boy — my baby — caught in it." She lunged for him, pulled him to his feet and nearly crushed him with a fierce hug. "Of course I love you and Phil. No matter what you think you have seen, never forget that."

She thrust him back and held him at arm's length. She was smiling. A sad, wise, knowing kind of smile that wrinkled the corners of her eyes. "You can't possibly understand this Mike. From your perspective I am the bitch of the century who is betraying her husband and son. I'm so sorry that you have become involved."

Mike stood still, amazed and somewhat in awe of her strength. She was good, unbelievably good. He had her dead to rights and yet she still hadn't conceded defeat. It shook him, that sad-happy look on her face. It didn't seem like an act. He'd never heard her swear, yet the "shit" and "bitch" were genuine. He found himself buying it, almost buying it. If he hadn't seen it with his own eyes, didn't have the pictures in front of him, he would believe her. Her sympathy for a mistaken notion that she was unfaithful was brilliant, tactically.

"Nice try, Mom." Damn, he had to stay with Phyllis, not Mom. "These are real, not Photoshopped." He pulled away from her and tapped the pictures. "Angie said you still loved us and that part I can accept, I guess. But don't try to manoeuvre this into me being somehow confused. The deal still stands. No more Janos, or I go to Dad — Phillip."

"Who is Angie?"

CRAP! What was wrong with him? Oh, crappy, shitty, crap! How had he let Angie's name slip out?

"Who?" He laughed, unconsciously taking a step backward.

"Angie. You said Angie thought I loved you and Dad."

"Did not."

She stared at him. How had this happened? He was on the defensive and no way to explain Angie.

"No more Janos, Mom . . . Phyllis" He picked up a photo and held it in front of himself like a shield. "Or this goes to Phil."

"Fine. Agreed. No more Janos." She said it deadpan, emotionless.

"That's it? No tears? No regrets?" He didn't believe this but it might be a way to get past his Angie blunder. "One moment I'm all wrong and the next suddenly you give in?"

She didn't answer him. She pulled out a chair and sat, as though deep in thought.

"All right, Mike. I'm going to tell you everything I can right now. I promise on my life." She fixed him with a clear eye. "I promise that I will tell you the *whole* story of Janos and me and your father after this Tuesday."

"Tuesday? What? Why?"

She held up a hand and he fell silent. There was more here than he had suspected.

"Your father's new project."

"The Genesis thing," he said.

"Yes. It's brilliant and it will rock the physics world if it is approved for use. He'll find out Tuesday. In the mean time I have reason to believe Janos Teleki plans to sell your father's project to the highest bidder before Tuesday's approval." She rattled this off quickly then paused to let Mike comprehend it. "If CLS approves, then its value will drop because it will become part of the scientific community, eventually available to everyone. If the idiot McCulloch gets it rejected, then the new, illegal owner will be able to sell it for ten times its cost to another country smart enough to use it and claim the glory and subsequent international attention and money that accrues to it."

"Industrial espionage." Mike felt the little hairs on the back of his neck bristle up. "Who is McCulloch?"

"A troublemaker at CLS who wants to sink your dad's project out of jealousy."

"So Janos will be a middleman. Good money for certain. But the buyer will be taking a gamble on McCulloch's powers of persuasion, hoping to make the really big money."

"Yes. You figured that out quickly."

"And Dad thinks Janos is his friend but really he's just using Dad . . . "

"Not quite," Phyllis said frowning. "It is much more complex than that. Janos does want Phil to be approved and succeed. He needs him and I believe he really likes him. They have to work together to make the Hungarian project succeed, using the Genesis procedure. Janos will get his black market money *and* get to use the Genesis if CLS approves."

"Yes, yes! Of course! Classic." Mike's brain rushed with the revelation. "Agent must develop relationship with target but can't help truly befriending target. Agent also needs target to NOT know he has been spied on. Right out of the manuals. Classic! And you are using the honey trap to watch Janos and stop it. But you haven't yet been able to catch Janos selling it."

"Honey trap? Manuals?"

"Sex for information and control! MI5, KGB, CIA manuals." He said it before he realized what it truly meant.

The rush faded. Phyllis was having sex with Janos in order to get close to him, to discover who he was selling Phil's project to.

"So you are whoring to protect Dad's Genesis?" he asked incredulously, not knowing if she would slap his face or cry.

"I promise you don't have to worry about Janos and me anymore. I am asking . . . " She touched his cheek with the back of her hand. Not a slap then. " . . . begging you to wait a few more days. Don't go to Dad. I'll stay away from Janos, and after Tuesday I'll explain everything to you."

"Deal." He sighed, relieved for a way out. "I'll hold off."

"But don't lose those pictures, I may need them."

"What?"

She looked away. "I'll not go near Janos. But then I'll need you and Badger and your sneak camera to go for me. We have to watch him, for Phil's sake."

"You want me to keep the pictures of you and Janos?"

She nodded, lips clamped tightly as though she was biting them from the inside.

"And you want me and Badger to spy on Janos. Expose him to protect Phil from any complicity in the illegal sale."

She nodded again. "You really do understand these things. It took me some time to calculate the importance of exposing Janos. At first I thought it best to just stay out and let Janos take the risk — couldn't see the impact on Phil."

"How did you get suspicious of Janos when Phil didn't? And why not just tell Phil of your suspicions?"

She shrugged. "Phil is too close, stressed incredibly high by the Genesis thing. He can't see outside of that. But things he said about the Hungarians over the last few weeks — being under-funded — paying extra for Genesis research — being audited by Bucharest. Then Janos' behaviour towards me, being overly friendly, and being excessively supportive of Phil. It made me uneasy. I talked to Janos the night of the welcome dinner and he seemed suddenly relieved of his money worries, even talked about making an arrangement that would solve his troubles, things like that." Her neck flushed red. "There is more, that left me in no doubt . . . but that's really all I can tell you until Tuesday."

"I don't need details," Mike said quickly. "Just needed to know if we are working on solid intel or supposition."

Phyllis gave him a funny half-quizzical look, but said nothing. Her adventures with Janos could be veiled and his knowledge of whether intel was solid or weak seemed best left unexplored. If he had been asked to come up with a thousand possible outcomes of this confrontation, Mike thought, spying on Janos Teleki for his mother to keep her from having sex with him to protect his father would not have been one of them. At least it wasn't an affair of the heart.

"And who is Angie?"

"Badger's new girlfriend," he said, suddenly inspired.

"That's nice for Badger. Why hasn't he mentioned her before?" She paused. Mike said nothing. "This Angie knows everything?"

"Nearly."

"Trustworthy?"

"Very."

The back door opened. "How does a guy get a cup of fresh French Vanilla coffee in this joint?" Phil bellowed.

"We'll talk later," she whispered. "There better be a cherry-cheese Danish coming through that door if you want coffee, buster!"

"Has it occurred to you that she made up the whole industrial espionage thing to get you off her back?" Badger asked.

"Not at first." Mike admitted. "But later yeah, after I phoned you guys. Then I thought it through and it's unlikely."

"Couldn't be." Angie said. "She was telling the truth there."

"How can you be so certain?" Badger got out of the easy chair and crossed the living room. His parents were gone as was his brother. The Badger Den was theirs for the afternoon. He sat down close to Angie on the couch.

"Her first defence was the fake anger — to scare Mike off. The pictures were more of a shock that she let on. Once she realized she couldn't make it go away, why would she come up with a second lie to get three more days? I mean, there's no advantage. Either she walks out on her family or she gives up Janos. A mere three-day extension to her affair would be irrelevant, so she must have been telling the truth about the industrial spying."

Badger put his arm around her. "No wonder you get the best marks in class, honey." He kissed her cheek. "Just so you know, your brains don't threaten our relationship. I'm pretty secure in my own identity."

"Get OFF!" She straight armed him and jumped up from the couch. Badger stretched his arms out and made kissing noises, smacking his lips.

"Oh, Kitten. Don't play hard to get."

Angie flopped into the easy chair. "What an ass you are Bertram." She laughed. "Why did you have to make me Badger's girlfriend?"

"Because Phyllis wouldn't believe that I had a girlfriend," Mike said honestly. The others rewarded him with an awkward silence and he realized that the unspoken assumption was that Angie really was his girlfriend and oh, shit. He'd said the wrong thing again. The right thing for spying — always stay plausible — but the wrong thing for real–life, high-school people.

"Listen Angie." He studied the carpet pattern at his feet. "Sorry. Didn't mean to imply that you are, you know, that you and I have become, you know."

"Fer Chrissake!" Badger cut in. "It's like watching a car crash. Just shut up and let it go."

Mike exhaled and stole a glance at Angie. She was fiddling self-consciously with the band on her ponytail, looking out the picture window at nothing on the street.

"Besides," Badger said with a small laugh. "Spymaster and genius Bond Girl hooking up — not a big stretch, is it?"

"I told you not to call me Bond Girl."

"Oh yeah, must have forgotten, Bond Girl."

She had anticipated his answer because she sent a décor pillow from the chair whipping across the room and it struck his face before he could dodge. "Why don't you make yourself useful and get us something to eat and drink."

Badger threw the pillow back at her, missing wide, then sauntered toward the kitchen. "I guess the honeymoon is over, eh, sweetie?"

"Just get the drinks."

"Drinks coming up. Shaken not stirred, I assume?"

Angie fired the pillow again and nearly cleared a row of Badger's mom's china figurines from a corner shelf. "Hey! Settle down!" Badger retrieved the pillow, tossed it on the couch and left the room.

Mike was still watching her when she turned quickly and made eye contact.

"I got it, you know. Better to keep Phyllis as far as possible at arm's length. Me being Badger's girlfriend keeps me cut out. Phyllis doesn't need more emotional involvements."

"Geez," Mike said, again too honestly, but with the usual disregard for spy craft that Angie seemed to engender. "You really are smart, too."

"Too?"

"Yeah. You know a person doesn't always have both brains and, ah, I guess plumage."

Angie fluttered her eyelashes at him and laughed out loud. He laughed with her and imagined her warm hand in his again.

"Like Badger said, it's not such a stretch, is it?" She asked.

"None at all."

"But like I said at the ravine, leave all that for a better day, when your parents are back together." She tossed her head and yelled "Honey! Bring some chips too, will you?"

"Anything you say, darling." Badger's voice came down the hallway.

"So, how do we watch this Janos guy?"

Mike leaned forward eagerly, pad of paper and pencil to hand. "I'll sketch it out. It would be best as a two-car watch, but Badger's folks have both cars out tonight. I can get Phyllis' car. Can you get one?"

Angie shook her head. "No, sorry," she said tersely, as though this was an unreasonable demand.

"It's okay." Mike thought she looked relieved. "The hallmark of a good watch is flexibility. We'll cope." Why was she worried about not getting her mom's car? He was happy to be back in spy logic. He'd save the notion of being Angie's boyfriend for later. Bring it out and enjoy it after the watch. Also try to figure out why the car thing upset her.

# The Source of Light

~

Mike tore off a piece of duct tape and pressed the light switch on the car door frame.

"Light's off," Badger said.

Mike taped over the switch then reinforced it with another strip. He moved clear of the car door.

"Duct tape, the spy's secret weapon," Badger said, opening and closing the door several times. The interior stayed dark. Mike knelt and checked the tape. No lifting. Good.

"Phil and Janos are working for two hours this afternoon, quitting at five." Mike flipped his notebook open, going over the plan again. Badger leaned up against the car beside him. Angie stood, arms folded, opposite him. "We pick up Janos when he leaves CLS. If he goes to a public place to meet his customer, then Angie follows." He looked her over, professionally. She wore the same faded jeans and beige sweatshirt from this morning, the only addition being a grey, long-billed ball cap. Average, unremarkable and non-threatening to even a nervous Hungarian spy. "If he is crazy enough to sell in a direct meet, you'll have to get a couple of pictures but that will be risky. Stay well back, use the zoom, get the customer's face, don't worry too much about focusing on Janos."

She nervously bobbed her head.

"If you think they're aware of you, it's best to just turn casually and walk past them — never walk away — keep your face tilted slightly down. Open your cell and smile while you talk into it."

She practiced it a couple of times, walking up and down the garage.

"Then use a bush, tree, wall, any solid object to wheel around and pick them up again. If he doesn't meet, but does a dead drop as I suspect, then you just have to stay out of his way, hold tight to the drop, and call us. We'll come in and wait for the customer to pick up."

He looked at his notes. This was just excellent. A proper watch on a proper spy. For long minutes he was able to forget that Phyllis and Janos were lovers, but then it came back, damping down his enthusiasm. He sighed and looked up at Badger. He was dressed in black sweats and T shirt, with dark boots, and a navy ball cap.

"If he goes into a private house or his own home or the woods then Badger has to follow, covertly. No lights, no sound."

Badger grinned hugely and tugged his cap down tight. Not the best arrangement, Mike knew. But Badger did know how to move quietly under cover and he was keen — too keen — but you can't have everything.

"Can't say much more except to repeat again. Meets a customer, take a chance and get the picture, then get out. Leaves a dead drop, stay tight and call us."

Badger made a sudden move toward Angie, then darted backward on the balls of this feet.

"Like a cat, that's me. Reflexes, grace, predator instincts."

Angie rolled her eyes.

"When it goes wrong . . . "

"Maybe it won't." Angie said.

"Assume something always goes wrong," Mike said forcefully. "Try to be flexible — remember the main aim — call me if you get the chance and I'll try to coordinate something."

"What if he's already sold the package?" Badger asked the question that had been nagging Mike ever since he had started planning this morning. His confrontation with Phyllis seemed like days ago, not hours. "He's had the final version ever since Friday's meeting."

"If the Genesis project was handed out on a flash stick or CD, then maybe he already has moved it. But I think it was in paper format on Friday. Then he went directly to the Keg with Phil, so he couldn't take it with him. We left about midnight." Mike went through his best-guess answer. "He'd had to have gone back through security at CLS very late, suspicious, to get the project and copy it to a disk. So likely he went in today to do that, then see Phil for the meeting this afternoon — nothing out of the ordinary. That would mean he is likely to sell it this afternoon, or tonight, or tomorrow or even Monday, but that would be late. Likely tonight. Hold the stuff as briefly as possible is the norm."

"There's a norm for this?" Angie grunted. "Nothing normal about any of it."

"I think my scenario has a good chance of being true. You can't cover all the eventualities. You can only play the highest percentage possibilities."

"Why wouldn't he just email the report to his customer instead of using a paper copy or a CD," Badger asked.

"More secure, safer. Better deniability believe it or not." Mike was reassured by their questions. They were thinking and learning. If things crashed, they'd have a better sense of the op and improvise accordingly.

"Walking around with an actual copy of the report is safer?" Angie cut in. "Everybody at CLS know the project is restricted to the building right?"

Mike nodded.

"So anybody sees Janos walking out with it . . . "

"But they won't. He just tucks it under his arm or puts it in a bag. And if he is caught with it, he simply says: 'Gee, I forgot it was in my briefcase'. Deniable. And once it is sold, a three-ring binder is untraceable. But." Mike wriggled his fingers tapping an invisible keyboard. "If Janos emails it to somebody and is caught what can he say? 'Gee, I typed in this guy's address, attached a file, and sent it by mistake?' Or if the buyer is caught later, they trace the file directly to Janos's email address. And any half-assed IT security team can source an email attachment. Then you are nailed twice."

Angie smiled at him. "And I suppose it is as easy to burn and flush paper as it is to crush a CD or flash stick."

"Easier," Mike said, happily absorbing her implied praise.

Phyllis opened the garage door and held out a knapsack. She nodded quickly. "Hello, Badger." Her body pulled back into the doorway, embarrassed that Badger knew of her affair.

"Hey, Mrs. S." Badger, to whom sex was a function of nature and nothing extraordinary, shifted awkwardly from one foot to another. He still felt for Phil even though it shouldn't in theory matter who Phyllis mated with. "This is my friend Angie."

Angie tilted her cap back and waved. "Hello, Mrs. Smith."

"Hi, Angie, pleased to meet you." Neither of them crossed the garage to shake hands. "I made something for you to eat, maybe a long night and . . . " Her voice tailed off weakly. Mike strode to her and took the bag. He smiled his thanks. No point in friction now, keep it easy and smooth. She could have left the food for him earlier. He guessed she had forced herself to say hello to Badger and Angie, acknowledge their help even if it meant facing their judgmental stares. She did have guts.

# CHAPTER 10

"THAT'S ABOUT IT, DONE EARLY." PHIL SAID, leaning back in his chair, pushing away from the desk. Janos scribbled a few lines in the margin of his copy of the Genesis Report. As usual, he found himself collegial, content and yes dammit, friendly with the man who was ruining his life.

"It is good, excellent." Janos turned and put his face in the crook of his elbow, sneezing loudly. "Pardon me. I seem to be coming down with a cold. I am exhausted and it being not even four thirty."

"You sound pretty plugged up, sinus. Tired as well, eh?"

"Very tired. Like a kitten is weak." Janos coughed.

"You should have said something. We could have done this later." Phil couldn't suppress a genuine sympathy. Janos was a hard driver but there was no urgency for this refinement meeting.

"No, no. I'm fine. We are done early so that is good. I'll lock this up in my office then go home and to bed."

"Should drop into emerg, see if they can give you an antibiotic."

"Always, my friend looks out for me." Janos shook his hand. "I am so glad this illness came after the Keg. I enjoyed the meal most tremendously."

"Yes, yes, very nice," Phil murmured. Janos returned to his office. Phil locked up and waited for him, the morning still running through his thoughts. A delight in most respects. Sleep in, no tension with Phyl, coffee, papers, pastry, and a long chat with his wife. Then just before lunch, he'd noticed Phyl in Mike's room, her back to the door.

She had been running her fingertips over his bedspread, smoothing it. Then she stood back, looking at his bed and bent forward to touch his pillow. Something in her manner, so quiet and deliberate, kept him from joining her. She turned to his desk, picking up a book, setting it down. Tidied some paper into a pile. A picture in a small frame of the three of them outside Banff Springs hotel two summers ago was on the desk. She lifted it up, studied it, then gently kissed it. The side of her face reflected to him in Mike's mirror. Quiet tears, only a few, slid down her cheek. He'd hesitated, then crept away, unsure if he'd acted wisely or cowardly.

"Let us be off, my friend," Janos called from the floor. Phil descended the catwalk and joined him. They walked past the Hungarian beam-line hutch and around the ring. Phil sensed the electron stream only a couple of metres away, encased in its massive concrete cave. Soon he'd use that miracle to look at life and fulfill a destiny. Move humans away from Atwood's dark forest of survival into real light. The thought warmed him. They separated in the parking lot. Phil pulled away, conscious of the Hungarian minivan in his rear-view mirror. Mike was out with Badger tonight. Maybe he'd get Phyllis to talk about their son. They'd both seen it at the Keg. Happy teenager one second, desperately unhappy loner the next. Her tears in Mike's room meant something. Suddenly Janos did not seem to be so important.

～

"I knew it, there's Phil already and we're not even in position. Christ, we'll drive right past him; he's bound to spot us!" Mike tried to say it as an unruffled professional but he failed. "Badger down! Angie slide over next to me!"

"It's not even four thirty yet. We're half an hour early," Badger said, undoing his seatbelt and rolling below window level.

Phil's car approached rapidly, Angie put her arm behind Mike's shoulders and leaned toward him.

"Not too close! Don't draw attention. He might not recognize me if he sees a couple in the car, but don't make him look." Phil's car slipped past. His head never moved.

"Okay, we got away with it. Hopefully the target hasn't left. Damn. I think that's his van now."

Mike slowed. There was a field-access approach just ahead. He could let Janos go by then, do a U-turn, but that was horribly conspicuous. Only one road into CLS. Their plan had hinged on being tucked up in the car park before Janos left, but nothing goes to plan on real ops.

"Look, he's pulling over," Angie pointed. The van swerved across the road into the widened approach. Mike accelerated and shot past him.

"We'll lose him." Badger popped up from the back seat.

"No," Mike said quietly. "This is good. Just keep an eye on him while I get us turned in the parking lot."

"He's turning around, coming after us."

Mike checked his mirror. What the hell? No chance they'd been spotted. He drove into the lot and pulled over at the far end, behind the row of white CLS vans. Janos parked and hurried into the building.

"Do I follow?" Angie had her hand on the door handle, her voice pitched high.

He leaves with Phil, then doubles back. To meet his customer inside CLS? Highly unlikely.

"Mike?"

He ignored her, following the logic. Why leave if your customer is already inside? Could Angie follow him? Only to the front security desk.

"No," he said. "Sit tight."

"Why did he go back in?" Angie asked, her voice normal again.

Mike shrugged.

"Likely forgot something; went back to use the can. Or maybe he didn't want Phil to see him staying at work," Badger said.

"Probably something like that." Mike nodded. "Speculation isn't of value here. Just keep focused and watch him when he returns." He sat back, clearing his mind. Fifteen minutes later, Janos reappeared.

"He's got something, a binder, in his hand." Badger was first to spot it.

Janos descended the front steps.

"Yup, binder." Badger had the binoculars to his eyes. "Black with a red design on it. Could be the Genesis Report."

Mike grinned, God, this was fun. "Angie, call Phyllis at home. See if she knows . . . "

" . . . what the cover on the report looks like?" Angie finished his sentence and hit the speed dial on her phone.

Mike waited till Janos was in his van then started his car.

"Got the map ready?"

"Roger that." Badger dropped the binoculars and spread a city street map over a clipboard on his knees. Janos pulled away and drove quickly. Mike followed but kept well back, only the two of them on the out road.

"That's it. Black binder, red design of a sun. He's got the report." Angie snapped the cellphone shut.

"Janos, you naughty boy," Badger said. "Confidential material strictly forbidden to remove from CLS premises."

They never needed Badger on the map. No alternate route or lost target option calls were required. Janos drove directly to a mobile home park and just over ten minutes later pulled up in front of a double wide unit. Two men were lighting up a barbecue on the patio adjacent to the house. They waved to Janos as he walked past them. No report. Maybe hidden inside his jacket. Mike drove past them, circled around the crescent. It contained a mixed batch of neat, well-maintained homes alongside several ramshackle trailers running red with rust, their yards festooned with debris.

"Janos lives here?" Badger asked.

"Yeah, I recognize one of the BBQ boys from the Hungarian Light Team. Been to our house with Dad," Mike replied. "They are on a tight budget so I guess this is their best accommodation option. But man, this is the skids."

Badger giggled. "Trailer Park Trash! I wonder if they're growing dope in the back?"

Mike allowed himself a smile. "I don't think Janos will be selling physics secrets to any of these high achievers."

Badger guffawed.

"If we get a good spot to watch the road out, we'll be able to pick Janos up when he leaves to meet his customer." Mike turned back the way they had come in.

"What if the customer comes to the slums?" Badger asked.

"Very, very unlikely Janos would do business out of his own address, with the other team members there. Besides, he left the report in his van."

"Okay, I have to tell you this." Angie jerked her thumb in the opposite direction. "There is a second road out the other end of the park. Connects to Wiggins Avenue. He could go that way and we'd miss him."

"Good call, Angie." Mike kicked himself for being so slack. "We'll have to watch both."

"She's right," Badger said, finger tracing a line on the street map. "How did you know that, Ange?"

"I live here."

Mike's fingers tightened on the steering wheel. Badger coughed.

"Take a left," Angie said quietly. She directed them to the other exit and got Mike to pull over near a patch of gravel choked with scrub and weeds. She got out of the car and stooped to look back in.

"Got my cell turned on, I'll call if I see him. There is a good spot for you guys about fifty metres out the other way." She slammed the car door and disappeared into the bushes. Mike turned the car and drove back through the park.

"Shit," said Badger.

"Shits." Mike corrected him. "Both of us, long runny ones."

~

The cell rang a half hour later. "He's coming now." Mike started the car. Neither he nor Badger had said much. Mike had stopped blushing over their insults to Angie's home, but it was hard not to think about her, living here. They stopped for her and she hopped in, smiling.

"Got him! My first operational kill. I hope you bastards haven't eaten all the food — I'm starved — it was getting cold out there."

Mike breathed a huge sigh of relief. Badger nearly tore the backpack open and threw a sandwich at her.

"We wouldn't start without you! What do you take us for?"

"A couple of . . . " She chewed and swallowed, " . . . guys with weird hobbies and strange ideas of social behaviour. Both intelligent but very immature in many ways. Should I go on?"

"Enough." Badger put his hands up in surrender. "It was a rhetorical question, you know."

Janos drove to city hospital, parked and went in, empty-handed.

"Report might be inside his coat. Stay with him, Angie."

She left the car white-faced, but nodding, she felt for the camera in her sweater pocket.

"A hospital," Badger said as Angie passed through the front doors.

"Smart," Mike said. "Lots of people. Lots of places, cafeteria, waiting rooms. Lots of noise. Pretty good place for a direct meet but lousy for a dead drop. This could be it, all over at once."

The phone rang.

"He's gone to emergency. I heard him say he had a sinus infection," she said. "I'm sitting in the emerg waiting area. He's on the other side of the room."

"Good work. Might be a legit visit. Is he still wearing his jacket?"

"No, just took it off. No black and red binder that I can see."

"Okay, relax. Follow him out. Call if you need me."

He clicked off, then dialled home.

"Hello?" Phyllis answered on the first ring.

"Hi. Dad home yet?"

"Yes. Just came in."

"Can you find out if Janos had a cold or felt sick at work today?"

Within minutes, Phyllis called back to confirm Janos's illness. They waited for Janos and Angie to come out of the hospital and followed Janos to a drugstore then directly back to the trailer park. Moments later, the Hungarian lights went out.

"The guy is sick and gone to bed with a prescription. Almost no chance tonight is the night." Mike said this with more conviction than he felt. "But I still think, if you guys are up for it, we should stay."

"Don't worry. We can do the all-nighter as planned," Angie said. "We've got the sleeping bags, and my house is just a block away so I can at least sneak home for a pee. You guys go outside." Mike grimaced at the thought of her alerting her family to their presence.

"Mom sleeps really heavily and my sisters are at the far end of the house." She answered his grimace.

"Sure, that'll work." Mike let it go. "And it's plenty dark. We can park just down the street. Two sleep, one watches. No need to cover both exits."

A light came on in the target house, then extinguished a minute later. Mike pointed like a bird dog. Janos was moving. His cell rang.

"I just called Janos," Phyllis said.

"WHAT! Mom, Damn it!" Mike barely controlled himself.

"Calm down. Your father insisted I phone to offer him some of my chicken soup, for his cold. I couldn't refuse."

"Sorry, what did he say?" Mike relaxed his grip on the phone.

"He sounded terrible. Asked could I bring the soup at noon tomorrow as he was too sick to leave home but he," she paused. "Get this Mike. He said he had an urgent meeting tomorrow afternoon that he had to attend. Hoped the soup, and my company, would perk him up for it."

Dirty, horny, son-of-a-bitch, Mike thought.

"That must be the sale," she prompted.

"Almost for certain that's it. We'll stand down tonight. But Phyllis?"

"Yes, Mike."

"I will deliver the soup tomorrow."

# CHAPTER 11

MIKE IN HIS ALB, CALMLY ARRANGING THE flow of ritual surrounding the priest, appeared almost holy, Phil thought. Too good to be true. It didn't reduce his fears, it fed them. What seventeen-year-old boy happily supervised Catholic mass? He tried to keep his dark thoughts at bay and concentrate on Fr. Fitz's excellent homily, but he could not. Instead, he saw the newspaper headline: *Loner introvert was a good Catholic boy before he snapped. Parents at a loss to explain behaviour of shooter.*

He glanced at Phyllis. Another good Catholic: Weekly Confession, daily Rosary, fully-absorbed by the sermon — yet fouling the sacrament of marriage. Phil was a lapsed protestant and lukewarm Catholic who had not yet converted to the Mother Church. Yet he was the only one in the family unlikely to commit adultery or murder. Well, when he actually caught them at it, who could say about murder? The blackness would win out, but whether he'd faint or kill was a question he still hadn't answered. His pathetic effort to control Phyl and Janos's next meeting with the chicken soup had failed.

Pimping his wife with soup to a sick man. He snorted. Phyl looked over, and the pair of white-haired ladies in the next pew glanced back at him. He pretended a cough. Phil had offered to accompany Mike with the soup, but Mike had insisted he go alone. Almost an angry insistence that caused yet another tense, stubborn silence. Wanted to apologize to Janos for his rudeness Friday night, he'd said. Phil said it was okay, leave it, but Mike had flared up. Phil began to run Friday's meal at the Keg through his mind and at the same time replay this morning's soup event beside it — make some logical sense of his son's fluctuating behaviour. He traced them back and forth over the remainder of the service and finally put it out of his mind, unresolved, at the final benediction.

He sat back in the pew while Phyllis knelt for even more prayer. What could she be thinking, praying for? The congregation drained out and Fr. Fitz, handshaking duty discharged, walked back up the centre aisle, waving. Phil smiled and waved back. Had Phyl confessed Janos to Fitz? Was that a priestly smirk? Phyl's eyes were still closed. Just as Fitz reached the sacristy Mike came out. They talked and laughed briefly. Phil nudged his wife.

"He's ready to go."

She nodded but remained on her knees. Phil stood, stretched, yawned and began tapping his trouser pockets for the car keys. Mike was gone. Phil shuffled right a metre and craned his neck, just gaining a view of the south transept. Mike stood very close to a slim girl. She was talking, gesticulating, making a point. Mike was laughing. His body seemed to slouch, visibly relax. She touched his arm; he made a sudden move and she began laughing too.

"Phyl!" he whispered urgently. "Phyl, look at this." His whisper changed to a hoarse shout. She glanced up. Phil hurried toward her, caught his left foot on the end of the extended kneeler and received a red hot bolt of pain from his sore toe. He tried to correct, overbalanced and fell, flipping himself sideways at the last second missing Phyl but sprawling like a clumsy seal full length on the pew.

"What on earth are you up to?"

"Damn toe! Jesus, it hurts."

"Potty mouth!" Phyl sat back on the pew, her thigh near his head. "Not in church Phil. I told you that toe has a hairline fracture — you have to see a doctor."

"Mike." He struggled up, using her arm and shoulder for support. "A girl. Mike and a girl, quick, over there."

⌁

"Sometimes it is like that. There's a guy who must be sixty-years old there and his trailer is a hydroponics marijuana field," Angie said.

"How do you know?"

"Two weeks ago, he left the water on too long and it must have overflowed because it started leaking out his door. My little sisters were out on their bikes and I was riding behind them to keep an eye on them."

She swept a lock of hair behind her ear, stifling a laugh. "So anyway, we see water dripping out this guy's front door so we slow down to look and suddenly . . . Wham!" She flung her arms out wide. "The door bursts open and a miniature tsunami whooshes out."

Mike laughed out loud, leaning back against a corner pillar.

"He is bald, with a fringe of long grey hair, scraggly grey beard, with a tie-dyed shirt and he comes flailing out like a senior citizen surfer."

"No, come on. Really?"

She reached forward and touched his wrist. "I swear to God. An old hippie body surfing in Mary Jane water."

"It wasn't Flashpoint doing a chemistry experiment was it?" Mike asked. She burst out laughing and slapped his shoulder. He watched her face, bright and shining. "Will you forgive me, us, for those stupid, stupid things we said?"

She turned serious quickly. "I hate living there, but I'm not ashamed of it — anymore — and you guys were ignorant. But to be fair, I likely would have said the same things a couple of years ago, out of ignorance." She folded her arms defensively.

"Is that when you moved there? When your dad left?"

She looked away and he wondered for a moment if he'd gone too far, too personal.

"More complex than that." She sighed.

A loud thud echoed from the nave followed by a scrambling series of thumps and a raised female voice. They both peered around the pillar. Angie's shoulder touched his. He caught the scent of her shampoo. Phil was pulling himself up out of a pew. Phyl was laughing and helping him.

"What now?" Mike said.

"Think he saw us and fell over?" Angie nudged him.

"Quite possible. Look, I'll have to get going but I'd like to talk about your trailer-park stuff — maybe become less ignorant."

She turned her face to him, only a few inches separated her grey eyes from his. She wore a trace of eyeliner and mascara. She didn't need it.

"I know you're Badger's woman, so this isn't a date. I just thought if the watch goes well this afternoon that we could, you know."

"Sure. I've never been out with a schitzo, head-case before." Her breath was peppermint scope or something like that. "Will it be you or Arthur Guthrie taking me on this non-date?"

"More complex than that." He sighed, hoping to God his breath was okay.

Her eyes flitted away. "Your folks look like they are trying very hard to stare at us without staring at us."

Phil and Phyl were ostentatiously studying the coloured sunlight coming through the south transept stained-glass window.

"Better go." Mike pulled away from her. "See you in a couple of hours with the soup." He wheeled around the pillar and gave a small wave.

"Mike," she called.

He paused.

"When are you or Arthur going to take me on our first non-date?" She lowered her voice so it wouldn't carry.

"Monday night, pizza?"

She shook her head. "English test Tuesday. I'll be studying and you should be too."

"Oh, yeah. How about Tuesday."

"Good. Don't tell Badger yet, eh?" She made a pleading face. "Just us two for now. We can tell him later."

Mike could not have grinned wider. "Just us two," she'd said. How could he be so happy so suddenly? He nodded vigorously. She waved and left for the south exit. He watched her ponytail sway back and forth. She was wearing a loose skirt and blouse. The hem of her skirt swirled around her slim legs. It was great. Everything was just great. He turned, quashing a sudden urge to pump his fist into the air and tripped instead over the foot of the altar stairs crashing full-length to the floor. A squeal came from behind. He bounded up, red-faced, and saw Angie slip out the door, laughing again.

Badger and Angie waved through their windshield as he pulled away from the curb and drove into the trailer park. They would wait at the main exit — invisible in Badger's mom's Astrovan. They were the least likely to be spotted by Janos and thus had to be primary chase. He would deliver the soup and take up post on the back entrance to the park. He would be the tag in Phyl's car, following on parallel streets or farther behind to pick up the target if they had to drive by to avoid suspicion. They had practiced for an hour this morning following cars picked at random and it had worked well. A two-car watch — dream come true. Angie and Badger, not pros of course, but really quick and surprisingly well-disciplined. He'd given them copies of *The Watchers Manual* from CSIS to read, but practical ability and book knowledge were two different things. Once more he felt his own professional detachment slipping as he thought of his friends. Strange to find two real friends after nearly thirteen years of casual school acquaintances. Especially when he had reached the point where he'd thought Arthur Guthrie was the only real friend he'd ever need.

He put on his apologetic face, checked it in the mirror, then wheeled into the Hungarian double-wide parking space. One of the Hungarians waited at the door for him as he carried the hot soup tureen and a bag of buns from the car. The door opened onto a large living room dominated by two folding tables, computers and file cabinets. A smallish TV and a couple of easy chairs were parked in one corner. The team, except for Janos, appeared to be hard at work even though it was Sunday. They took the soup into the kitchen; each one shook his hand, exclaimed at Phyllis's generosity; wished they were sick so they could get such delicious food.

Janos, white-faced, red-nosed, and swathed in a housecoat, walked unsteadily into the kitchen. The team members fluttered around him as they seated him, poured soup, buttered a bun and exclaimed all over again how fortunate he was to be treated so generously by Mrs. Smith.

"Yes, yes." Janos leaned over the steaming bowl, bathing his face in the aroma. "I am lucky as a skunk," he croaked.

*Phil's favourite expression*, Mike thought.

The three other members of the Hungarian Light-Source Team had good morale. Janos seemed to be the informal, popular leader as well as the formal lead scientist. His men liked him, Phil loved him and Phyllis, well that made for a successful spy, didn't it? Others do your bidding without knowing it.

Janos dipped a spoon into the bowl and came up with noodles, a big chunk of tender white chicken and a pool of broth, half of which seemed to disappear up his outrageous moustache.

"Ah, heaven." He immediately took two more mouthfuls. He munched the whole-wheat bun, butter colouring the tips of the stash, and murmured his delight. Then he broke into a racking cough. Mike edged out of the way as the others clucked and sympathized. Janos waved them off and continued eating. They drifted back to their work in the living room. Mike sat opposite Janos.

"Doctor Teleki, could I say something?"

"Naturally, dear boy. Say whatever you like. I am in your debt for delivering this nectar to save my sickness." He smiled in such a way that the fatuous little speech seemed genuine.

"I brought the soup today because I wanted to apologize for my rude behaviour Friday evening at the Keg."

"Not necessary!" Janos waved his spoon and sucked at his moustache. "It was nothing. No offence taken, I can assure you." He stretched his arm across the table.

"Thank you, very kind." Mike shook his hand making a mental note to wash his own as soon as possible. "I know my father greatly appreciates your support for his project and I would hate to jeopardize your relationship with him."

"You are smart, no, wise for one so young." Janos's eyes, red and runny, narrowed alertly. "I don't know," he coughed harshly but his eyes stayed on Mike. "Excuse please. I don't know many seventeen-year-old men who could or would make such an apology."

Mike kept his poker face, but he tensed nonetheless. This guy was very sharp. He knew there was something here other than a tub of soup and an insincere apology.

Mike smiled. "I practiced a bit before I came here."

"Your mother made you come! I see it now." Janos grinned. "But really there was no need. Phyllis looks out for my feelings, always."

A drop of soup wriggled out of his moustache and dropped onto his housecoat. Mike watched it, trying not to react to the reference to Phyllis. The thought that she was with Janos in a sick honey trap was awful, but better than the thought that she loved the jerk.

"Yes, she does. Very thoughtful is my mother."

Janos, satisfied now by Mike's presence, began slurping soup again.

"She, ah, was concerned about your feeling fit enough for an important meeting today?" Mike raised his voice inquisitively and Janos stopped slurping. His head came up slowly.

"She told you? About my meeting today?" His eyes had gone on the alert again, searching Mike's face.

"Sure." Mike pointed at the tureen. "She hoped this soup might give you some strength back. You know, so you could attend a meeting."

"Important meeting." Janos corrected him thoughtfully. "You may tell her my great thanks and not to worry. I am so ill and weak that I postponed till tomorrow afternoon." He watched Mike as though waiting for a reaction.

"She'll be happy to hear that." He kept his face perfectly composed, bland.

Janos inspected him. "Perhaps if I am very lucky, she would make me soup for tomorrow lunch as well?"

"I'll be in school so I'd have to run it over on my break." Mike's mind was leaping ahead to take this in. Was it a ruse, a test? Did Janos suspect him? Real meeting today but throw me off the scent? No. This guy was truly too sick to go out today.

"Not so much trouble for you again, Mike. Do not disrupt your day. Phyllis has no work tomorrow and my colleagues will be at the synchrotron so she would be the most logical to come. Give me some company too, maybe." He smiled, more a leer than a smile. Not too sick to make a date with Phyl.

"All right." He said evenly. "I'll ask her to make more soup to fortify you for your very important meeting. Tomorrow afternoon, you said?"

The leer spread across Janos's sallow face. "Yes, perfect. If not too much trouble. I eat, take a short nap, then leave at two o'clock for my meeting."

"I'll pass that along." Mike stood. "I'm certain she'll be happy to come at noon and leave you time for your," he nearly choked with anger but managed to get the words out, "your nap."

"Pleased to meet you. Any friend of Badger's and all that."
Phil shook Angie's hand. "I thought you kids were out for the
afternoon?"

"Change of plan," Mike said, herding Badger and the
skinny girl with thin brown hair toward the stairs. "We'll
hang out here, watch a movie downstairs, if that's okay."

"Fine, sure, great. How was Janos?" Phil walked with them.

"Death warmed over," Mike replied.

"Hope you guys don't catch it."

"Not me, Mr. S," Badger said. "I've got the immunity of a
wild animal. No preservatives in my feed, lots of exercise, you
know."

Angie, poised at the top stair gave Badger a playful shove.
Phil wished she was Mike's girlfriend; longed for his son's
banter to cause a young girl to give him a playful shove.

"You eat Doritos by the bushel," Mike protested. "It's
because you're full of preservatives that you never get sick."

"Full of something," Angie said, glancing at Mike, a cute
smile emerging on her angular face. Phil looked to Mike and
saw an answering grin. Badger was busy making growling
sounds and snapping his teeth. He missed the smiles just
exchanged. They thundered down the stairs leaving Phil
wondering about teenage boyfriends, girlfriends, and his own
antiquated notions of dating. Phyllis came through from the
kitchen and stood at the top of the stairs.

"Snacks? Drinks?" She called.

～

Phyllis set the tray down in front of the TV. Angie and Badger
paused their video game. Mike looked past her, up the stairs.

"Phil?"

"Living room, with coffee." She shook her head. "We can talk for a few minutes."

"Right then. Same two-car watch tomorrow as we planned for today. Phyllis delivers the soup and gets away quickly, passes her car onto me outside the Mobile Home Park, then she takes a cab home." So strange giving his mom orders that were tailored to keep her out of another man's bed. "Foresee any trouble with that, Phyllis?"

She shook her head emphatically. Both Badger and Angie looked away.

"Good," Mike said briskly, trying to sound professional but feeling like an extraordinarily pompous prig.

"What should we do about school?" Angie asked. "Is there any way of not just skipping?"

"A half-day absence won't ruin your honour role," Badger said impatiently. Angie nodded acceptance. Mike left it at that but felt a tug of loyalty to her, wanting everything be good for her.

"Sorry. Maybe we can come up with something. But for now, we skip."

"It's all right, Mike. Thanks. This is more important."

Mike lost his concentration for a moment, allowing himself to remember *just the two of us.*

"Where to meet?" Badger prompted. "Same equipment? What's the plan, man."

"Meet in school parking lot half hour before school. Badger brings a tripod for a second camera, his zoom bird-watcher rig, but I'd like it in my car to start."

They focused on him. He was briefing a full-scale watch. He had a girlfriend, or would have one by tomorrow. He'd nail a case of industrial espionage and he'd put an end to the worst of the parental distress. Tomorrow could be the best day of his life.

～

"Is it just me or did you see something between Mike and Angie?" Phil asked.

"Wishful thinking, probably." Phyllis sipped her coffee looking at him over the cup's rim.

"Just Mike then, nothing on Angie's part?"

She shook her head. "No. I meant wishful thinking on our part. I try so hard to accept Mike for who he is, but I can't help wanting him to be . . . normal."

Phil couldn't contradict her. She'd said out loud what they'd both been thinking and now it was something of a relief to hear it spoken.

"Lord, that sounds terrible." Phyllis waved her hand as though to erase the thought. "I meant I just want him to have friends, be happy, be a bit rebellious. He seems so . . . I don't know, bottled up."

"Don't apologize. I feel exactly the same. That *über* self-control he uses, no emotion or at best, contrived emotion." Phil felt encouraged to keep going, expose everything. "I was so happy to see him make friends with Badger, go to a party, do their crazy experiments. It seemed to cancel that whole loner, secretive, religious-tightly wound spring that we thought would explode one day."

"That was my paranoia scenario," Phyllis said. "A boy reads John le Carré spy books, and I go strange with Columbine theories."

"But it fit the facts and I was worried as hell. I could see it, Phyl. In my mind's eye, I could see him in a school wearing that black leather coat and exploding with rage."

"Not now, surely. Badger and Angie change all that." Raucous laughter bubbled up from the rec room stairwell followed by some kind of owl hooting. Phyllis nodded toward the noise. "He's fine. And if Mike is connecting with Angie, that is a good thing. It's friendship — Mike and Badger wouldn't fight over her."

"You could be right there. And really, she seems to be a nice enough kid. She needs to put on a little weight though, don't you think?"

"Phil!" Phyllis glanced over her shoulder. "Don't you dare even mention her weight. Teenage girls can be hyper-sensitive to such things. She's quite attractive — or could be with a bit of work on her hair and makeup — I wish my problem was being too thin."

"Women need curves and you're perfectly curved Mrs. Smith." Phil felt almost light-headed when he made the compliment. But the image of his wife's body swiftly connected to his own lack of performance, which in turn clicked to Janos's full capability to appreciate Phyllis physically, and the darkness edged in.

"Not everyone has your tastes." She smiled. No tension, no hidden jab. Just like Saturday morning. Perhaps she was so happy with Janos she no longer even considered the possibility of bedding her own pathetic husband.

"Then what about the Keg?" He gave into the encroaching gloom. "Tell me that was normal."

Phyllis's smile dropped. She drank coffee and swallowed loudly.

"I saw you in his room. Holding the picture of the three of us at Banff Springs. I saw you cry." He didn't want to be so relentless but he was unable to stop. "I saw you cry over a boy we probably don't really even know. Can you explain that, Phyllis?"

She stood and turned her back to him, then hurried upstairs to the bedroom. The door clicked shut. More tears? Phil stood to follow her. What to do? Apologize for being angry that she was cheating on him? Because that was a big part of it. He sat down. Wisdom or cowardice; again he just did not know. More laughter from the family room. Phyl must be right. Mike was fine. He stood, apology ready, and made his way to the bedroom.

## CHAPTER 12

AT FORTY MINUTES BEFORE SCHOOL TIME, THE city bus was nearly empty. Mike watched, clutching his arms to his sides, hands jammed into coat pockets. His breath puffed white in the cold spring air. Angie's ponytail and ball cap silhouette moved to the door and got off. She waved as she walked quickly toward him. He wished she wouldn't be so obvious — not that they were trying to be covert in the school parking lot — he'd just become so accustomed to being invisible that a wavy, cheery girl was unnerving. She smiled as she got close and he suddenly realized that after tomorrow night's date, she would expect him to behave like a boyfriend. Meet before classes, lunch together, hold hands. They would be noticed by every inmate from Vanessa on down the penitentiary pecking order. Mike shivered, it was a sobering thought. Less than two months to go before parole and his cloistered world of nearly thirteen years would be cracked open.

"Hey, Mike." She punched his shoulder. He had to steel himself to not pull away.

"Morning."

"Where's Badger?"

"Late." Mike held up his cellphone. "Just called. He had to take the van to haul his little brother and some other kids to drop off at a fieldtrip. He can't make it till just before bell time."

"So do we wait here for him or . . . "

"No." He cut her short. "We wouldn't have time to transfer the kit then we'd all be running to make the first class. Too obvious."

"Who would notice three students hurrying to class?" She shrugged her shoulders.

"I would." He looked past her. "I would notice. It's poor field craft." That was better. His feelings for Angie had already caused some sloppy procedure. He wouldn't give up his old life quite yet. He set his neutral face into place and looked at her.

"Something wrong, Mike?"

He blinked. "No, just can't afford any mistakes today."

"You sure nothing is wrong?" Her voice was soft, concerned. He felt her fingers touch the back of his hand. He side stepped clear.

"If I wasn't sure I wouldn't have said so," he snapped. "Badger is late. We have to rethink, which is what I'm trying to do right now."

"Well obviously I'm mistaken. I thought I was talking to Mike Smith but clearly Arthur Guthrie is running the show today." She walked to the rear of Phyllis's car. "Let me know if Mike shows up."

*Goddamn it to hell.* He kept his face. He didn't go to her but he felt sick. He had to stay firm, in control, didn't he? He risked a glance. She was perched on the rear bumper facing away from him. Her long soft neck and brown hair caused a surge of affection to well up. He swallowed it. He envisioned

Vanessa and her pack watching their every move, putting them in some king of weird, social spotlight. "See my old friend Angie finally got herself a guy? Don't they know how lame they look? Wonder if he shares her with Badger? Bet she goes Columbine with them."

He wasn't the only one taking a risk. He had respected her for busting him on the phone tap. She wasn't just some chick, girlfriend. Maybe she wouldn't demand anything. "Just the two of us." Oh, for God's sake — now he was going in circles. Figure out a new plan and behave decently to Angie. Even if just for the sake of the operation. None of le Carré's handlers ever upset their people unless it was absolutely necessary. What was he thinking of, snapping at her like that? Talk about sloppy field craft. He'd worry about being socially outed later. He walked to her, put his hand on her shoulder.

"Arthur said you wanted to talk to me."

She smiled but didn't look at him.

"Sorry Angie. Little tense — Badger late — should have been more professional. No plan ever goes without a hitch."

"I didn't want professional." She looked now. "Just Mike."

Ah crap. He tried to pull away from her clear-eyed stare but all he did was squeeze her shoulder and smile.

～

"Badger here. Go."

"New plan," Mike said, shielding his cellphone with his free hand. "We'll cut at the eleven o'clock break. Not twelve. Lots of kids in the parking lot at eleven going for the early lunch so we shouldn't be noticed. Load the car, get changed, then go to the Kinsmen park and wait there until noon."

"Angie aware of the change in plan?"

"Yes, she's right here."

"Roger that. Badger out."

⌇

Flashpoint's chemistry class was interminable. Then Garchinski was repetitive and tedious. Not wanting to give away tomorrow's quiz questions but afraid not to because the class average was already low and it didn't need another anchor tied to it.

At the 11:00 o'clock bell they filed out, each one careful to keep a couple of other students between them — professional separation, Mike noted with satisfaction. They flowed into the parking lot, and one by one, appeared at the back of Badger's van. Quickly but calmly they dressed in their warm clothes. Badger in brown camo pants and khaki bunnyhug. Angie in a dark polo-neck sweater and knee-length canvas poncho. Mike back into this leather coat — a bit too conspicuous if he had to leave the vehicle but warm and plenty of pockets. He liked to ensure all the details were right. They might spend hours in a hide while it was cool and overcast. The morning's near frost was gone but not by much. Any fool can freeze and lose his focus. A pro dressed for the weather so he wasn't distracted by it.

A dark mane of hair appeared from behind a Toyota in the row directly behind him, then disappeared. He watched the spot. The same head slowly reappeared, peeking up over the trunk. Mike turned his own head slightly away but swivelled his eyes to keep contact. Dark flowing curls, sunglasses, bright red lipstick. Mike turned abruptly and stared directly at her. She shot down out of sight.

"What's up?" Badger followed his line of sight.

"Vanessa." Mike pointed. "Playing Peeping Tom behind that Toyota."

"Is that a problem?" Angie asked warily.

"Not really. We did good but somebody like Vanessa is pretty hard to defend against," Mike said confidently. The Vanessas of this world could certainly cause him trouble in the Big House but out here on a real watch she was nothing. "She's a joke. Ignore her."

"With pleasure," Angie said.

They began transferring the camera kit and tripods. Badger showed them a roll of sacking wrapped around a series of sticks taken from his bird blind. Maybe not needed but great if they had to watch from a country hide. Mike congratulated him on his initiative. He put the tripod bag into his car and stepped back, mentally ticking off the preparations. They were ready.

"Maybe nerves or whatever but," Badger's teeth chattered briefly before he clenched his jaw. "Maybe it's this cold wind."

"What?" Angie asked.

"He has to pee." Mike said. Angie chuckled.

"And now that he has suggested it I guess I should go too," Mike admitted.

"We're going to wait in the park before we get Phyllis right? In that case I might as well go too. Do we have to move separately?"

The parking lot was emptying. A clutch of students were heading into the school.

"We'll be alone out here soon. Let's go in with those guys then make your way back to the cars separately. We should hustle up so we're not stuck in the hall when classes start."

They walked quickly and just caught up with the other students at the main entry on the steps leading up to the glass doors. The fire alarm sounded. A series of short blasts — silence — then a series of short blasts. Mike stopped, puzzled, looking at Angie and Badger. Each of the doors clanged loudly, glass vibrating. One of the nearest students tried it. Locked.

Short blasts — silence — short blasts — silence.

"Holy shit, it's a lockdown!" Badger exclaimed. Just like a bad comedy movie, they all stood still for a two-second heartbeat, then turned and ran.

"Back to the van!" Mike shouted, taking Angie's hand. She shook loose, sprinting ahead of him. Badger had the presence of mind to hit the unlock button on his remote. They piled headlong and breathless through the sliding door into the back of the van.

"Unbelievable. A lockdown!" Badger crawled to the front seat and peeked up. Distant police sirens wailed.

"Do we get out?" Badger asked.

"I don't know." Mike's thoughts were scrambled. "No! If we peel out of here the cops may stop us. Start her up and be ready to move quietly once we see how this is going to shake out. We've got lots of time."

"Now I really have to squirt," Badger said, forcing a brave grin.

A blue and white patrol car shot into the parking lot then braked, showering an arc of gravel. The siren was doused abruptly but the strobe lights atop the roof flickered a warning. The car crept slowly forward nosing first toward the school then away from it like a dog sniffing for scent. Mike was centre, Angie right and Badger left, pressed shoulder to shoulder, crouched in the front of the van, eyes peering over the dash.

Two officers were visible in the front of the car, one talking on a radio, both heads swivelling, scanning the school. The car slowed, stopped, then started again, angling to the front steps.

It pulled up parallel to the entry and stopped. The passenger door opened, both cops scrambled out the same door and disappeared behind the car. A moment later, the head and shoulders of one policeman appeared above the hood, arm extended, pistol in his fist. The other one popped up over the trunk, same pose but aiming a shotgun.

Badger whistled. "Serious, serious shit."

A second cop car, siren screaming, rocketed up the entry ramp then performed a Hollywood half doughnut stopping in a cloud of dust perfectly astride the ramp.

"Looks like we're stuck here," Angie said.

Mike dropped down out of sight. This could last forever. Could they get out on foot and into another vehicle? Maybe Phyllis could get Phil's car from work. Meet them down the street. One car watch — wait outside the trailer park?

"Mike?" Angie nudged him.

"What?" He bit off, 'I'm thinking, don't bother me.'

"Something is really odd about this There are no students or staff or anybody leaving the school. It's so quiet."

Mike looked out and it struck him immediately. The TV images of Columbine and Virginia Tech: students ducking and dodging as they streamed away from the school; armed cops weaving past them to get into the school; chaos and screaming and crying. But not here. No movement. No sound. Not even any lights on in the classrooms.

"The shooter is out here, with us, in the parking lot." Badger got there before him. "The cops are defending the school, not searching it."

Mike physically shook his head to clear the preconceived idea that killers were in the school. Of course, that was the anomaly. The police crouched behind the cars, guns and heads moving in a continuous surveillance, were facing the parking lot, not the school.

"Did you hear any shots out there?" Badger asked, turning to them, his eyes wide on his face. They shook their heads.

Another siren, then another took Mike's gaze to the entry. A patrol cruiser pulled in parallel to the one blocking the exit. A grey van stopped beyond them and figures in dark blue jumpsuits sprang from the side and rear doors. Blue helmets, rifles, armoured vests. They split into two teams. One group moved swiftly to the first row of cars in the lot by leaps and bounds. Three covered, rifles aimed and alert while three others ran forward. These then stopped to cover the first three in their dash. Four others used the same game of tag to reach the police car guarding the school entrance. There was a hurried conference then a man appeared inside the school doors, unlocked one and was quickly hustled out to the police car and thrust down behind it.

"That looked like Garchinski," Badger said.

"That's what I thought," Angie replied.

"Seems like the SWAT team are going to work their way through the lot to the shooter, wherever he is." Mike strained to look past Angie at the police skirmish line at the end of the cars. "So our best bet is to let them evacuate us when they get to our van. Make sure we've got the cameras in deep pockets. Leave the tripods and camo nets behind."

"Unbelievable," Angie said.

"What?"

"There is a psycho killer out here. Cops armed to the teeth are coming to shoot it out right in front of us, and you are thinking about Janos?"

"Of course." He was in control. No matter what, maintain the aim. Stay on goal. "I'll take that as a compliment." He smiled at her.

"I'm not sure it was meant as one." She crawled into the back of the van and squatted on the floor. Mike tapped Badger's arm and they followed her. Mike put the small infrared camera in a long pocket sewn into the liner of his coat. Badger removed the lens and big camera from their case and tucked them in under the bunnyhug.

"Got the digital, Angie?"

She patted a crease on the poncho, nodding.

"I'll call Phyllis when we're clear and tell her where to meet us. Until then we sit tight."

The rear passenger seats had been removed and they sat on the floor, feet touching, backs propped against the van walls. They fell silent except for Badger who hummed a tune and moved his head rhythmically.

Mike congratulated himself on his cool-headed attention to detail. He relaxed, half closing his eyes. He allowed his thoughts to wander over his friends. Less than two weeks ago, he'd been trying to decide if Badger was his friend or his agent. Angie had been the skinny, academic overachiever he'd met once at a Halloween party. Now, he couldn't contemplate going on without them.

"We'd have heard shots in the parking lot." Angie spoke slowly, breaking the quiet.

"And if somebody was shooting, there'd have been a panic. But those kids ahead of us . . . " Badger tapped his knuckles nervously on the floor. "Those kids out there would have been running *everywhere*, not just poking along."

"So there was no shooter, no psycho." Angie sat up. "False alarm?"

"School's locked down. Cops are here ready to rock."
Badger continued to tap his knuckles. "There's a psycho, just
maybe got spotted before he could go nuts."

"I don't know. Does that make sense?" Angie knelt, looking
out the back window. "Badger, do you have to keep up that
knocking? It's getting on my nerves."

Badger stopped tapping and began to flap his knees
together, then out, then together as though doing a frog-kick
swimming stroke.

"Can't see anything." Angie sat down. "Now what's with
the dance thing?"

"I'm controlling my bladder by a very, very slim thread,
Angie." Badger began tapping again. "If I don't distract myself
there could be waterworks. I wonder if there's an old slurpy
cup in the garbage."

"Great. Please let those cops get us out of here quick."
Angie knelt up to the back window again.

"I wish I hadn't said slurpy." Badger began squirming. He
crawled onto the passenger seat and pulled a plastic bag from
under it.

"No cup," he said tensely. "Really sorry guys but I've got
maybe five minutes. I'll have to use this bag, hope there aren't
any holes in it."

Mike's previous smugness was gone, replaced by a growing
horror. Of course there was a psycho in the school parking lot.
His own bladder became urgent.

"Aw, come on, get a grip. Hey, wait." Angie stiffened at
the back window. "Two SWAT guys just ran past the Toyota.
Hang on, Badger."

"Angie, get down!" Mike rolled across the floor and
wrapped his arms around her hips pulling her back. She was
so light. Her body folded into his, fitting him, joining him.

They rocked back onto the floor. She didn't struggle, she trusted him.

"We are the shooters," he said. "Stay down. Those cops are after *us*."

Angie turned her face, her cheek brushed his as she tried to roll away. He let her go.

"What the hell?" Badger vaulted from the passenger seat, landing one knee on Mike's arm. "Are you serious?"

"Black leather coat, camo suit, poncho, tripods and brown sticks that look like guns, and," Angie said, grey eyes on Mike, "and Vanessa."

"Mike?" A mellow loudhailer voice penetrated the van. "Mike this is detective Allan Southland. I work for the city police." It spoke slowly.

"Will they shoot?" Angie curled up into a ball, eyes now scrunched shut.

"Mike, nobody has been hurt and nobody will be hurt. This can all just go away if you and Angela and ... " The loudhailer clicked off, then a moment later back on. "And Badger will just talk to us."

Angie opened her eyes. "Thank God," she whispered.

Badger knelt, unzipped his pants and held the plastic bag up to his crotch. "Time's up, sorry guys."

~

When the police arrived at the synchrotron, Phil's assistant, Fran, had to literally take him by the hand and lead him out of the office. But she stayed in the police car when they got to the school. He'd nightmare-dreamed it so many times yet now that it was actually here, he'd been shocked to near incapacity. He was still shaking but he walked through the school without help. Detective Southland seemed to soak up the insane tension and breathe out calmness. He kept his hand lightly in contact with Phil.

"Nothing fancy. Just talk to them." He said it for the tenth time although each time he repeated the simple instructions it seemed to Phil that he was hearing them for the first time.

They hurried to the police cruiser in the parking lot and knelt behind it. "Can you handle the loudhailer?" Southland's breath was cigarettes and wintergreen mints

"Loudhailer?" Phil's foot began to throb. He shifted so that he was kneeling on his right knee, bracing himself against the car.

"Ask Mike if he can hear you." Southland's radio show host voice betrayed no impatience. "Ask him to tap the van horn if he can. Then ask him to honk the horn once for yes and twice for no."

"Of course, yes, you told me that several times already — sorry." He must concentrate. He had to get this right. God, where was Phyllis? "No word from my wife yet?"

"Her cell is shut off and she's not at home." Southland looked at a police officer holding a radio handset. "Anything from Mrs. Smith?" The cop shook his head.

Southland gripped the bell shaped megaphone and clicked the switch a quick on and off. "We shouldn't wait any longer for her."

So much blackness closing in. Phil's realization that Phyllis was likely with "sick" Janos nearly blinded him. The memory of Mike's clutching hand in the Keg was the only sliver of light keeping him rational. He pulled that memory to his mind's eye.

"Let's go."

Southland stood. "Mike? Mike, this is Detective Southland . . . "

⁓

Southland finished his talk, urging calm on the kids in the van then he turned and looked at Phil. Phil held out a shaky hand. The loudhailer was heavy, its handle slippery in his fingers.

"Go slow, Phil." Southland stood at his side.

"Mike. Hit the horn once for yes. Twice for no. Do you understand?"

Toot.

"Are you and Angie and Badger all right?"

Toot.

"Whatever is wrong, we can fix it. I know you are upset but can we just talk it through?"

Toot.

"Can I come to the van so we can speak face to face?"

Toot.

"The police would like you to throw your guns out of the van first. Then we'll talk. Can you do that for me, please, Mike?"

A long silence followed. Phil looked at Southland. He smiled reassurance.

Toot, toot.

Phil's heart sank. His legs went soft and he staggered. Southland put an arm around him. "It's okay if he says no. We'll just keep talking. Nobody is going to attack them."

Toot.

Toot — toot — toot.

Phil stared at the van. The side door cracked open and Badger's voice yelled in a falsetto yodel. "We don't have any freaking guns to throw out! We just want out of here. Mike's gotta pee and the bag is full!"

⁓

Mike had never been in the principal's office before, but it did look like the warden's office in the movies.

"Clearly this has been an unfortunate miscommunication but I don't apologize for acting on the side of caution." The Warden was already practicing his press quotes. Mike sensed Angie stiffen beside him. "And of course there was no harm done apart from an afternoon of suspended classes."

Mike sighed. Why couldn't he just be quiet and let them go?

"No harm done other than publicly humiliating us." Angie opened her hand and began ticking points off on her fingers. "Wasting police time and resources, nearly traumatizing Mr. and Mrs. Smith, *and* my mom, plus scaring me so badly I curled into the fetal position." She glared at the principal.

"Mr. Swanson has a duty as principal to act in the best interests of all the students in a situation like this," Phil said. He and Phyllis sat near Mike, clutching each other's hands.

"Angie, you are young." Swanson condescended, one palm thoughtfully stroking his chin. "Mr. Smith is right; he sees that one must act on the facts available at the time."

"Facts?" Angie cut him off. "Vanessa comes in here shooting her mouth off with some line of vindictive bullshit. Making up horrible stories about me and my friends just because I wouldn't do what she said — and you take that as evidence to call police and lock down a school?"

Mike tried to catch her eye — shake his head — make her see it didn't matter, but she was brimming with a cold fury and wouldn't look at him.

"CCTV." Swanson gestured to a monitor on this desk. "Vanessa's story plus this." A blurred image flickered across the screen. Mike with a long, black, leather coat carrying a metallic tube. "Camera tripod or rifle?" The Warden mused.

Then Angie in a poncho and Badger in camo gear and bunnyhug handling a similar brown lengthy object. "Sticks and rolled cloth or a shotgun?"

"Oh for God's sakes," Angie spluttered.

"And we should remember, Vanessa was profoundly affected by this event. To her, it was real. She did see you and Michael playing a suicide game with a handgun at a party. But she overcame her fear and acted properly in going to Mr. Garchinski. He, in turn, was concerned about a recent creative-writing project written by Mike that involved a revenge fantasy." Swanson leaned forward over his desk. "The fact that she was mistaken about a deadly assault . . . "

"Bird-watching cameras and tripods! Bird watching!" Angie ground the words out. "And it was a water pistol, not a handgun."

"To her it was a lethal danger," the principal retorted. "Out of all involved, she will most need our understanding and possibly professional help to recover from the trauma."

"I was the one huddled in a van waiting for the cops to open fire while Badger emptied his bladder into a plastic bag."

"Angie, whoa there, enough," Badger cut in. "I think we can all agree Vanessa needs professional help, eh?"

Mike burst out laughing. It wasn't that funny, but his friends, the school, even Vanessa were in this mess because of him. Yet Angie and Badger were fighting for him. He raised his hand, something he never did in class, and Warden Swanson reacted instinctively as a teacher.

"Yes, Michael?"

"It's all down to me. I'll apologize or take whatever rap has to be taken. But couldn't we just leave it be for now and go home?"

Swanson smiled benevolently. "No blame, Michael. Like I said, a *miscommunication*. The police have their statements and seem to be satisfied. Detective Southland even complimented us on our efficiency in the lock down. Naturally you may leave. I would prefer that Bertram and Angela remain here until their parents arrive but . . . "

Angie and Badger stood as if on command. "We've talked. Parents are cool," Badger said. "We can go with the Smiths."

# CHAPTER 13

PHYLLIS HUNG UP THE PHONE. "I'LL TAKE the soup to Janos in forty-five minutes. He's still got time before his meeting."

In a day bursting with dark stress, this was nearly the last possible straw. Phil stared at Phyllis as though she was a stranger. How could she still be concerned about her boyfriend's chicken bloody soup when their world had nearly crashed. The principal was right. The fact that it had been a false alarm didn't just erase the distress. His hands were still trembling with the aftershock of it all. To Phyllis it was clearly nothing more than a wrong number. She crossed the living room and sat beside him on the couch. Her hands, warm, dry, picked his cold damp paws from his lap and held them.

"Phil honey, I have to tell you something now. Things that I wanted to wait for, ease into, but after this morning I can't delay."

"Damn right." Phil pushed her away. "Our worst nightmare." He shot a quick glance at Mike. Go on? Leave it till later? He plunged onward. "Our worst case scenario and you're okay with this? No sweat? Just so long as it doesn't upset Janos's lunch? What is happening to you, Phyl? To us?"

"I knew it was a false alarm. I knew what Mike and Angie and Badger were doing."

Phil shook his head. Was this how it would be then? The darkness wins and everybody speaks gibberish?

"Janos is going to sell the Genesis Technique on the Black Market. I was trying to stop him — the kids found out — we were working together." Now a plot from a Hardy Boys book, yet Phyllis said this so cleanly that he almost found himself believing her. He looked to Mike, expecting wild-eyed Keg restaurant anger and denial. Mike nodded.

"True, Dad, sorry. It is true. We're watching Janos this afternoon, so cameras, coats, tripods and stuff."

He wasn't wearing his bland face. His son was speaking to him, or so it seemed, not a psycho teenager. Phillip had wanted to pull Mike back from the brink at school. He'd learned that much this morning. Even when Mike had double blasted the horn refusing to throw out the guns — even when he'd been certain his son was a killer — he'd only wanted to save him. Love him. At least he knew that.

"Mike, there is something you have to know." Phil said it, trying now to pull his boy back from Phyllis's brink. "Your mom and I . . . " He looked for Phyllis at this last second, to say something to save them. "Are not doing well. I suspect that she and Janos Teleki . . . "

"I know about that too, Dad." Mike interrupted crossing the room. He sat between them and put his arm around his dad's shoulder. "Badger and I saw them, you know, the CLS van two weeks ago in the alley? And Angie got some pictures of them together at the theatre on Thursday."

Phillip Smith touched bottom. He registered the pity on Angie's and Badger's faces. He felt Mike's arm. He breathed noisily. Full darkness would settle now and it might never leave.

Phyllis left the room. Silence remained. What could be said? What could be done?

Phyllis returned carrying a Kodak envelope.

"I hope this is the right thing to do. I pray it is," she said softly. "I don't know what else is left."

She spread a handful of photos across the coffee table. Phil looked. Pictures of his wife grotesquely kissing Janos Teleki.

"Mom!" Mike reached for them. She deftly pushed his arm away.

"That is me." She tapped one fingernail on her face in the first shot. "And that," she said pointing at the man's face, "is you, Phil, not Janos Teleki."

Phil goggled open mouthed at the pictures. Back row cinema four. Janos never had shown up. Phyllis hadn't been with anyone; he'd watched her with his own eyes the whole time. *Time gone by as though he'd slept*, he remembered. He picked the photo up and held it nearly to his nose. The man in the picture had a moustache but half of it was twisted up and smeared across his cheek — a phoney moustache.

'Janos has a fake moustache?" he asked. Nobody answered. He examined another picture. It wasn't Janos kissing his wife. It was some clown in a cheesy disguise, an evil twin brother.

"Do you think that was me? I mean, I was there but I don't remember seeing you with anyone."

The self-evident contradiction in what he'd just said hung in the air around him. He wriggled his left foot and his toe burned. Yes, he had kicked the car in the cinema parking lot. He touched his upper lip. His glued-on 'stache had gone loose. He'd pulled it off. It had stung. Could there have been another man with half a stage moustache kissing Phyllis?

Virtually impossible. He looked at the photo again and this time he saw himself. It made him terribly sleepy, as though an internal tumult had suddenly calmed and drained his energy. Confusion clouded his thinking. He was desperate to close his eyes, surrender to an overpowering lassitude. There was no darkness. All round him was light and that was nice, but he was exhausted. He recognized this feeling — he'd experienced it once before, long ago, doing his masters. Something inside him, stealing his energy, but he couldn't make sense of it right now.

"I'll go to bed now. Need a nap." He stood, felt giddy, and stumbled forward. Phyl darted to his side, her hands strong and sure.

"I'll help you." She sounded just like Fran when he asked her for assistance in prepping his PowerPoint slides. "Can I get you anything?"

He walked to the stairs. "A cup of tea when I wake up would be nice."

"I'll be right here, honey. Tea it is. Sleep as long as you like."

She stripped him to his shorts and he slid into bed. The pillow felt heavenly. Phyllis tucked him in and kissed his cheek. He closed his eyes. The sheets were cool, clean, delicious on his skin. He'd made love to Phyllis in these sheets on Saturday morning. Then he'd been frightened of her when she went to shower. Why was that? Oh well, not frightened now. Maybe when he woke up and had his tea they could make love again. He smiled and slept.

~

"Man, did you see that?" Badger asked as Phyllis and Phil disappeared up the stairs to the bedroom. "That was the creepiest, craziest — no offence, Mike, I like Phil — but that was the scariest thing I've ever seen."

Mike picked up one of the photos. Phil wearing a silly theatrical moustache in profile. Phil's eyes and forehead. His father clear as day, yet he'd not seen him. It had been Janos in that picture just five minutes ago. Now it could not be anyone but Phillip Smith, PhD, brilliant particle physicist. He handed the photo to Angie.

"Phil or Janos?"

"Phil. How could we have all been so wrong?"

"We weren't wrong," Badger said stubbornly. "Our expectations were Janos, we were looking for Janos, so Phil became Janos. You saw him just now. The hairs on the back of my neck are still erect. My hackles are definitely up, aren't yours?"

Angie dropped the picture as though it was hot. "God, yes. He was Phil, then when your mom showed him the picture, did you see his face change?"

"Even without the moustache," Mike said. "His cheeks became — I don't know — tight. His whole face seemed to pull back, go smooth, young."

"His forehead went wider. He actually made his head grow." Badger stared at the pictures again. "Look, he's doing the same thing in this shot. How'd he do that?"

"Changing your lips, jaw, will do it to a certain extent," Angie said, hugging her arms to herself as though she was cold. "Actors can do similar things, but that was out of this world."

"Phyllis." Mike said slowly, each word having to be forced out of a labouring logic. "Was having an affair with her own husband — who was pretending to be Janos Teleki."

"A sex game. Remember I said that when we listened to the tapes — fantasy for old, burnt-out, married people. But we thought it was Phyllis and the real Janos, not Phil."

"And," Mike went on, "and Phil was so immersed in his Janos fantasy that he now actually thinks or thought he was Janos?"

"Split personality." Angie said. "Two people in the same body."

Neither Badger nor Mike replied.

"That was it, boys. We all saw it. Two faces, two sets of mannerisms, just for a second. Phil has a copy of Janos living inside him."

"I don't even know my own father. Is Phil really Phil or what?" He was frightened now. Afraid of what was in that bedroom. Angie took his hand. The fourth time. No thoughts now about covert or overt, he clutched it gratefully. They sat on the couch and she pulled his hand onto her thigh.

Phyllis came into the room. She looked at Mike and Angie. *Just who was together here?* Then she looked at Badger for an answer.

"Them, not me. Cover story." Badger explained. "Keep you from asking questions."

"Who is that upstairs, Phyllis?" Mike asked, ignoring Badger's exposure of their miniscule deception. "I'm afraid. Really afraid."

"That is Phil," she said. "Janos is gone."

"Well then, who is Phil?" Mike persisted.

"He is the guy you have known for your whole life. Physicist, hockey player, father." She crossed her arms. "Never doubt it, Mike. He is the man who has always loved you and you don't have to be afraid of him."

"Come on!" Mike shouted. "We all just saw two people, split personality or whatever. Is he crazy? Are you? You had sex with that other thing inside him! Don't be afraid? It's not that simple."

"Of course not, it is extremely complex," she said quietly in response to his shouts. "You should know first off that everything I did with your father these last two weeks was to help him overcome a real psychological problem. It should never have involved you — I had hoped it would remain between just the two of us."

Mike relaxed his grip on Angie's fingers and rubbed his eyes, trying to order his thoughts. "So Phil isn't crazy. Sorry, I shouldn't have said that. But what kind of psych problem are we facing? Will he ever get over it?"

"Phil has a disorder." Phyllis adopted her nurse's voice. "He had a mild case of it when he was doing his master's thesis — terrible stress — acted out the part of his tutor. It only occurred a couple of times, lasting minutes each time. It's called Multiple Personality Disorder or Dissociative Identity Disorder. I helped him through it and he never relapsed again until the night of the Hungarian dinner two weeks ago. I thought maybe the dinner would just be one isolated incident. But with the ongoing stress of the Genesis project it got worse rather than better. I role played along with him during the episodes of personality split to avoid any catastrophic conflict. I hoped that once the Genesis stress was over the split would heal naturally."

"So he could wake up as Janos?" Angie asked.

"Not now. He saw himself in the picture and disconnected very briefly to become Janos. You saw it. It was a risk on my part to force that conflict but I felt I had no choice after the school lockdown. He needed the full truth so he could make sense of the situation. Once he knew that the D.I.D. was recurring I hoped he could overcome it. That takes a huge mental adjustment and terrific will power but he is a really intelligent man."

"Yeah, awesome scientific brain," Badger said.

"His sense of logic is so strong," Phyllis clenched her fist. "I believe it overpowered the anomaly and let him see his own disorder."

"What about the future?" For himself, Mike just wanted to stay with Angie on the couch, hoping nothing would happen or need to be done in the future. But his dad was another matter.

"I'm not leaving him. I want to be here when he wakes up. You three will have to catch Janos selling the Genesis Project and then Phil will have to expose him to CLS. I don't really give a darn about the Backlight Techniques being stolen. But if Phil can see Janos for what he is and turn him in, then I feel certain it will permanently cleanse the Janos personality from his body."

Mike understood. Phyllis the cheating, self-indulgent bitch had been Phyllis the self-sacrificing angel who'd played a covert game infinitely more complex than he could have imagined. It was a sick game nonetheless.

"Okay, Mom. We'll get him." Mom, not Phyllis. That felt good. Then in spite of it all, he asked, "Was that really you and Dad in the CLS van in the ravine?"

His mother blushed. Badger coughed loudly. Angie pinched the back of his hand. Really, it had been Mom and Phil and Janos. Just like her confession to Fr. Fitz. Nobody was clean in this. Janos was being used and he didn't even know it.

Phyllis called Janos again and cancelled the soup, saying she had been called into work on short notice. Angie and Badger in his mom's van picked Janos up going out the back road at two o'clock. They pulled in behind him and called Mike. The two-car watch was on. Mike had his cell open, on speaker, wedged and taped into the ashtray. Janos drove straight north on Wiggins Avenue. Angie and Badger stayed a hundred metres behind him. Mike paralleled them farther back and a block west on Cairns Avenue. One block short of the intersection with 8th Street, Badger's voice came tense and quick over the cellphone.

"He's doing a U-turn. No warning, no signal."

Mike smiled. A simple but effective way of spotting a tail. Janos would slow down, scan his rear view mirror to see if anyone mimicked his U-turn.

"He's going really slow." Badger's voice dropped quieter. "He's watching all the cars ahead of us. Do you think he's onto us?"

"No. He's just hoping you'll expose yourselves."

"Angie's cool." Badger's voice, loud again. "Didn't change her speed; he's just driven past us now, going in the opposite direction."

Mike had spun his own U-turn, accelerated back down Cairns to intercept Janos's path. A few seconds before he reached the intersection, Janos drove through it, heading south. Mike carefully turned right and got in behind him.

"Got him on Wiggins. You guys shift over to Cairns and come south."

"Already there. What's your location?" Badger, excited now.

"Just coming up on Hilliard Street."

"Roger that. We're two blocks behind, closing fast."

Janos made a quick left, then a right and continued south. Mike followed the left but ignored the right and called Angie to take over the tail again.

"Got him, we got him! This is outstanding." Badger's voice up another octave.

Mike turned right at the next corner and resumed his parallel trail. He grinned and did a small fist pump. It was outstanding. Janos made one more left at Cascade Street then slowed.

"He's pulling into the park — Tatler Park — off Cascade. He's stopping and, holy crap, he's getting out. Quick! Angie get past, get past!"

Mike sped up and crossed over. If Janos moved rapidly into the park he might lose them.

"Hurry Angie, hurry. He's going to . . . "

"I see him!" Angie's voice now, shouting Badger down. "I'll go to that bush and hit the brakes, you jump and get after him!"

The phone clicked off. Mike slowed down, breathing deeply. Out of his hands now. Badger and Angie would do it — or not.

~

"How long?" Angie asked. Her body language was calm. They leaned against the sunny side of the van. Phyllis's car was just ahead. They were parked at the curb just around the corner from Janos's vehicle.

"Ten minutes," Mike lied. He'd only noted the time five minutes ago but that had to have been another five since Badger had gone after Janos.

"Hope he doesn't blow it with all that predator crap," Angie said, voicing Mike's inner nerves.

"He is pretty good at the hide-and-seek stuff." Mike replied.

"Well he definitely doesn't have the cat-like reflexes he brags about."

Mike looked at her, raising an eyebrow.

"He jumped out the side door of the van like a drunken squirrel, arms and legs flailing away like this." She swooped her limbs in large circles. "Then he hits that lilac bush and cartwheels a few metres before he does a face plant."

Mike grinned. "Damaged the camera, do you think?"

"Surprisingly no. Landing on his face cushioned the blow to the rest of his Badger body and that protected the camera." They laughed together, in the sun.

Mike's cell rang, he clicked on.

"Home base, this is James Freakin' Bond Badger."

Mike smiled. "Go, Bond."

"Dead drop like you said. I got two good zooms of him hiding the file. He left a second ago. Never saw the Badger. Never heard the Badger. Not a sniff."

～

The Genesis Project Report was underneath the plate covering a cluster of underground sprinkler-control valves. Mike took a couple of photographs of its open lid. Establish the dead drop's validity. There was an L shape of bushes and hedge on two sides of the control site, about fifteen metres from it. They simply stood amid the foliage. Badger with his camera in the hedge. Mike and Angie with Mike's camera in the bushes. Mike checked his watch. Likely to be a quick mark up and retrieval if the sprinklers were supposed to be turned on overnight. And it was. Two hours into the watch, a slim blond man, middle-aged, no hat or glasses or disguise of any kind, rode across the open lawn on an old, three-speed bike. He stopped, put the bike on its stand and flipped the cover plate off the sprinkler taps. Mike took four shots: one of him standing full-face beside the bike, one of him kneeling and two quick ones of him holding the file. He put the binder into a saddle bag on the rear fender and rode off.

Badger got similar shots from his angle. Mike felt somehow let down. The lockdown, Phil's split personality, the car chase, had all been so wild, exciting. Yet in the end, it had been a simple photo shoot.

"Very professional, I'd call it," Angie said, reading his face. He brightened. "It was."

## Chapter 14

Phil studied the clock in the car dash. He was late — unheard of tardiness for Dr. Smith — nine forty-eight A.M. His meeting with Len Edwards was scheduled for two P.M., today, Tuesday. Exactly two weeks since he'd first followed Janos, then turned into Janos, then taken Phyl to the ravine. It had been painful going back over all the events with Phyllis, listening to her explain his behaviour as 'Janos' — behavior he could not remember. But it had been necessary and in the end he knew he was back in control, no hidden demons. He would be told that Genesis was go or no-go at fourteen-hundred hours today. He subtracted 14 from 948 and got 934. Then did it again and got 920, 906, 892, 878, 864 . . .

"Phil, honey . . . " Phyllis was driving him to work.

"Yes?"

"You're counting by fourteens."

He was startled. "How did you know?" Janos inside him was unsettling enough; he didn't need Phyllis tinkering with his brain.

"Out loud."

"Oh, sorry."

The Source of Light

"It's okay, kind of soothing in a way." She pulled into the CLS parking lot. "But not out loud at work."

"No, no. Of course not."

She wheeled smoothly into a painted slot then stopped, but she didn't look at him. He reached into the back seat and picked up his briefcase.

"Kids did well yesterday," he said.

"Yes." She still didn't look at him. "Excellent photos."

"Won't show them to Len until after the two o'clock meeting."

"I think that's best."

They had discussed it well into the night. She'd been terribly apprehensive about the whole Janos industrial espionage thing. Worried that he'd relapse into his Janos persona and go off the rails when he saw "himself" selling the Genesis Project to a black marketer in Mike's pictures. But he hadn't. 724-710-696-682. He actually felt as though he'd physically lost weight. He felt fit, trim, lively; suddenly alert and clear of any lingering dark depression. He'd agreed to see a professional. Phyllis would get him in to see a shrink at the University hospital, but he was sure it wasn't necessary.

Janos's invasive personality was gone. He had pangs, even now, of betrayal and hurt. Janos for all the imagined trysts with Phyllis had been his professional friend. Now it turned out to be the opposite. Janos, innocent of seducing his wife, but guilty of betraying the Smith backlight technique. The lesser of two evils — still very evil, and it hurt.

Phyllis released her seatbelt and turned. She straightened his tie and fussed with his shirt collar. "I know you have a high regard for Janos."

Have, *not* had, Phil noted. She did see clearly.

~ 237 ~

"But you have to go through with it. If not for you own career's sake, then for our sake." She put her palms on his cheeks and held his head gently. "We need to be clear of him. He can't come into our bedroom again, Phil."

"I know." He'd do it for her.

"Why do I feel, like this?" She laughed quietly.

"Like what?"

"Like I'm sending you off to your first day at school." She pulled her hands back from his face and placed them in her lap. "You're a genius. You're an experienced leader in a world-class facility. You're a hard-edged hockey player with a forty-nine point season. Yet right now I see my Phil as somebody I should be protecting as though he was a child."

"I'll take a stab at answering that," he said, wanting more than anything in the world to protect her. She who had been through so much. "Because I've spent two weeks in a half-crazed, delusional state chasing my own ass in circles. Close enough?"

She kissed him. He got out of the car and stood on the sidewalk while she drove away, waving.

～

"Is he in yet?" Len Edwards' voice surprised Phil. He'd been listening to Fran's keyboard clicking — 234-220-206-192 — and reading Genesis Verses 3, 4 on the wall.

"Yes, he's in," Fran said.

Len stepped into but not through Phil's office door. Phil looked up. If it was good news he'd have waited until the meeting. Bad news would force him here early so Phil could have his meltdown in private and behave with some decorum in the formal meeting.

"Doctor Smith," Len said, deadpan. "It looks like the decision — in the end — was unanimous."

*For or against?* Phil wondered momentarily.

"Unanimously approved!" Len shouted and burst into the room hand outstretched. Phil stood and let his hand be shaken. Len laughed and slapped him on the shoulder.

"Even chainsaw? I mean McCulloch?"

"Of course. Once he saw the vote going heavily your way, he jumped on board. Bad form to be the lone recorded naysayer. He does his work behind the scenes."

Phil wobbled as Len pummelled his shoulder.

"I couldn't be happier Phil. I shouldn't be here, but I had to tell you now, couldn't wait for two o'clock."

"But I was such a jackass at the meeting," Phil protested.

"Your presentation was solid and a game winner." Len paced enthusiastically in the small office. "And you did behave like a horse's ass but Doctor Teleki pulled your horse's ass out of the fire."

Phil glanced down at his briefcase and its cargo of spy photos.

"Once you got past your sparring match with McCulloch and made it to the hard science, well, it was almost what the kids call a no-brainer."

"But it was Janos who let me get to that point." Phil already knew he'd never have turned Janos in. He knew he'd been lying to Phyllis this morning, and lying to himself. He couldn't destroy the man who had saved his science with a true act of friendship and unwittingly refilled his testosterone tank. Sale to the black market be damned. Sure Janos wanted the procedure approved for his own benefit. Nonetheless, Phil could feel it in his backbone — Janos had saved him because he loved the backlight too.

At least now he had a reason to take to Phyllis. Couldn't betray the man who had saved the Genesis Procedure. True, he sold it for cash, but that was now almost moot. It had limited value for the buyer; the slim blond man couldn't resell it after the announcement today.

"You owe Teleki. Now for pity sake, act surprised when you go into the meeting." Len wheeled around. "Fran!"

"Yes, Doctor Edwards?"

"I assume you're eavesdropping out there?"

"Of course, Doctor Edwards."

"Well keep a lid on this till after the meeting."

"Naturally, Doctor Edwards."

Len pumped his hand one more time then rushed out. Phil followed him out of the office onto the walkway. He bent over and leaned his elbows on the top of the railing. The Hungarian beam line spoked off the ring to his right. The hutch was empty. The ring was closed for two days maintenance. Janos and his team would be hard at work prepping for their next session.

He still had no recall of the theatre or the van or even the night of the welcome dinner. Phyllis had told him — in needlessly graphic detail — of his performance on those occasions. He did remember Saturday morning as a daydream that turned out to be reality. But of the others, nothing came back to him. Perhaps for the best Phyl had said, especially the movie-theatre episode. He'd waited for himself to appear, changed character and made out with his wife, then chased himself out the front door. As though he'd lost his soul and gone to look for it in the parking lot of a Galaxy Six. What would Fr. Fitz have to say about that? One thing seemed clear in all this clutter. Janos was his man. He was Janos's man, and he had let "Janos" make love to his wife. He'd talk to Janos now. He knew what to say and he didn't really need a shrink to explain it to him.

～

They left the two o'clock meeting together, Janos tenaciously shaking his hand again as they proceeded toward the ring.

"Got time for a chat?" Phil asked.

"Yes, of course."

Phil pulled up in front of the bank of vending machines and plugged loonies into them receiving two Cokes and two Eat-Mores. "Let's walk." Phil nodded at the ring.

They sipped and chewed in companionable silence as they crossed the main floor. The massive doors that usually sealed the metre-thick concrete walls stood open. Inside, a crew was working near the end of one of the straight sections, adjusting a dipole magnet. Phil led the way, passing around corners of two more sections till they were hidden from the technicians. He spread his arms out, Coke on one end, chocolate bar on the other. He tilted and swooped like a bird in flight.

"You fly the ring very well," Janos said behind him. "You see the electrons in your head, yes?"

Phil slowed, dropping his arms but not losing the extraterrestrial surge of emotion and insight that made him happy. Here, in this concrete tunnel, were the shining steel rings making light. Here was the habitat of Phil Smith's soul, not a cathedral chancel.

"Yes," he said simply.

"Not just science is it?"

Phil stopped and turned slowly. "What do you mean?" He asked this, knowing exactly what it meant but wanting to see how far Janos would go.

Janos tapped his chest. "The heart. This is our heartbeat.
Yes of course, sub-atomic particles and protein crystals. They
are the scientific process. But if that was all, we could not love
it. And this is our love, is it not, Phil?"

Phil examined Janos's dark eyes and curly black hair. He
and Janos really were similar except for the grand moustache
and their chronological age differences. They both loved this
ring of light and Phyllis. No wonder Janos had been able to
creep inside him and hide there without him knowing.

"You're selling the Genesis Project on the black market."
He watched Janos's face closely.

The moustache moved up and down as though Janos was
eating these words — chewing and digesting them.

"I have pictures of your drop site in the park off Cascade, at
the underground sprinkler box."

Janos nodded.

"You don't deny it."

Janos shook his head.

"Have you nothing to say?" Phil wanted this betrayal to
disappear. Somehow Janos could explain it.

"I am the Judas, Phillip," he said quietly. "I must not beg.
You will say what is to happen."

"Nothing will happen." Phil was happy to hear his own
words. "The Genesis is really not worth much in itself, now
that Canada and Hungary have approved it and will use it
publicly. Without the follow-up data, it's actual black-market
application is almost nil."

Janos inclined his head to one side but remained mute.

"Do you plan to sell the results of our work?"

"No need. You are right. The Genesis sold for an exact but
modest amount that the buyer saw as a speculative gamble.
I was desperate for that modest amount, and now it is over."

Phil let thoughts like gambling habit, drug addiction, blackmailing hookers flip through his head. None of them matched the man opposite him.

*Twenty percent.*

Excess testing costs paid by the user team from their twenty percent funding were automatically authorized. He remembered Janos's calm voice in the meeting. The man and the money that saved Genesis.

"You didn't have enough for the extra tests in your twenty percent. So you hid the shortfall from your budget reports to Hungary."

The moustache curled into a smile. The dark eyes blinked. Phil followed the logic forward. "Budapest noticed the discrepancy and put your feet to the fire two weeks ago today. You left early to see a buyer for Genesis — that's why the first meeting was cancelled."

Janos shrugged, moustache still curled.

"You weren't seducing Phyllis, I know that now."

Janos stiffened. "What? The word seducing," he stammered, his sang-froid shattered. "Surely not what I think it means. I find Phyllis, the expression I believe is, extremely hot. But I would never try to steal your woman."

"You really do think of Phyllis as . . . " An unexpected tremor of jealousy quivered in Phil.

"Extremely hot," he confirmed. He put his hands together as though praying. "Never, never, ever would I act on those feelings."

"No. Of course not. So you risked your professional reputation and perhaps criminal charges back home to do the extra testing needed to validate my theory."

"Not likely criminal — a bit too dramatic." Janos demurred. "But yes, I took a serious risk."

"And raised the money to cover the deficit by . . . "

"Yes, again, shameful." Janos dropped his praying hands limply to his side. "I covered the deficit by selling your beautiful theory to an animal who cares only for resale profit."

"A bit too dramatic," Phil echoed his words. "Why did you do such a thing, take such a risk? Just to prove my theory?"

Janos tapped his chest. "Not just science, eh, Phil?"

"No." Phil walked to him and put his arms around him. He felt Janos's arms wrap in reply. He rested his chin on his shoulder, smelled him. Janos's warm chest pressed against his and they stood, together, in their beloved concrete ring of light.

"Come home with me for supper tonight." Phil whispered. "You and I and Phyllis will eat and talk. Mike is out with a friend."

# CHAPTER 15

HE WAS EARLY AT TWO GREEK GUYS. Adele the hostess remembered him and gave him a table by the window. He polished the lenses of his Arthur Guthrie glasses, watching the door, keen for their reaction when he met them as Arthur. It was the first opportunity they'd had to get together since the operation against Janos. It would be fun to debrief the team over Greek food and wine — Arthur paying the bill.

A moment later Angie came through the entryway, followed by Badger. She looked for him, he waved and got to his feet. She wore a slick shiny silk top and snug fitting jeans. As he approached he saw how good she really looked — lipstick, eyeliner, hair down in soft brown waves to her shoulders. Composed — mature — beautiful. He grinned, almost giddy at the sight of her. This could have been their first date, but they had to invite Badger — he couldn't be left out of the debrief.

She didn't return his smile but she did lean forward and kiss him quickly on the cheek.

"Hi Mike, what's with the glasses?"

"Mike?" Adele materialized at his side. "I understood your name was Arthur Guthrie — what it says on your driver's licence."

"Nickname, Adele — I'll take it from here, ta." He handed her a five-dollar bill and hustled them toward the table.

"Excellent." Badger slapped him on the shoulder. "Arthur Guthrie — let's get a carafe of wine, Art." He turned to Angie. "Red or white?"

Angie ignored him, staring out the window.

"What's wrong?" Mike asked.

"I thought we established that Art G. was an insensitive control freak," she snapped. "I don't want him buying me wine — or supper — or anything."

Mike nearly broke the glasses as he tore them off his face. "A joke — just a prank, Angie. I wouldn't let Guthrie ruin our first date." He stammered.

She looked at him, a smile on her face. "Date?" Then she glanced at Badger.

"Hey — I'm gone if you guys want to go all lovey-dovey here." Badger said, without moving. "I mean . . . if you *really* want me to go that is . . . and miss out on supper."

"Oh stay." Angie laughed — taking the glasses from Mike's hand. "You two really do need a lot of instruction on social behaviour."

Badger's face fell. "No, Arthur — no wine?"

Sunlight came through the window and caught the side of Angie's face, shining from her hair. "You look absolutely fabulous." Mike said a trifle too loudly. He realized that he couldn't have played the restrained Guthrie character tonight anyway. But one part of his brain made a mental note to get the glasses back — he wasn't going to abandon Arthur completely.

"Yeah, finally, some decent plumage." Badger agreed as he perused the menu. "How about we eat first, then debrief. I'm starving."

Angie slid her hand halfway across the table. Glossy fingernail polish Mike noticed — she really had done the plumage. He put his hand over hers.

"Do we *have* to debrief?" she asked. "Can't we just enjoy ourselves?" She threaded her fingers through his. "A spy debriefing seems so unnecessary now. Your parents are good, right?"

Mike nodded.

"Then let it go. Spying on people can be a dirty business but it all came clean. Can't we just leave it at that?"

Badger looked up from the menu. Angie fell silent. Their hard truth stared him in the face. They were clean — he was not. He was still lying, concealing that one bit of dirt that simply would not scrub clean.

"I'm not going to confession tomorrow."

They waited expectantly.

"Why not?" Badger prompted. "You always go to confession."

"I can't." He pulled away from Angie and slumped back in his chair. "It won't work."

"Finally came to your senses?" Badger grinned. "It never worked — it's not real."

Angie elbowed him. "He means there's something he wants to say but there's a rule . . . or regulation against it I'm guessing."

"Kind of like that." Mike shrugged. "I did something at the start of the operation that was way beyond dirty business and I need to confess it but I can't so I'll be lying in the confession which means committing a sin to cleanse my sins." It came out in a rush. "So . . . It won't work, see?"

"No," Badger said. "I don't see at all. You're a good guy Mike except you let all this Catholic — God — Jesus guilt tie you up in knots." He slapped the menu down with a bang. Mike flinched. "We're your friends. Tell us what you did — not some priest."

Mike picked at the edge of the tablecloth. Badger couldn't get this. He shouldn't have mentioned it.

"You know," Angie ventured quietly. "Much as it pains me to say this . . . the Badger is right. At least partly. We are your friends. We stuck by you. You should tell us. Face us. If we can help you get clean, we will. Surely you believe that."

Believe? Mike's head snapped up. What did he believe? How could he believe in God but be afraid to confess to Him? He shook himself, took a breath. He did believe in God and forgiveness. He also believed in Badger and Angie — maybe start with them — a test run.

"I needed to know if Phyllis *was* cheating on Phil and I figured she might confess it to Fr. Fitzpatrick." The words settled on the table like overturned playing cards — revealing his hand.

"I took my directional receiver to church and . . . "

"You didn't!" Badger lifted a hand, palm out. "Awesome man. Straight out awesome. You've got bigger stones than I ever would have guessed, Smith. Give a high one."

Mike stared at Badger's hand. He looked at Angie for some kind of embarrassment — shame even. But he saw a tiny smile of hope.

"You took your receiver to church and you . . . " She repeated for him, pulling Badger's hand down. "Let's hear the whole thing."

"I bugged the confession. Heard enough to convince me that my mom was having an affair but she never actually said Teleki's name so I got it wrong. But I broke the Sacred Seal of the confessional."

"I say again, awesome, man. Feel better now?"

"No." Mike hugged himself tightly. "I feel like I did then — like a total shit."

"Well, you need to go see Fr. Fitz tomorrow and fess up. To him and God — although I don't know how God doesn't know already." Angie said this calmly, prying one of his hands loose, holding it again. "I know you've got the . . . "

"Stones," Badger supplied.

"Heart," she continued. "And faith to do it." Her grey unblinking eyes held him.

Spying, he thought — you just never knew what you'd discover in the world of espionage.

∿

Mike stood quietly, arms loose at his sides and gazed at the coloured light streaming from the stained glass onto the altar. Would Fr. Fitz forgive him for bugging a confession? Could he? What kind of penance do you give for that? Is there a special prayer — an Act of Contrition — for such a violation?

The confessional door clicked open loudly behind him. He entered and knelt. Fr. Fitz cleared his throat on the other side of the screen.

"I confess to the Blessed Virgin Mary and all the saints and to you Father that I have sinned." His own voice surprised him. It was calm, clear and filled the cubicle. "It has been three weeks since my last confession. I've been deceitful. I've spied on people — invaded their privacy."

Fitz was silent. Mike shut his eyes and put his arms out, hands braced on the walls. He saw Angie and Badger. Felt them here with him and God and the priest. He smiled. Badger in a Catholic church — awesome. He would force the admission out quickly — that he had broken Fr. Fitzpatrick's Sacred Seal of the Confessional — disgraced it.

"My mom and you. Spied on you, that is."

"What?" Fitz was normally ice calm in a confession but there was shock in his voice "You don't mean in here?"

"Yes, Father. I do. I listened to you on a special receiver."

"In God's name why? And how many times?"

"Once. I thought my mom and dad were headed for divorce. I had to know why. I thought she'd tell you."

"Are they? Divorcing?" Fr. Fitzpatrick's voice was concerned now, not angry.

"No. They're fine — it's more complicated than just the confessional but that was the worst and I had to tell you."

"Have you told your mom about the confession?"

"No. Not yet. But I am going to. I have to get clean."

There was a long silence. Mike bore it, trying to be strong, not cringe.

"I agree." Fitz said. "You have to get clean. I can't pretend this doesn't hurt me personally. Yet you have shown a certain courage . . . "

Angie's voice came to him — heart and faith, she'd said.

" . . . you have a strong faith from which you can draw courage and I am glad of it."

Mike's eyes blinked open. It seemed like Fitz — God — had read his thoughts.

"I think that a full admission to your mother will be mandatory as a part of your penance. I trust you to follow through on that. For myself — for the church you've wronged — I honestly don't know what penance is appropriate. Prayer, I suppose. A full rosary recited with a true spirit of remorse must be enough. May God grant you pardon and peace; I absolve you from your sins in the name of the Father, Son and Holy Spirit."

Mike made the sign of the cross. He left the confessional and walked toward the coloured light to say his penance. He felt clean, the dirt would wash away after all. And more than that — he was not the grey boy — not a jackrabbit crouched in front of a snowback refusing to be flushed. As le Carré had taught him — use the facts at hand to make your plan, then go forward without second guessing. Mike was no longer hiding beneath the surface. He was now openly a good son, a trusted friend and most surprising of all, a lover. You just never knew where particle physics and espionage would lead you.

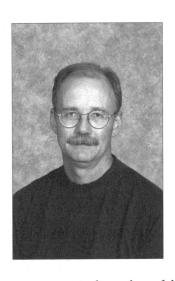

DAVID RICHARDS is the author of three novels: *Soldier Boys* (Thistledown Press 1993), *Lady at Batoche* (Thistledown Press 1999), and *The Plough's Share* (Thistledown Press 2005). *The Source of Light,* focuses Richards' attention, research, insight, and storytelling on science and technology — subjects close to his learning and his heart. David Richards lives in Moose Jaw, Saskatchewan.